When **Virginia Heath** was a little girl it took her ages to fall asleep, so she made up stories in her head to help pass the time while she was staring at the ceiling. As she got older the stories became more complicated—sometimes taking weeks to get to their happy ending. One day she decided to embrace her insomnia and start writing them down. Virginia lives in Essex, with her wonderful husband and two teenagers. It still takes her for ever to fall asleep.

THE DISGRACEFUL
LORD GRAY

Virginia Heath

Leabharlanna Poiblí Chathair Baile Átha Cliath

Dublin City Public Libraries

MILLS & BOON

First Published in Great Britain 2019
by Mills & Boon, an imprint of HarperCollins*Publishers*
1 London Bridge Street, London, SE1 9GF

© 2019 Susan Merritt

ISBN: 978-0-263-26898-0

MIX
Paper from
responsible sources
FSC® C007454

This book is produced from independently certified FSC™ paper
to ensure responsible forest management.
For more information visit www.harpercollins.co.uk/green.

Printed and bound in Spain
by CPI, Barcelona

For Claire Sayers, who gave Gray his name,
and for Trevor, my adorable, naughty Labrador,
who made the perfect hero's sidekick.

Chapter One

July 1820

There was no doubt about it. Lord Fennimore was going to have his guts for garters. Especially after the unfortunate shredded underwear incident of last night. The commander of the King's Elite had no discernible sense of humour which didn't bode well for Gray's newly discovered, but no less coveted ambition.

'Trefor! Give it back. *Now!*'

There was no point in chasing him. The blasted dog saw everything as a game and had been in a state of playful overexcitement ever since they arrived in Suffolk yesterday—and who could blame him, really? Aside from a few brief weeks after his birth, Trefor had always been a city dog. If one ignored Hyde Park and St James's, vast open spaces of green were completely alien to him. But the green here was never ending, filled with flat fields to dash across, abundant trees to relieve himself against and sticks aplenty to chase with impunity. Doggy paradise. And Gray's mischievous mutt seemed determined to reach this strange, alluring new horizon at lightning speed with curmudgeonly old Fennimore's slipper clamped firmly between his jaws.

To tease Gray, the dog dropped the stolen booty at the boundary to their rented property and eyed him mischievously, his powerful tail wagging nineteen to the dozen, his floppy ears pricked and his enormous pink tongue lolling out of one side of his mouth like a juicy slice of ham.

Gray examined his cuffs, looked at the sky, some trees, anything but his dratted hound while he slowly edged his way forward, hoping to convince the animal he wasn't fixated on his superior's now slobbery shoe at all. Mere inches away he lunged like a panther, only to growl as the dog snatched up the blasted slipper again before he could reach it and raced towards the tree-lined horizon once more.

'Trefor!'

This time Gray did give chase, not only because of his dour superior's footwear, or because the animal had disappeared into a small wooded copse, but because a couple of sheep had also appeared in the distance and his dog had even less experience of sheep than he did wide open spaces. He needed to make a good first impression on the Viscount Gislingham. He needed to befriend him. Ingratiate himself. Be the perfect neighbour and work his way into his small, intimate social circle. More than anything, he needed to impress Lord Fennimore if he was ever going to stand a cat in hell's chance of getting that coveted promotion. Something unlikely to happen if his out-of-control canine injured one of the flock and the Viscount banned him from entering the grounds; the mission shot in the paddock before it had even started.

Not that Trefor was violent; he was a licker, not a biter. He adored everyone and everything and loved them enthusiastically. Something the dim-witted sheep would not know as he came bounding towards them intent on saying hello. Why had he insisted on bringing his dog along? All his lofty claims that a proper country gentleman would have at least one loyal hound at his side seemed to be doomed to be ruined by the said hound from the outset because, while Trefor was exceedingly loyal, he was also completely untrainable.

The dog failed to materialise out of the clump of trees, their trunks so densely packed Gray had to skirt around them before he encountered the unexpected steep bank of a deep yet narrow stretch of water which cut through the flat pasture.

Marvellous.

There had to be water.

Trefor's absolute favourite thing in the world bar footwear, sticks, balls and sausages. There was no point hoping he hadn't found it or wasn't fully immersed in it. Some things were as inevitable as day following night or another carpeting from his furious superior about his unruly, destructive pet mere hours since the last. This morning, more than Lord Fennimore's slipper would be going home soggy—not that Gray blamed Trefor for that either. The summer sun was already blazing in the sky and it was only eight o'clock.

Last night, thanks to the sticky heat, the huge weight of the new responsibility on his shoulders, his overwhelming desire to show old Fennimore that he was exactly the right man for the job and the strange bed, he had slept so fitfully he would have dunked himself in this convenient stream in the small hours had he known of its existence. Because of his unexpected morning sprint, the cold wash he had revelled in a scant few minutes ago in his new bedchamber was now wasted and his meticulously ironed shirt was clinging to his hot skin in a manner no gentleman would allow to be seen in public.

Not that he was much of a gentleman. Not any more at any rate, although that was all of his own making so there was no point being angry about it. He was over it now. Nearly a decade after his life had imploded, he was actually rather philosophical about the experience. Life was too short for regrets, especially when he had racked up so many.

Gray had come a long way since those dark days of his youth. He shared little in common with the reckless, needy adolescent he had been that fateful summer. Or the aristocratic brother he hadn't seen since his heart had been ripped in two by betrayal. Betrayal that had come courtesy of the cold, unfeeling father who had instigated it behind Gray's back and the woman who hadn't truly loved him at all. Nor did he have any regrets about what might have been. The wife and immature, romantic and ultimately futile dreams of the future he had once believed should have been his now rarely crossed his mind. It was what it was. Done and dusted. And fate had sent him hurtling down a very different path, one he was pleasantly surprised had led to adventure instead of matrimony.

He was now older, much wiser and was clearly what he had been born to be. A spy tasked with bringing the enemies of the Crown to justice. A man who had seen and done more than most. Experiences that had made him hardy, resourceful and tenacious. Aside from having his childish heart shredded and creating the mother of all scandals, he'd had an interesting life since. Travelled the world. Seen and done some amazing things, met a variety of fascinating people, both eminently good and outrageously bad. Temporarily dallied with considerably more women than the single one he had originally pledged to spend eternity with, and he now worked for His Majesty's government instead. How many of his former peers could say that?

If he, or his incorrigible mutt, didn't make a total hash of this mission, soon Gray would also command the Invisibles—the highly trained, most covert and most important branch of the King's Elite—answerable only to Lord Fennimore, the Home Secretary and the King in that order. Not bad going for a man disowned by his family for losing his entire fortune in the gaming hells at the tender age of twenty-one. He had craved adventure and entertainment far more than he wanted to conform.

Still did, truth be told. Ten hard years and a brutal betrayal still hadn't managed to dampen his mischievous zest for life or his tendency to live entirely in the moment. Life was too short to ponder what might have been. If it was meant to be, it would have happened. It was as simple as that. There was no point lamenting the fickle finger of fate or wasting time being angry or crippled by remorse. Better to live his life much like Trefor did. Enjoy the here and now, forget the past which couldn't be changed and let tomorrow sort itself out.

Gray craned his ears until he heard joyous

splashing and the dog's trademark swimming grunt. A cross between a cough and snort, muffled slightly no doubt by the obstruction of the stolen slipper betwixt his teeth. Gray tracked it several yards along the bank, then stood and glared at the animal deliriously paddling in a happy circle below.

'Well, I'm in for another blistering lecture thanks to you. Were the old man's drawers not enough? I thought he would have an apoplexy when you shredded them, but at least he brought spares. I'm fairly certain he only brought one pair of slippers.' He put his hands on his hips and channelled the disappointed expression his father had always worn when addressing him. It felt odd on his face. 'I hope you are proud of yourself, young man?'

Judging by the joyful wag of Trefor's fierce whip of a tail in the water, he was. Happy and proud and gloriously cool. It took around five seconds to decide not to attempt to drag the dog out. The slipper was ruined. Beyond hope. Lord Fennimore's lecture was now unavoidable, yet the day was young, the spot secluded and the water enticing. A nice, refreshing swim would certainly take the sting out of the tongue lashing and it would be a terrible shame to waste the opportunity. Especially when the hopelessly wayward part of his character still couldn't resist the seductive lure of the moment even now.

His dog saw the indecision and swiftly dropped the slipper as he climbed up the bank. It took approximately three seconds of foraging in the undergrowth before Trefor found a suitable stick, then he sat like a good boy and gazed at his master winsomely, the invitation to play clear in those manipulative, soulful dark brown eyes. As resistance was futile, and before he did anything remotely sensible like reconsider, Gray tugged off his shiny new boots, stripped off his newly tailored aristocratic clothes and waded happily into the water.

'We should probably find a little shade to set up your easel.' Thea gazed up at the clear blue sky and the unobstructed sun and frowned. Much as she loved the sunshine, it didn't love her. Pale, sensitive skin was the redhead's curse. Any more than twenty minutes' exposure and she was guaranteed to look like a beetroot for days.

Harriet rolled her eyes dramatically, greatly put upon despite dragging Thea out of bed at the crack of dawn to chat to her while she attempted to paint. Watercolours were Harriet's new hobby and, like all her hobbies, destined to be abandoned because nothing truly held her wandering interest for long. 'You wouldn't burn if you'd wear a bonnet.' Not that she was wearing one either, or a lace cap—when everyone expected mature widows of good breeding to wear one of those at all times.

'You know a hat in this heat will only make my head hot and then my dratted hair will turn into a big ball of frizz.' Thea began to stride towards the trees, knowing her companion wouldn't really begrudge her some shade as long as she kept her company. They were an odd partnership, separated by thirty years in age yet the very best of friends as well as neighbours. Probably because Harriet was basically naughty and devil-may-care by nature and didn't give two figs about it, while Thea feared she was exactly the same, but worked hard to control it. A classic case of opposites attracting. Or birds of a feather flocking together. Living within spitting distance, and in the absence of any other local ladies who held either of their interests long, they had formed an unlikely bond shortly after her friend had been widowed.

'Aunt Caro has invited half the county for tea this afternoon and for once I'd like to look a little less of a disaster than usual.' Although the humidity was already playing havoc with her coiffure. Despite all the pins and plaits her maid had used to tame it this morning, Thea could still feel a great many of the unruly strands making a determined break for freedom from their tight shackles and twisting themselves into their preferred upright corkscrew shape.

She castigated the Almighty daily for saddling her with vertical, twirling, wayward hair. While she rather liked the colour—the red was unique and gave her a touch of dash as well as giving her the excuse not to wear the insipid pastels other unmarried girls had to wear—the unpredictable curls were a menace. When all the other young ladies had artful, bouncing ringlets framing their face, Thea wore a veritable halo of fluff.

'Will a certain Mr Hargreaves be there?'

'Lord, I hope not! The man is such a dreadful bore.' And an obvious fortune hunter who Thea suspected was one of her aunt's cast-offs, not that she would ever admit such a thing even to Harriet. Her suspicions about her aunt's infidelities were hers alone and, no matter how many times her friend pumped her for gossip, she kept her counsel. While she loved her uncle to distraction, he wasn't a particularly good husband and had neglected his fragile second wife abominably over the years. At times his tone towards Aunt Caro was overly antagonistic and bitter, and if he was in the mood to be ornery with her then it was uncomfortable to watch. Poor Caro, in turn, had sought comfort elsewhere over the years and, although Thea didn't condone it, she tried not to judge. Theirs was the unhappiest of marriages and a stark warning of what could happen if you settled for the wrong person.

Mr Hargreaves was one of several who might have warmed her aunt's bed on her frequent forays out. The pair shared far too many knowing looks when they assumed nobody was watching them. 'All he talks about are his superior connections—as if the fact he knows Lord and Lady So-and-So should impress me.'

'He's handsome though. If one has to be bound to a man for all eternity, it's best he is easy on the eye. I insisted upon that when I had to marry. Crudge, God rest him, was exceptionally easy on the eye and liked to ride. Such pursuits do wonders for a gentleman's buttocks. In my humble opinion, there is nothing better than a pert pair of cheeks encased in tight buckskin.' Her incorrigible older friend had a wicked glint in her eye. 'Did I ever tell you I seduced him first?'

'Repeatedly.' And in intriguing detail. Practically all of Thea's knowledge of procreation came from Harriet's detailed confessions.

'I was already falling in love with him, was certainly in *lust* with him, and saw no point in beating around the bush with a long and protracted courtship. Obviously, it all turned out for the best. We married in haste and got to enjoy seeing each other naked a great many more times than we would have done had we adhered to the fashion for protracted courtships.' She sighed again. 'And, by Jove, did that man look good naked… Mr Hargreaves has a pleasant posterior. Or at least I think he has. I haven't managed a thorough scrutiny yet to be completely sure, but I did catch a *hint* of a glimpse at last month's hunting party. Decent thighs—which usually are a good sign. They suggest a certain robustness. Although, in truth, I want more for you than him. I want you to have some adventure and excitement first. Your life is far too predictable and regimented for one so young. It's a crying shame… wait… Is that a dog barking?'

They both paused and listened. After a beat of total silence broken only by the chirping sounds of the morning chorus, a succession of rapid, high-pitched woofs could be heard coming from the trees.

'That doesn't sound good.'

'No, it doesn't.' The bushes beyond rustled violently and the dog barked again, setting her vivid imagination whirring with possibilities. 'Do you suppose the poor thing is in distress?'

Thea adored animals. The thought of one in pain was too awful to bear. More barking set her heart racing, but answered her question. With images of a poacher's trap and a grisly death in her mind, Thea picked up her skirts and broke into a run. Twice this last month her uncle's gamekeeper had found snares on the estate and evidence that someone was helping themselves to his pheasants. If the poor dog's paw was caught, it would panic and injure itself in its quest to free it.

Thea plunged into the trees, following the sound, then skidded to a halt at the top of the bank at the unexpected sight of an exceedingly pert pair of male buttocks.

Very nice and very naked male buttocks.

A pathetic squeak of shock popped out of her mouth before she covered it with her hands and the buttocks disappeared beneath the water a second before the owner of them turned around, his own hands covering the most important part of his modesty. Which was now quite submerged, but leaving little else to her imagination. Her eyes travelled upwards from those hands to the flat abdomen bisected by an arrow of intriguing dark hair which widened over a broad chest. Muscled shoulders. A gloriously strong set of biceps. Twinkling blue-grey eyes stared cockily right back at her, clearly amused and set in one of the most outrageously ruggedly handsome faces she had ever seen.

'Good morning, ladies.'

'Er...' For the first time in her life, Thea had no words at all. Her cheeks were glowing scarlet and it took all her strength to stop her eyes wandering back to where they had just feasted, making her blink and gape like a hooked fish. Because it was the right and proper thing to do, she immediately averted her badly behaved eyes and stared off into space, mortified.

'Good morning, sir,' said Harriet's voice over her shoulder, then she unsubtly nudged Thea with her elbow. 'I take back everything I said about buckskin, Thea. It is *vastly* overrated.' Shamelessly, her friend barged past—no doubt to get a closer look. Harriet would never avert her eyes. 'And who might you be?'

'Lord Graham Chadwick.' In her peripheral vision, the naked man executed a courtly bow with one hand still clutching his unmentionables, apparently completely comfortable and unrepentant in his nudity. 'But do call me Gray. I am new to the parish.'

'Ah, yes! You have recently rented Kirton House, have you not? Why—we are practically neighbours, my lord.' Typically, Harriet was not lost for words. Evidently, she felt the situation warranted small talk, no doubt to prolong the encounter for her own outrageous reasons. 'I am Lady Crudgington of Exley House and this is Miss Theodora Cranford, your new landlord's ward.'

'His *ward*?'

Hearing herself mentioned by the naked man himself, Thea guiltily looked up, heartily ashamed that her eyes had scandalously manoeuvred to his impressive chest again when she had been trying so hard to keep them properly latched elsewhere. After a valiant battle with the wayward, impetuous inner Thea, her eyeballs reluctantly flicked to his. The cocky smile was gone, replaced with an expression she couldn't quite fathom.

'The very one, although Thea has long passed the milestone of her majority, so is technically just his niece now.' Harriet shot her a loaded glance. 'Content to wither in her uncle's house until Cupid sends her a worthy knight in shining armour to finally whisk her away.'

Before her interfering friend began matchmaking in earnest, something she was prone to do at every available opportunity, Thea had to interrupt despite having no earthly clue what she should say. 'Mr Gray... I mean, Lord Graham... Er...'

Could this be any more mortifying?

'We heard a dog... I came to rescue it... I didn't mean to interrupt your... Um...' Gracious, now she was waffling like a ninny and her silly eyes were darting every which way possible. It probably looked as though she suffered from an uncontrollable facial tick. One which explained why no knight had thus far bothered saving her. Her face was so warm and doubtless so very red with guilt that one could toast crumpets on it if there happened to be some handy.

To save herself from further embarrassment and to give her naughty eyes something suitable to do, Thea rapidly turned her back and stared resolutely at the trees. 'Put some clothes on, sir! You are a disgrace. What do you think you are about, cavorting naked in my uncle's stream?'

Hopefully that let him know in no uncertain terms that she did not consider him shining-knight material and was horrified by his total lack of propriety rather than itching to stare unabashedly at his wet body. His shirt and breeches lay in a heap near her feet, so she snatched them up and without turning around wafted them in the general direction of her friend. 'Give him these! Immediately!'

She could hear him wading towards the bank and, if she turned her eyes slightly to the right, could see Harriet holding his shamelessly discarded garments in such a way that Lord Whatever-His-Name-Was would have to rise out of the water to reach them. She shot her friend a pointed look which was, of course, completely ignored.

'Tell me, my lord, how exactly did you come to be naked in Gislingham's brook? Are there no bath tubs in Kirton House?'

'I apologise wholeheartedly for shocking you, ladies.' She saw his big hand grab the proffered clothes, then heard the water move as he sunk back into it. 'But I blame my dog. He led me astray. Trefor is a *very* bad influence. It is entirely his fault you caught me cavorting.'

At that, something fast and as black as pitch emerged out of the foliage with an enormous stick in its mouth. He took one look at Thea and simultaneously dropped the stick and shook himself, sending a spray of muddy water all over her favourite green-sprigged muslin, before wagging his tail cheerfully.

Then he lunged.

Two big, wet paws hit her squarely on her belly and she lost her balance. Arms waving like a windmill in a gale, she struggled to stay upright. Instinctively she threw one foot behind to steady herself, only to realise too late that she was stood on an incline. Thea tumbled clumsily backwards, her feet lifting from the bank as gravity took over. To her utter horror, she landed with a huge splash in the water mere inches from the irritating naked man's groin.

Chapter Two

Judging from her furious expression after she emerged coughing and spluttering from the water, Gray shouldn't have laughed. Especially as she was, unbelievably, Gislingham's ward and he needed to make a good impression. But with Trefor already swimming in excited circles around her, her vibrant hair plastered over her face and her blush so ferocious she practically glowed, he couldn't help it. It had been a spectacular fall.

'Here… Let me help you up.'

She slapped away his proffered free hand. 'No, thank you! I know where *that* has been!' Outraged and delightfully flustered, she dragged herself to her feet, shooting daggers at her companion who was also snorting with barely contained laughter, as she tried and failed to climb up the slippery bank. 'Don't just stand there, Harriet! Do something!'

Keeping his *filthy* hands to himself and wondering exactly how he was supposed to fix this mess before Lord Fennimore had him lynched for his carelessness, Gray watched the older woman brace her legs and heave the fuming redhead out of the water. Despite his now-subdued mood, it was a wholly pleasant sight. Miss Cranford's soaked, thin summer dress was stuck to her shapely body like a second skin, moulding wonderfully to reveal a gorgeous peach of a bottom, and because she had to hoist her dripping skirts up to scramble up the incline, he saw a great deal of a very fine pair of legs from ankle to mid-thigh. He had always had a thing for bottoms and legs. Hers weren't covered in stockings, giving him a splendid view of her pale alabaster skin, which nicely filled in some of the blanks in his suddenly rampant imagination.

She would be wonderfully pale from top to bottom, and, like a Titian, that paleness would perfectly set off all her riotous hair. Although darker now that it was soaked, Gray remembered how it had popped and crackled in the sunlight when he first saw her, like the dying embers of a warm winter fire. Evidently, he now had a penchant for redheads as well as bottoms and legs. Who knew? It was these surprising, unforeseen revelations which made his meandering life interesting. That and the enormous potholes it consistently threw in his path.

He did a quick flick through his many happy memories, disappointingly sparse these last two years since ambition had come unexpectedly knocking, and came to the unfortunate conclusion he had never bedded a redhead before. Something he needed to remedy—but not yet. It was a crying shame he couldn't bed this one, because she was a tasty morsel if ever there was one, but Gislingham's ward wasn't his mission.

Gislingham was.

For the foreseeable future, Gray had to be on his very best behaviour. But he would store it in his mind for future reference and try to repair whatever damage he had done, making a mental note to seek out a suitably willing redhead as soon as he was able as a reward *if* he miraculously managed to save things.

While the ladies were occupied on the opposite bank, he swiftly pulled on his shirt then sank down in the water to wrestle on his breeches. Something much easier said than done. Only once he was semi-decent did he risk scaling the bank.

Miss Cranford was striding across the parkland by the time he had grabbed his boots, her fists clenched tightly at her sides and her lovely legs tearing up the ground, oblivious of the already besotted Trefor trotting along beside her. Gray didn't bother calling his hound back, instead he sprinted bare foot to catch up with Lady Crudgington, who was still grinning, intent on eating an enormous slice of humble pie.

'My sincerest and humblest apologies, ladies.

My lack of propriety was unforgivable.' Yet another thing for Lord Fennimore to justifiably rant about and one he couldn't blame on his dog. 'I feel dreadful.' Which was true, but for entirely different reasons. He blamed the spectre of ambition which had unwelcomely crept up on him and simply refused to go away no matter how much he tried to tell it that he was a wandering gypsy at heart. With every passing moment, that coveted promotion was slipping away, as all things he coveted tended to do if he wanted them too badly. And as per usual, it was all his fault. He really did need to work harder at being a better spy. Especially as his tendency to live in the moment had created this moment—one he would much prefer not to have happened at all.

'A bit of water never hurt anyone, my lord, and it was *very* funny.'

'Traitor!' Miss Cranford's head whipped around and she positively glared at her companion.

'Well, it *was* funny, Thea. You'd think so, too, if you weren't in a snit about your hair.' The older woman dropped her voice conspiratorially, while clearly intending for her delicious friend to hear. 'It takes for ever to tame the natural curl, poor thing, and she wants to look her best for Mr Hargreaves this afternoon.'

'I most certainly do not want to look my best for Mr Hargreaves!' Miss Cranford stopped so abruptly, Gray almost walked into the back of her.

The flecks of copper in her dark eyes matched her hair. They narrowed in accusation. 'Look at the state of me!' Noticing the two muddy paw prints on the front of her dress for the first time, she rubbed at the stain ineffectually. 'This will take hours to repair!'

'It would be my honour to buy you a new gown, Miss Cranford, to replace the one my dog has ruined.' On cue, Trefor nuzzled her thigh with his head and began to wag his tail so fast the whole of his gangly body shook, gazing up at her in canine adoration. Gray watched her eyes drop to the animal and soften and in that second found himself liking her a great deal. And his dog. She clearly had a weakness for the mutt, which might be the only hope he had. 'Trefor is very sorry, too, if it's any consolation. Look at his eyes.' Only the most hardened of individuals—or Lord Fennimore— could not be seduced by those sorrowful eyes.

Her hand dipped down to tickle the dog's ear. 'You're a good boy really—aren't you, Trefor? Just boisterous is all. I don't blame *you* for what happened in the slightest.' He heard the intended dig as she glared somewhat half-heartedly at him, and he did his best to look contrite. She was calming down and seemed in no hurry to stop petting the dog.

'Miss Cranford, I really do feel wretched. I should have behaved with more decorum. In my defence—although I am well aware what you witnessed was wholly indefensible—the park-land was quite deserted when I ventured into the stream. Trefor loves water, you see, and he especially loves it with me in it. Had I had any inkling that somebody would stumble across me so early I would never have sullied your delicate sensibilities with the sight of me *cavorting* in my birthday suit.' He felt his lips twitching again and bit down tightly on the bottom one to stop it. Good spies didn't ruin contrition with laughter. 'I can assure you it will never happen again.'

'Well, I for one enjoyed it immensely, my lord,' said Lady Crudgington with a wicked grin. 'Do feel free to cavort in my presence whenever you see fit.'

'Harriet is incorrigible.' A vibrantly blushing Miss Cranford was crouching down to tickle Trefor's suddenly skyward-facing tummy, rather than looking directly at him. He silently willed his dog to remain prostrate and adorable for as long as it took to earn her forgiveness.

'That I am, young man, and proudly so. I behaved myself for thirty years and *that* was quite long enough. I keep hoping a little of me will brush off on Thea, but alas, she is too buttoned up nowadays for her own good. She has become one for rules, Lord Gray, whereas I am one to break them. Which are you?'

Most definitely the second. Obeying rules for his first twenty years had ultimately left his life in tatters. 'I shall allow you to work that out for yourself, my lady. I couldn't possibly comment.'

'A kindred spirit! How marvellous, Lord Gray.' She whacked him with her elbow.

'His name is Lord Graham.'

'Which doesn't suit him at all. Gray is his preferred name and it matches his eyes, so he shall be Lord Gray to me now for evermore. It sounds so much more romantic than Graham. Do you have any objections to your new name?'

'Not at all. You may call me what you wish. I've never been particularly fond of it.' It reminded him too much of his unfortunate links to his father and brother.

'Splendid! Then it is decided. An exciting new name for an exciting new gentleman! It is just as well, for the society hereabouts is very staid, my lord. With the notable exception of my lovely young friend here and her charming uncle, I can barely tolerate most of them. However, I think I shall enjoy having you as a neighbour. I even approve of your dog.'

So did Miss Cranford, who had happily turned into Trefor's willing slave as she petted him, all the previous fraught tension in her delectable, damp body beginning to disappear in the thrall of his dog's spell. 'Is Trefor a mongrel? Only I've never seen a dog that looks anything like him.'

Gray stared in mock affront. 'Cover his ears! Don't let him hear that, Miss Cranford! He will feel inferior.' He bent over to scratch the shameless mutt's belly, enjoying the way her eyes shyly locked with his for a second before she hastily returned them to the dog. 'In actual fact, he is the result of two centuries' worth of careful breeding. He is a St John's. Rather aptly, bred to be a water dog to help the fishermen of that smelly port haul in their nets. They are excellent swimmers with the most amiable of temperaments. He's come all the way from Newfoundland.'

'Really?' It was obvious she was a dog-lover. She had barely taken her eyes off Trefor since he had cosied up against her.

'Indeed. Many moons ago, I was in the merchant navy.' Gray had run away to sea within days of the momentous scandal exploding and had happily stayed at sea while it blew over, the dust settled and society quite forgot about him. 'My ship was docked in that very harbour and one of the fishermen was offloading a litter of puppies, intent on drowning any he could not rehome that day. As Trefor was the runt of the litter, none of the other fishermen wanted him.'

'And you took him?' Her lovely eyes left his dog's belly and locked with his, impressed. It had the strangest effect, almost as if he was suddenly bathed in sunshine that he never wanted to leave.

'I couldn't let the poor fellow die.' The truth. Seeing Trefor's tiny puppy face buried in a wrinkly bundle of black, fluffy fur, Gray had been smitten from the outset. He'd been the runt and empathised.

'That is very noble of you, my lord.' The softness in her eyes which had been wholly and exclusively for his dog a few seconds before was now directed at him. Bizarrely, it made him feel taller. 'Why did you name him Trefor?'

'Because it reminded me of home.' Good grief—more truth and one he had never shared. Gray blamed the hypnotic copper flecks in her eyes. Eyes that were coincidentally exactly the same shade as his dog's—minus the alluring copper, of course. 'I grew up in Wales. As a child I played on Trefor Beach.' With Cecily. Always with Cecily. The girl who had lived next door. The deceitful, conniving love of his life who had brought about his youthful downfall. 'I adored it.' As he had adored her until she had shredded his heart and stomped all over the remains.

Cecily's treachery aside, life had certainly been simpler then. Back when he was able to avoid his father because his mother kept Gray out of sight. The beach had been his mama's favourite place and she had been his absolute favourite person. Certainly the only member of his immediate family who hadn't found him wanting. 'I haven't been back there for years.' Not since his mother had passed, in fact, and had left him feeling like a cuckoo in a nest with only his overbearing father and equally staid and pompous elder brother for company, regularly disappointing the both of them simply by breathing.

That was when everything in his life had started going downhill—but at least he'd still had Cecily. Still clung to her and all they would have one day, biting his tongue and trying to please his father. An endeavour which had been ultimately pointless in the grand scheme of things, when Gray had never wanted to join the army or the church as good second sons were supposed to do. From his earliest memories, all he had ever wanted to do was raise horses. As a child he had lived in the stables. He'd loved animals. Had a way with them.

He found himself frowning at the buried memory, wondering why it had chosen today of all days to pop into his mind. Routinely, he avoided the past as a point of principle. It couldn't be changed, so why ponder it? Especially when the moment always held more promise. Or disaster. That wish for a farm filled with the finest horses he could breed was nothing more than all those carefully laid plans had been. A disappointing mirage of a future fate had never intended for him. One he would have loved if things had been different and a fine example of why he preferred now never to look too far ahead or too far behind. He had mourned the loss of that dream almost as much as he had Cecily.

Yet there was something about Suffolk which

reminded him of home. Ridiculous, really, when home was more than two hundred miles away and nothing in the universe could ever tempt him to return there. He ruthlessly pushed the memories away, knowing the unwelcome spectre of his past would not help salvage this mission. 'Please allow me to compensate you for the dress. It is the very least I can do.'

'It's only a bit of mud. Nothing that won't come out in the wash. I have plenty of other dresses to wear this afternoon.'

'For Mr Hargreaves?' A faceless man Gray suddenly, and irrationally, disliked.

She smiled and his breath caught. She was pretty beforehand, in a classic English rose sort of way, but that smile did something miraculous to her features. It turned pretty into beautiful. Achingly, uniquely beautiful. 'For my aunt's tea party this afternoon.'

'She has invited half the county,' said Lady Crudgington with mock solemnity, 'which in Thea's world means less than twenty. Aside from being staid, the local society is also distressingly small. The tea will be nought but a hot, claustrophobic room full of dullards. Unbelievably tiresome.' Lady Crudgington wound her arm through his, her eyes twinkling with mischief. 'You should come, too, young man. Introduce yourself. Meet your other neighbours and see first-hand how dire they all are, while keeping me entertained with your scandalous maritime stories. Shouldn't he, Thea? I shall happily vouch for his *credentials*.'

Her hair was an unmitigated disaster. So horrendous it had made its way on to her unwritten list of her Worst Hairstyles of All Time. Not quite as bad as the epically awful Fuzzy Chignon of Eighteen Nineteen, when the combination of cold winter rain and Colonel Purbeck's stuffy drawing room had created a gargantuan tangle of fleece-like spirals that had soared towards the ceiling—but dangerously close. Thea had caught Mr Hargreaves staring, perplexed, at the top of her head three times in quick succession as he sipped his tea, as if he couldn't quite believe what he was seeing either. Hair shouldn't be vertical. Especially when it had enough pins in it to secure an elephant to the ground.

She resisted the urge to excuse herself to circulate among the other guests, knowing at best it was a flimsy excuse to wander past the mantel mirror and witness the mounting disaster for herself, as she had several times already. With every passing minute her wayward hair became even more wayward and the sight of it would only depress her. If she couldn't fully tame her hair, how was she ever going to tame the streak of wayward selfishness that ran straight through her? The older she got, the harder it was becoming to behave when the urge hit and Impetuous Thea bubbled back to the surface.

She glanced at the door for the umpteenth time instead and tried to tell herself she was relieved that their new neighbour was not going to make an appearance. Another flimsy lie when she had spent most of the morning, all of luncheon and the entirety of Mr Hargreaves' conversation thus far thinking about the way Lord Gray's bronzed skin and intriguing muscles had looked, slicked with water.

Thea had never seen anything quite like it. Even as he had insisted on accompanying them to the boundary of the garden, the thin, wet shirt had been practically and gloriously translucent as he had chatted amiably about his dog and the navy and his utter wretchedness at what he had inadvertently done. When her eyes had begun guiltily wandering to his chest again, she had hung back to play with Trefor and been subjected to the equally enthralling sight of the damp linen clinging to his broad shoulders and back. Like her wayward hair, the wayward part of her character then refused to catch up, so it could feast on the sight for the rest of the way home—and feast it had. Thea was heartily ashamed of herself. Proper young ladies shouldn't be ogling disgraceful scoundrels. Or worrying about the state of their hair for them either.

It would almost be a relief to see the man fully

clothed. But then again, another part of her—the prim, proper, sensible part—never wanted to see him again, in the hope the memory of his body would quickly fade and her silly, flustered pulse would beat again at normal speed. Merely thinking about it all made her cheeks hot.

'Can I fetch you some more tea, Mr Hargreaves?' Which she would collect by way of the retiring room and dab mercilessly at those same cheeks with a cold flannel until they became decent.

'You are most kind, Miss Cranford.'

As she took the saucer from him, she felt his fingers purposely brush against the back of her hand in an obviously flirtatious manner and immediately gritted her teeth. There was something about Mr Hargreaves and his blatant, ardent pursuit of her when her aunt wasn't looking that raised her hackles, but ingrained politeness made it difficult to call him out on it in a room full of guests. Instead, Impetuous Thea broke free for a moment and she pretended to catch her slipper on her skirt. With more force than was necessary, she sent the cup flying, spilling the last dregs of the tea deliberately in his lap. 'Oh, I am so sorry!' She grabbed his napkin and passed it to him, enjoying the way the lukewarm stain quickly seeped into the pale kerseymere fabric. 'Will you have to go home to change?' She certainly hoped so.

'Not at all, Miss Cranford. It is just a drip.'

As was he.

No matter how many times he pressed the match, Thea could not imagine an eternity shackled to him. A lifetime of spinsterhood would be more appealing—not that she was resigned to the shelf just yet. At three and twenty, she wouldn't make a fresh-faced bride, but neither would she be a matron. As Aunt Caro frequently reassured her, there was still plenty of time to find the right sort of husband. Preferably one who regarded *her* with a heated look in his eyes, rather than her aunt, and wasn't solely after her money.

He would be respectable and trustworthy, not a scoundrel. Noble in both thought and deed, and—and this part was not negotiable—in possession of enough of his own fortune that hers merely complemented it rather than supplemented it entirely. He didn't need to be handsome and wear his breeches well. Both would be nice, of course, but they were in no way essential. Thea wasn't Harriet, after all. No indeed. She enjoyed stability and discipline nowadays far more than the pleasing aesthetics of a broad pair of shoulders. Once bitten, twice shy, and all that. Since the soldier, she had vowed to be sensible and suppress the impetuous, wayward part of her nature that acted on impulse and got her into trouble. Because that same day, while being taken for a fool, she had also learned the hardest of lessons. Her selfish pursuit of forbidden fruit had consequences.

Dire ones.

After she had self-righteously stomped out of the house to dally with that soldier, the worst had happened and her poor uncle had paid the price. Just as her father had all those years previously when he had slammed out of the house, justifiably at his wits' end with his precocious daughter, and had failed to come home alive. Common sense told her it was an unfortunate coincidence. That fate wasn't punishing her for two isolated and immature outbursts, done in the heat of the moment many years apart, but she secretly carried the burden of guilt regardless. And while her rational, sensible brain often dismissed her fear as silly, superstitious nonsense, the similarities were too eerie to be coincidence. Two momentous temper tantrums brought about by her own selfish desire to do something quite contrary to the will of others and the two people closest to her heart had unfairly paid the price.

Since then, Impetuous Thea had been locked in a box just in case she was tempted by forbidden fruit again and was only rarely, and cautiously, given an airing when the situation warranted—and never to satisfy one of her own selfish whims.

It had proved to be a constant battle between her rebellious character and her stubborn will, but for the most part she kept a tight lid on the destructive elements of her personality. Since then, her world had been calmer. A trifle repetitive and safe, perhaps, but she was content. She had Harriet and her uncle. Aunt Caro and Bertie. She rode Archimedes. She visited the village and her neighbours. Occasionally allowed Harriet to drag her out to shop. Her world might be small, but she read voraciously, losing herself in exciting romances and adventures in the absence of any of her own. All worthwhile and proper pursuits for a gently bred young lady.

Heavens, even to her own ears she sounded dull. Three and twenty wasn't old yet, although frequently she felt positively middle-aged. An older, staider, duller version of Harriet who had half as much fun. Nothing dreadful had happened for years despite Impetuous Thea's constant escapes. She had argued with her uncle at least three times since that night and he was still as robust and full of life as he always was. Of course, without proper supervision, Impetuous Thea would have probably argued with him a thousand times in the last three years if she hadn't practically chewed through her lip to stop the words coming and then silently seethed in her bedchamber for hours until she was calm again. Maybe it was all that suppressed emotion that was making her feel so unfulfilled?

Or maybe it was her increasing habit of dissatisfied introspection because there were simply too many hours in the day to fill with the proper pursuits she allowed herself. No wonder the disgraceful Lord Gray's buttocks were taking up so much space in her thoughts. The sight of them had been the highlight of her year!

With an irritated sigh she wandered to the sideboard, conveniently located next to the door and blissful escape, and picked up the teapot. A maid could deliver the beverage back to Mr Hargreaves while Thea avoided him and his wandering hands for the rest of the afternoon.

Horrid man! While she was not averse to a suitor some day, and Lord only knew decent men were thin on the ground in this sleepy corner of Suffolk, she didn't want one who fitted none of her sensible criteria or who made alarm bells clang in her mind.

Mr Hargreaves had a paltry annual allowance and a decidedly dubious past. He also shared heated looks with her aunt. Three very sound reasons to cross him off her list. The flesh-crawling bit made four, although that was more of a feeling than fact so hadn't thus far made the list at all. Henceforth, it would be added. There had to be some attraction, or at least the potential for some eventually. As Harriet said, if one had to be bound to a man for all eternity, it was best he be easy on the eye.

Perhaps Harriet was right and she did need more excitement in her life before she settled down with the sensible, independently wealthy husband she would spend eternity with. Then perhaps her life wouldn't feel so dull even if her choice of husband did. Each day did tend to feel exactly like the previous, blurring and merging into one homogenous infinity of sameness.

Infinity of sameness! Now she was in danger of becoming pretentious to counteract the dullness. Could one be a pretentious dullard? Mr Hargreaves certainly was...

'Hello again, Miss Cranford.'

At the sound of his deep voice so close to her neck, Thea jumped and poured half of Mr Hargreaves's tea over the sideboard. 'Mr Gray... Er... my lord. I'm so sorry, you startled me.' And despite the fine suit of clothes he wore with impressive aplomb, her errant mind had immediately stripped him of them. She knew exactly how impressive those shoulders were beneath that jacket, and she had seen his bottom. Valiantly, she willed her cheeks not to combust, yet they heated regardless just to spite her.

'I'm an informal fellow—as you have unfortunately seen. Gray will do just fine.' He was smiling. Amused. Little crinkles fanned out around his silvery blue eyes. Eyes which were almost wolf-like in their colour.

'Gray suits you.' Heavens—she had said that out loud. How frightfully impulsive and bold. Clearly, after her perfectly acceptable run-in with Mr Hargreaves, Impetuous Thea was not safely locked back in her box. She forced her gaze to shift from his hypnotic stare and came face to face with another man. Significantly older. Salt-and-pepper hair and a scowl that could curdle milk.

'Allow me to introduce you to my second cousin Cedric.' Gray grinned as the older man bristled. 'He *is* a very formal man and prefers to be called Lord Fennimore at all times. Even by family.'

Chapter Three

The rampant disapproval at the use of his Christian name was coming off Lord Fennimore in waves, but Gray was unrepentant. The old man had insisted on accompanying him on this mission because Gray was apparently new to his precious King's Elite. Two loyal and highly eventful, successful years chasing criminals wasn't new in Gray's book, but his commanding officer was a stick-in-the-mud who took for ever to impress. With Flint guarding his new bride and their key informant in their investigation in the wilds of Scotland somewhere, Warriner and Hadleigh minding the fort in London and Lord and Lady Millcroft on a similar mission in Norfolk, Lord Fennimore had reluctantly drafted Gray into front-line duty to prove his mettle, dangling the carrot of the yet undiscussed promotion temptingly in front of his face.

'Let's see how you do, young man, and then perhaps we shall talk.'

Hardly a blood-sworn promise, but the best anyone could hope for from the wily, manipulating, tenacious commander of the King's Elite.

But it was that tenacity which had served them well. Espionage was a long and patient game. After two years of covert, dangerous investigations and far too many deaths, the King's Elite had severely weakened the dangerous smuggling ring. Thanks to the new Baroness of Penmor, the French ringleader was dead, and his co-conspirators scattered in chaos. There was no longer a chance of them restoring Napoleon to power any time soon. However, despite having the names of the high-ranking British traitors who had sold the contraband on the black market, they still had no clue about the identity of The Boss—the elusive, faceless mastermind who had run the English side of the vast operation. So vast it had threatened the British economy as well as its security. The government wanted the traitors rounded up and tried as soon as possible, but without tangible proof of their guilt, all the evidence they had hinged on the testimony of one woman.

Or, in legal terms, and without further proof, hearsay.

They quickly realised they needed more than the word of just one witness if they were to make the charges stick. The Boss had no interest in Napoleon, or laws, or lives. He only cared about profit. Under Lord Fennimore's guidance the King's Elite had allowed the dust to settle, watched and waited. A man like The Boss would be ruthless in repairing all they had destroyed and they didn't have to wait very long for the smugglers, suppliers and greedy distributors to begin to piece together some of the tattered remnants of the operation.

Already, more illegal brandy was trickling back on to British shores and, because they had been allowed to do so unhindered, the smugglers were becoming bolder.

The Boss didn't know they knew. Nor did he know the net was closing in and they intended to catch him red-handed. The Boss also did not know they had narrowed down his true identity to one of two men. He was either the Earl of Winterton in Norfolk or Gray's target—and the delicious redhead's guardian—Viscount Gislingham. Whoever he was, he would soon be rotting in the Tower, awaiting his execution. And Gray knew he spoke for all his comrades—both living and recently dead—that that day couldn't come soon enough. Too much blood had been spilled already.

'I hope you don't mind, Miss Cranford, but I thought it made sense to use your invitation to introduce the both of us to our new neighbours. Hopefully I shall make a better first impression on them than I did on you.' Fennimore had practically spat feathers when Gray had confessed to being caught in the altogether by Gislingham's niece. He had yet to appraise him of Trefor's hand in practically drowning her. 'Once again, allow me to offer my sincerest apologies.'

There were two pretty, pink circles on her cheeks at the reminder, but she held his gaze politely. 'None are needed. Let us draw a veil over it.'

She blinked rapidly, luring his eyes to her ridiculously long, brown-tipped lashes before her hand fleetingly went to her riotous copper curls. She had beautiful hair. Unusual, but invitingly tactile. The obviously natural ringlets were not uniform. Tight spirals and loose curls wove together, begging to be touched and properly examined. If he pulled one, for instance, how much longer would it be? Double? Triple? Perhaps quadruple the length? In sunlight it crackled like fire. Wet, it deepened to auburn. Here in this bright drawing room it was vibrant, but the lack of direct light brought out the other tones. Bronze. Gold. The merest hint of chestnut. What would the pale moonlight do to it? He was staring at her head and she saw it. A little wrinkle of annoyance appeared between her russet brows, no doubt at his impertinence, before she quashed it.

'Would you like me to introduce you to my uncle and aunt?' Of their own accord, his eyes had now dropped to her lips. They were very kissable indeed. Soft, plump, a deeper shade of pink than the blush that stained her porcelain cheeks. Why couldn't he stop gazing at her when he knew he needed to focus on being a better spy?

'We would like that very much indeed, Miss Cranford.' Lord Fennimore shot him a withering glance and inclined his head, giving away no indication as to exactly how much the pair of them were looking forward to meeting their potential nemesis. 'You are most generous in forgiving my *idiot* cousin. Rest assured we have had words about the incident.' His superior had said all the words, mostly in a very loud, agitated voice which had sent poor Trefor into hiding for hours. Unfortunately, they were all justified.

Lord Fennimore held out his arm and Miss Cranford took it, and for some inexplicable reason Gray felt a pang of jealousy. 'Please lead the way.'

He suppressed the errant emotion and focused on the job in hand. At his best guess, there were twenty or so people in the room, all regarding them with interest. The fact they did nothing to disguise it was refreshing. In town, showing interest was one of the Seven Deadly Sins and everybody schooled their features to look bored. Provincial society was very different and one Gray was surprised to find himself comfortable within. Once upon a time he had loathed it, couldn't wait to leave it and headed to the capital as soon as he was able. But it was actually rather nice to see what people were thinking for once. It made him oddly homesick.

Holding court on the striped damask sofa was an attractive woman of middle years wearing a fashionable day gown which must have cost more than a month's worth of his salary. French lace and silk. You couldn't spend your days catching smugglers and not recognise some of the spoils. She turned her head towards him, then smiled, her gaze flicking briefly to his reluctant new distant cousin, then sliding back to his. 'Strangers? How exciting, Thea.'

'Lord Fennimore. Lord Gray. This is my Aunt Caroline, Viscountess Gislingham. Aunt—these are our new neighbours, who have recently taken residence at Kirton House.'

As introductions went, it was very proper, yet he was convinced he detected some censure in her tone beneath all the politeness one would expect from a well brought-up young lady. A quick glance to his right and Miss Cranford's features were quite bland as Lord Fennimore stepped forward to take the Viscountess's hand.

'It is a pleasure to make your acquaintance, my lady. I hope you do not mind our unannounced arrival. We were keen to meet you all.' He was almost as keen to meet the wife of The Boss as the man himself. Wives were rarely innocent, in his experience.

'It is always a delight to make new friends, my lord.' The Viscountess's eyes slowly panned to Gray's again and held, making him wonder if she was saying more than hello.

As the old man stepped back, Gray stepped forward and bowed. 'You have a beautiful home, my lady.'

Her gloveless fingers grasped his. Squeezed softly. 'Thank you. One you are *always* welcome in.' A definite invitation. Unexpected, but interesting. Something which might come in useful for the mission. He felt the back of his neck prickle and was instantly suffused with guilt—even more unexpected, but there regardless. As he stepped back he tilted his head to investigate the source, despite already knowing in his bones it was she. Miss Cranford's face was still bland, but her eyes were not. They were disappointed. Was she disappointed in her aunt or him? Ridiculously, he hoped it was the former.

'I shall let Thea take you on the rounds to meet everyone and then you must come directly back to me.' The Viscountess smiled at Lord Fennimore. That smile morphed into something entirely different by the time it reached Gray. She glanced up at him through her lashes, then the tone of her voice dipped ever so slightly as she lingered over the vowels. 'I *absolutely* insist.'

It was a subtle invitation, purposefully ambiguous, yet to him—a man of the world who knew how the game was played—he was now left in no doubt. The Viscountess wanted to play. Something which should have excited him, because it gave the King's Elite a way into the Viscount's circle, but instead he found it distasteful because Lady Caroline was not her niece. More evidence of his lack of focus, no doubt, and time to be that better spy.

For the next few minutes, while his nostrils twitched at the alluring perfume Miss Cranford wore, they were introduced to the gentleman who seemed to hang on their hostess's every word. The local solicitor, Mr Partridge. The second son of the Marquess of Allerton. A local landowner who dabbled in stocks. They were soon joined by the very Mr Hargreaves that Miss Cranford had apparently worried about her hair for earlier, although it took all of three seconds for Gray to work out the cut of his jib. All were much the same age as he was. Good-looking and knew it. All were cloyingly sycophantic and clearly all had enjoyed the Viscountess Gislingham's exclusive *company* at least once, if he was any judge.

'Follow me, gentlemen.' Miss Cranford's voice held a hint of snippiness as she brusquely turned, that sultry perfume wafting like a siren's call to tempt him, and glided in the direction of a particular group of ladies, three of whom happened to be the wives of the men he suspected were the other woman's lovers. Was that deliberate? If it was, was the point directed at him or her aunt? And why did he have the overwhelming urge to tell her she didn't need to worry about him because he wasn't attracted to her aunt in the slightest? Gray had to bite down on his lip to stop the words coming out, knowing they would be a lie. If he had to seduce the Viscountess for King and country, then he would. Regardless of the beautiful redhead's disapproval and his peculiar, misplaced guilt.

What the blazes was the matter with him? He had waited two years for the chance to head up an important mission—he wouldn't let his uncharacteristic reaction to a hitherto unknown woman stand in the way. It was probably the responsibility and the heat. Despite the lighter coat, he could still feel the back of his shirt sticking to him. Nerves and the hot July sun would do that to a man.

Thea found Harriet on the terrace soaking up the sun. Because the whole world believed a woman's skin should be pale to be beautiful, her friend was determined to fly in the face of convention and was lounging with her head tilted back to capture every ray. Typically, like her rebellious streak, the healthy tan suited her. Thea wandered to the bench and plopped her bottom on to it, irritated. 'You left me with Colonel Purbeck.'

'Of course I did. The man spits when he talks.'

'A true friend would have promptly rescued me.'

'Ah…but I could see that Mr Hargreaves was

eager to talk to you, so I knew you would be all right.' Harriet cracked open one eye and then shuffled to sit upright when she saw Thea's miserable expression. 'I was only teasing about Mr Hargreaves. Aside from the breeches and his face, he has little else to recommend him.'

'I know.'

'What's wrong?'

'Nothing.' She huffed out a sigh. Watching Lord Gray flirt with her aunt had left a sour taste in her mouth. Not that she was interested in him. If one ignored the fine face and impressive body, the man had too much of a mischievous glint in his unusual eyes for her to consider him as anything more than a pleasant conversation partner. Not that they had had a pleasant conversation. Thea had introduced him to everyone bar her uncle, who had slipped away for a nap, and then had delivered him eagerly back to Caro all in the space of ten minutes. Without all those tiresome introductions and her irritation at her aunt's blatant interest in their new visitor, the errant yet persistent memory of him *sans* clothes made it difficult to think of anything remotely interesting or even banal to say and he seemed to have no desire to fill the void.

He had immediately come to life in front of her vivacious aunt, though, as soon as she had delivered him back. He had practically bent over backwards to charm her. Not that Thea coveted that sort of charming or approved of anyone who fell for the flirty façade her uncle's slightly self-absorbed and highly strung wife presented to the world.

Still, being so blatantly overlooked rankled when she was obviously younger and single. And deep down she was thoroughly disappointed that the handsome new stranger no longer passed muster.

'Do you think I've become dùll?'

'I despise dull people. We couldn't be friends if you were the least bit dull.' Harriet's eyes dipped to where her hands fiddled idly with the fabric of her skirt. A sure sign she was tempering her response.

'I sense a but…'

'But you *are* a little too buttoned up nowadays, truth be told. Subdued. Too concerned with etiquette and behaviour and being proper and doing right by your uncle.'

'Ladies are meant to behave with decorum.' The impetuous part of her felt trapped by those rules, while the greater part feared what would happen without those boundaries. 'Unlike you, I do not have the luxury of abandoning my good reputation. I still have to find a husband.' Not that she had really been looking. All her suitors thus far had failed to exceed her low expectations and all were fixated on the money she came with. It had made her jaded. Understandably so.

'I wasn't suggesting you become a scandal, Thea. Merely that you let your hair down once in a while. You used to be so bold and spontaneous—I wish you'd let all those scintillating aspects of your character shine again rather than tempering them. You would have such fun! I want you to have some excitement in your life before you settle down—if you ever deign to allow a gentleman to get past your iron-clad defences, of course. Believe me, the years fly past so quickly and I would hate for you to regret your wasted youth. It worries me that you rarely leave your uncle's grounds unless I drag you.'

'You know that Uncle Edward is unwell.' And her aunt abandoned the house for days on end *visiting friends* or *shopping*. Polite excuses for not wanting to be in her husband's hostile or uninterested company. Their marriage had been strained before his illness and, despite her aunt's utter despair at the thought of losing her husband in those grim days after his collapse, it was practically non-existent after. Both were always happier when at least ten miles of road separated them.

'I also know dear Edward is as desperate to see you happy as I am. He's repeatedly offered you a Season and I have repeatedly offered to be your chaperon in London—yet soon you will celebrate your twenty-fourth birthday and you haven't set one foot out of Suffolk in for ever. I can barely get to you attend even the local assembly any more. What are you afraid of?'

She wasn't afraid. Not exactly. Reluctant, more like. When one had the amount of money in the bank that she had, the vultures tended to circle. At least here, close to home, she knew all of them, had repelled most of them and didn't have to waste valuable time trying to identify them as vultures in the first place. London was the great unknown, stuffed to the rafters with wholly unsuitable men who had no scruples and who would move heaven and earth to get their hands on her fortune. Winnowing out the wheat from the chaff did not appeal. Especially when Impetuous Thea had such poor taste in men.

'I need to be close in case something happens.' That was at least a reasonable excuse. With a sham for a marriage, no children and a largely absentee wife, Uncle Edward was alone. If Thea wasn't there, then he would have nobody but his manservant, Bertie, to keep him company from one week to the next. She couldn't allow him to live like that. Not when he had taken her in after she had been orphaned, loved her unconditionally and been both mother and father to her for over half of her life.

So much so, he had transferred the bulk of his unentailed fortune to her while she had still been a child. Tens of thousands of pounds, cannily invested, continually multiplying and held in trust until she had reached her majority. He still managed her fortune for her and every year it grew bigger still, ever multiplying like the venomous heads of the mythical Hydra and twice as frightening. Not that she would admit such a thing to anyone, least of all her beloved uncle. He had gifted her a lifetime of financial independence and had never asked for anything in return. It seemed horribly ungrateful to loathe the generous gift he had saddled her with.

'Very noble—but exactly how many more years are you prepared to wait for the worst to happen? It has already been three.' Which coincidentally was the last time she and her uncle had really argued, when Thea had defied him to sneak out of the house past midnight to kiss the handsome officer who she had met at the assembly rooms the week before. With hindsight her uncle had been entirely correct in his censure. The man had been too old, too worldly and wholly focused on her fortune. He was taking flagrant advantage of her youth, her rebellious nature and her inexperience to further his own ends.

Unfortunately, at the time she had been too outraged at being forbidden to see him and too wilful to accept the edict. While Impetuous Thea was out, the worst had happened. If Bertie hadn't been there to save him, her uncle would now be as dead as her father.

'Edward's condition has neither deteriorated

nor improved. You need to face facts, Thea. While you sit around waiting, being the overly dutiful niece and the devoted daughter Edward never had, your own life is passing you by. Mr Hargreaves notwithstanding, you could be married already, living close by and still being the dutiful niece who visits daily, yet you have thwarted every potential suitor who has shown an interest.'

'None of them was suitable. They all just wanted my money.' She didn't want to end up shackled to a vulture. 'With great wealth comes great responsibility. I have to be sure I entrust it to someone worthy.'

'Or perhaps your exacting standards are too high on purpose? You are the most suspicious person I know.'

That stung. 'I'm an heiress! I have to be suspicious! Every fortune hunter, ne'er-do-well and chancer who ventures into Suffolk automatically seeks me out and plights his troth, keen to get his greedy hands on all that money. I have to be cautious.'

'Cautious, yes. Not overcautious and determined to denounce them all as villains. Lord Selwyn, for instance, didn't turn out to be a swindler as you suspected.'

'But he *was* a fortune hunter.'

'And Mr Taylor, the young widower, was in fact a widower and not a bigamist either.'

Thea threw her hands up in the air in exasperation. 'Yet he was in debt up to his eyeballs and hopelessly in love with my fortune, too.'

'Yes, granted, both saw the money before you, but Captain Fairway had his own fortune.'

'And three illegitimate children by two separate mistresses. I knew he was a philanderer!'

'There is always something wrong with them—fortune hunter, philanderer, scoundrel...what was the name of the chap you thought was a highwayman?'

'Chisholm Hunter? I'm still not entirely convinced that he wasn't. There was something very shifty about that man.'

Harriet glanced heavenwards and briefly closed her eyes before continuing in an uncharacteristically measured tone. 'Your overly suspicious nature has given you an imagination as vivid as your hair, darling. In the absence of any real reasons to discount them you now have a tendency to make things up.'

'You think I should have settled? For a man I have no faith in nor any true affection for? Leap first into marriage without any forethought or rigorous contemplation? Like my uncle did with Aunt Caro? Look how miserable that hasty decision has made them! Might I remind you, you also found fault with all those gentlemen, too, as I recall.'

Harriet rolled her eyes again. 'Only because you continually hammered home their faults and

I am a good friend and want to please you. However, while you continue to repel each and every gentleman who glances your way, the clock is ticking. In two more years you'll be well on the way to being considered an old maid. And I don't want you to leap into marriage. I want you to risk the leap of faith. It's the most splendid feeling in the world, darling. You stand on the precipice, not ever truly knowing what is the right course of action, but you take that chance. You abandon your fears and leap.' She sighed romantically. 'I adore leaping. It's the ultimate *grand gesture*. The test of true love is the grand gesture.'

'So I should abandon all hope of finding a decent, upstanding, *genuine* man to love, and simply settle?'

'Leaping isn't settling, darling. It's throwing caution to the wind and trusting your instincts and laying yourself bare in front of another in the hope they feel the same. But if you are seeking absolute perfection inside and out before you dare to jump, which I am coming to suspect you are, then you are doomed. It doesn't exist. Nor should you use your aunt and uncle's marriage as the benchmark to justify your exacting standards—or your fortune as a barricade to hide behind. Your uncle would never have given it to you if he'd had any inkling you would use it to shut yourself off. He despairs of your stand-offishness as much as I do.

'Every human has flaws, but unless you allow

yourself to properly get to know a gentleman, warts and all…and he, you…and cease being instantly suspicious or stand-offish, you will never come to know if they are minor flaws you can live with or major ones which will make you want to grind their face under your heel when they dare to say good morning. If you want to fall in love and be loved in return, then you have to give it a fighting chance to blossom. Nothing blooms in the desert. You have to take that gloriously abandoned leap of faith. Your greatest flaw is that you dismiss people out of hand instantly.'

'I do not.' Surely she wasn't that pernickety? 'I judge every man on his merit and give them all adequate time to show it. A little cautious suspicion gives them the opportunity to prove their mettle.'

'Adequate time to prove their mettle? Really? Then I assume you are prepared to give our new neighbour a proper chance? Youngish. Handsome. Solicitous and *local*. His appearance is very fortuitous, seeing as you have given up all hope of any of the other bachelors in the county meeting your high expectations. Perhaps he is the *one*? He seems…' Harriet grinned '…quite lovely.'

It was Thea's turn to roll her eyes. 'And typically, you judge a book solely by its cover.'

'Not at all! While I'll grant you he has a splendid cover, he was most pleasant after we caught him so magnificently naked—and his dog clearly adores him. We humans could learn a lot from dogs. Animals are rarely wrong.'

'He's a shameless flirt.'

'I didn't see him flirt.'

'Well, I can assure you, he was certainly shamelessly flirting with Aunt Caro a few moments ago.' Something which bothered her, despite her infinitely better judgement and professed lack of interest.

'He's here?'

'Indeed he is. With his frowning cousin in tow.'

Harriet was up like a shot. 'How positively splendid! Let's hunt him down and monopolise him. I'll dutifully extol your virtues like a good friend and you can probe with pertinent questions which matter to you. Start to get to know him... Why, we don't even know if he is married or betrothed! And a young man who voluntarily lives with an older relative would naturally be more sympathetic to your dutiful attachment to *your* uncle. How serendipitous is that? The fates appear to be miraculously aligned for once.'

This needed to be nipped in the bud. Especially as Harriet was beginning to sound reasonable. 'No, thank you. He doesn't interest me in the slightest. Nor I him. He made no effort to impress me, yet every effort to charm my aunt.' A lie; he had tried then lapsed into silence after she had been stand-offish because Impetuous Thea *had* been interested. 'I'm afraid I have his measure already—and he comes up woefully short. If I'm being brutally frank, I'm not even sure I like him.' Although she had, before she reminded herself of all the reasons why she couldn't entertain it. She still had a penchant for parts of him.

'Are you sure?'

'Until you mentioned him, I had forgotten he existed.' She held Harriet's gaze, determinedly ignoring the image of Lord Gray's pert, bare buttocks and broad, bare back which had apparently seared itself on to her mind.

'Hmm…' Harriet looked sceptical, then shrugged. 'Only I cannot recall a time when I have ever heard you sound so waspish over a mere man after such a *short* acquaintance.'

'That's because it's his fault my hair looks like this!' Thea petulantly pointed at her head, but she was already talking to her friend's retreating back. 'It might have been a short acquaintance, but it was certainly eventful. Cavorting in the brook in his birthday suit *was* disgraceful!' And thrilling. It *had* been quite the highlight of her dull year. Drat it all to hell.

'All I ask is that you give the fellow a fighting chance, Thea! This might be exactly what the doctor ordered!' Harriet stopped, spun and inhaled deeply. 'I can positively smell the romance in the air.' Then she was off again, striding with such purpose there was no point attempting to reason with her. There was nothing Harriet loved more than meddling. Especially in what she considered was for a person's own good. As a mark of protest, sensible Restrained Thea remained exactly where she was and would remain so for the foreseeable future despite the baking sun.

Chapter Four

Gray spent the better part of an hour with the Viscountess, being a very good spy, and learned nothing new whatsoever. She was amiable, if a little self-absorbed, her conversation mostly a ploy to receive a compliment. It was obvious she lived a small and inconsequential life. There was a brittleness about her, a need to be adored, which was quite sad for a woman her age and said a great deal about the state of her marriage. Gislingham himself had yet to make an appearance and his wife didn't seem to know or care if he was likely to. Clearly, they lived completely separate lives, which meant she was unlikely to know anything significant about her husband's nefarious business dealings. With Lord Fennimore the unwilling captive of the droning Colonel Purbeck and the deliciously smelling Miss Cranford mysteriously missing from the gathering, he found himself eager to move on as he extricated himself from the sofa.

If nothing else, he could have a little snoop around. This rose-covered mansion in the heart of the countryside, a good forty miles from the coast, didn't appear to be the likely lair of England's most wanted smuggler. Nor did the aged servants seem to be his criminal accomplices—but appearances could be deceptive. Look at Lord Fennimore. To all intents and purposes the world thought him a crusty old peer. One who turned up diligently at Parliament to vote and was a reliably reluctant guest at society events—yet for over twenty years had managed to hide the fact he ran the King's Elite. Not that anyone in society circles or outside of it would know about that organisation either. Therefore, where better to hide than here? Who would suspect a respected country squire of high treason? In another life, he certainly wouldn't.

Of course, in that other life he had no ambition either, other than to embrace whatever whims or pathways he took a fancy to and that had crept up on him unannounced. One minute he had been at a loose end on the cusp of leaving the merchant navy, the next he had accidentally fallen into working for the King's Elite. Up until then, he had had no concept of possessing either the valuable skills necessary for covert espionage or the burning desire to see justice done. Yet because of things he had seen and his nagging conscience, he had approached the Excise Men with suspicions about the particular shipping company he happened to be working for at the time and inadvertently soon found himself spying on them.

After the resounding success of that first mission, Lord Fennimore simply assumed he would continue and Gray hadn't corrected his assumption. For the last two years he had been working beneath Seb Leatham in the Invisibles, blending into the background, pretending to be someone else. Learning the trade and loving it. With Seb now working in a wholly different way alongside his new wife, Gray wanted more than anything to step into his friend's shoes, knowing they would be the perfect fit. After an aimless life of searching for nothing in particular beyond what was happening in the moment, he had finally found his place.

If only he could convince old Fennimore.

For the umpteenth time he huffed out an irritated breath at this morning's incident. His thoughtless lack of propriety had not helped his cause, but at least it had got him here, thanks largely to Lady Crudgington. Miss Cranford had seemed horrified to see him and had introduced him around the room most begrudgingly. He had made a much better impression on the Viscountess, although prudence dictated he be cautious with her. She liked male company. More than liked it, if his suspicions were correct, which made aligning himself too closely problematic.

If Gislingham was the jealous type, Gray risked alienating him. The first priority had to be getting closer to their chief suspect. Only once all hope of that was dead could he risk a dalliance with the wife to get what he wanted. Or the ward.

Miss Cranford was entirely off limits until he understood the lay of the land. For the sake of the mission, she had to be his last resort even though she was the family member he was most drawn to. As much as he was tempted to shamelessly flirt with her and was wildly curious to know whether her vibrant blushes ended just below her demure neckline or travelled all the way down those shapely legs to her toes, seducing a gently bred young woman tended not to go down well with protective male relatives with a cruel streak a mile wide. Doing so would not only alienate Gislingham, it would probably result in getting Gray killed.

He could pretend to properly court her, he supposed.

The errant thought caught him unawares. Not because he wasn't supremely confident in his abilities to thoroughly charm her, more because it terrified him to have even thought of it. He had willingly come within a hair's breadth of marriage once before and had ended up broken-hearted and deceived. From the tender age of ten he'd had his future with Cecily mapped out. They were going to wed as soon as he turned twenty-one when he finally gained his financial independence; they would buy a nice house near their favourite beach in Wales and raise fine horses and the best Welsh lamb alongside their bushel of children.

Then his father and hers had brokered a different deal, one Cecily had been given a choice in, and to Gray's horror the love of his life decided she would much rather be a wealthier marchioness wedded to his elder brother than live on that farm with him. It had been that same week that the walls of Jericho had come tumbling down. Blind with grief and convinced she would change her mind if only he could quickly enlarge his fortune to supersede his pompous brother's, Gray had taken every penny of the money his grandfather had left him in his will to London and the hells where the savvy owners, gamblers and card sharps had quickly relieved him of it. It had been the harshest way to learn his lesson—daring to dream was as pointless as regret, and risking your heart was for tougher men than him.

He now avoided all serious overtures of intent, even if the serious overtures would be just a ruse to infiltrate Gislingham's confidence. He couldn't bring himself to toy with another person's feelings as Cecily had done his. Heartbreak, it turned out, took for ever to get over. He avoided touching hearts with the same diligence that he avoided commitment and he wouldn't trifle with

Miss Cranford's no matter how much his body wanted her.

Assuming she would be interested, of course. Which she didn't appear to be in the slightest. She had barely said three words to him between all those polite introductions, so he had given up trying. Probably because he didn't have Trefor with him. She had *adored* Trefor… Good grief! Another pointless train of thought in the grand scheme of things. He needed to be a better spy, not jealous of his dog.

He rounded the shrubbery and stopped dead. The object of his musings was lying flat on her back on a stone bench, a gauzy shawl draped over her face like a shroud leaving her fiery copper hair to crackle in the sunshine. One hand rested gently on her belly while the other was thrown over her head. The artful pose, reminiscent of one of the epic tableaux of the Renaissance where some ancient Greek heroine had been cut down tragically in her prime, was doing wonders for her bosom. Her covered face allowed him to gaze longingly at it for a few moments as her chest gently rose and fell with her breathing in her splendid, fitted coral gown. Bizarrely, despite that unexpected bonus, he missed seeing her smile. That stunning smile combined with her current alluring position would be quite something to witness.

A sensible, dedicated spy would silently retrace his steps and take another route to continue his unhindered reconnoitre. But for some reason, his feet had already decided to head towards her as if pulled by some invisible cord. He was halfway across the lawn when he realised she wasn't asleep, in fact, and much to his amusement, she was talking to herself.

'Give *him* a fighting chance, darling.' If he was not mistaken, she was snippily mimicking Lady Crudgington. 'You are a little *too* buttoned up.' The hand that had been on her belly wafted in the air. 'I cannot recall a time when I have ever heard you sound so *waspish* over a mere man, Thea.' Gray suppressed the spontaneous snort which threatened to erupt as she blew a raspberry so fat the floaty shawl quivered. 'Settle for a *wholly* unsuitable man before you become so *decrepit* and wizened no one will ever fancy you and to hell with the consequences. Your exacting standards are *far* too high and your imagination is as *vivid* as your wayward, vertical hair. And while you're about it, become a total scandal, why don't you? Throw yourself at the fellow. Stand on the precipice and *leap*! The clock is ticking after all. Tick-tock, Thea. Tick-tock.'

He did laugh at the second raspberry, making her sit bolt upright, the delicate shawl slipping to puddle at her feet and her lush mouth a delightful *O* of embarrassed outrage. 'How long have you been there!'

'Long enough to know that Lady Crudgington

thinks you should give Mr Hargreaves a fighting chance, but that you are not so enthused by the idea.'

She was simultaneously blinking and blushing furiously. 'Yes… Mr Hargreaves…indeed… and you are correct. I am not at all enthused by the idea.' Primly, she straightened and adjusted her clothing. 'If anything, I am thoroughly unenthused.'

'I'm exceedingly glad to hear it. Having had to listen to him for the last half an hour, I found his conversation quite…'

'Sycophantic? Insincere? Grinding?'

He smiled at her accurate assessment. It was refreshing she didn't mince her words. 'Yes. To all. You can do much better than him.'

She beamed again as she had this morning and the sight of it did odd things to his heart. 'Thank you, Lord Gray! That is *exactly* what I keep telling Harriet, but she is determined to meddle.'

'Well, I dare say the meddling is necessary. You are on the cusp of decrepit.'

'You heard everything, didn't you?' The blush on her cheeks mirrored the deeper one staining her collarbone and disappearing beneath the lace edging her close-cut bodice. 'It's very rude to eavesdrop.'

'Surely eavesdropping involves listening to an obviously private conversation between two or more people. As you were loudly talking to yourself, out in broad daylight, I didn't think it counted. It gave me a very interesting insight into the young lady you are beneath that impenetrable exterior.' She looked attractively flummoxed and guilty at his assessment, which was very intriguing. 'Besides, like you, I sensibly came out here to hide and get some fresh air, so the eavesdropping was merely an unanticipated bonus. How could I resist it?'

'For a big man, you move with impressive stealth. Was it your intention to sneak up on me?'

'You credit me with too much talent, Miss Cranford. All I did was walk across the grass. If you hadn't been talking so much, you would have heard me. Do you mind if I sit—or is that grossly improper? If it is, I can hide somewhere else.'

She hesitated, then wrapped the filmy shawl around her shoulders, her jaw set and her eyes riveted on a distant spot across the lawn, feigning complete indifference politely. 'We are in view of the house and Harriet will be back presently.' Gray decided to take that as acceptance and sat on the opposite end of the seat to her.

'Why are you hiding? When I left you, you seemed to be having a high old time. My aunt appeared *most* enamoured of your charm.' He detected the hint of disapproval and decided to pry. These little rifts and obvious censures, leaked in confidence, proved time and time again to be fertile hunting grounds for spies.

'Your aunt obviously enjoys socialising.' A very delicate way of saying the woman basked in the glory of being the centre of attention, particularly when surrounded by a bevy of eager, much younger gentlemen.

'She does. More so than my uncle, so he indulges her.'

'I was hoping to meet your uncle before I outstayed my welcome. Will he be rejoining the party later?'

Her dark eyes clouded as they stared straight ahead. 'My uncle's health is not good, my lord, and hasn't been for several years. He managed much of the first hour, but prolonged socialising does take its toll on him. He needs his rest and sleeps like the dead most afternoons. I do not expect Uncle Edward will make another appearance today, I'm afraid. You shall have to meet him another time.'

He could tell by the worried look in her eyes she believed this to be the case and felt a rush of anger towards the man for his duplicity. Poor health was a convenient and ready excuse to disappear to do his dirty work. He'd wager every hard-earned coin in his purse that Gislingham was currently up to no good somewhere on this estate—or elsewhere—while his niece worried over him unnecessarily. 'That is a shame. Perhaps my cousin and I would do better to call upon him in the morning?' Before he left today, he needed to do a thorough reconnaissance of the grounds and as much of the bottom floor as he dare. His gut told him Gislingham ran his operation from this house and Gray needed to know exactly where.

'He is at his best in the mornings and enjoys small, intimate company. I know he is keen to meet you—especially as Harriet has already apprised him of this morning's unfortunate events.'

That didn't sound good. 'Should I expect a thorough telling off when I come calling?'

'Not at all. Uncle Edward has a very warped sense of humour and found the state of me upon my arrival home hilarious. I fear Harriet brings out the worst in him.' Gray sincerely doubted that. He had lost many comrades thanks to The Boss at his worst.

'Lady Crudgington is indeed a force of nature.'

'And very curious. She left me determined to give you a thorough grilling.'

'I suspected as much. But she was distracted by a fruit scone and clotted cream on the sideboard, so I managed to escape her clutches before I crept out. I can only cope with so much heat from the drawing room…and Mr Hargreaves.' Gray might as well take advantage of her dislike for the man. 'He brays when he laughs.'

The ghost of a smile played at the corners of her mouth. 'Colonel Purbeck spits when he talks.'

'Hence I stumbled across you shrouded like a widow.'

'I'm sorry about that. It was most improper.'

'Propriety is hardly a field it would be fair for me to judge you on and, anyway, it is vastly overrated. Don't you think?'

Her fingers played with the dangling edges of the shawl as she glanced up at the cloudless sky and, inadvertently giving him more clues as to her character, she avoided answering his question. 'Alas, I adore the sun, but it doesn't adore me. With my fair skin, I burn easily, so I have to ration it. Hence the shroud.'

'Then perhaps I should escort you back inside. The afternoon sun is always the worst.'

Prudence dictated that she should grasp the opportunity to escape inside seeing as he had offered it. It wasn't proper for an unmarried lady to be in such a secluded place in the presence of a gentleman without a chaperon and she knew Harriet had no intention of coming back outside and wouldn't be caught dead anywhere near the garden if she suspected Thea was alone in it with Lord Gray. But her friend's criticisms rankled and as much as Thea wanted to discount everything she had said, there was a great deal of truth in her words. She was becoming unacceptably jaded and had an ever-increasing suspicion of the motives of others. Since the smooth-talking soldier that dreadful night, she did make snap decisions about men and she did push them away. The fear of Impetuous Thea falling for a money-grabbing bounder, the huge responsibility of the unwieldy fortune her uncle had amassed on her behalf and the sense of responsibility and love she had for him had made her reluctant to consider anyone seriously.

To her shame, that reluctance had made her unacceptably stand-offish to the point where she risked never finding a decent man, and that simply wouldn't do. Because one day when the time was right and the gentleman perfect, she did want to live happily ever after. She wanted to be loved and adored. Wanted to love and adore back. Wanted to fill her home with the happy sound of children laughing, the closeness of family and the promise of a future she could look forward to. Uncle Edward had insisted she have financial independence so that she could marry the man of her dreams without having to compromise as he had done. True love, he often waxed after a bit too much brandy, was the greatest joy in the world and worth all the hideous turmoil in the long run.

Somehow, while waiting patiently for true love to come, she had allowed those alarm bells to start clanging well before she got to know a gentleman, which made a lifetime of spinsterhood a foregone conclusion. If she had created the vicious circle, she could jolly well unmake it.

'I suppose I can tolerate a little more sun.' In a concerted effort not to be stand-offish and judgemental, she would be cordial and properly get to know this handsome new gentleman beyond his compelling, wolf-like eyes and splendid physique. Harriet was right. Aside from the fact he was local, he did live with an older relative as well, so might understand her situation. He was the first gentleman she had met in for ever who had not actively sought her out to begin with. They had met wholly by chance without the allure of her impressive bank balance, so perhaps she should give fate a fair crack at the whip before she wielded the repelling Shield of Suspicion. 'Tell me something about yourself, Lord Gray.'

She could tell she had surprised him because his dark brows momentarily drew together. 'What would you like to know?'

'I suppose it makes sense to start at the beginning. Where did you grow up? Who are your family?'

'Very close to the mountains of Snowdonia. My father was the Marquess of Talysarn.'

'Was?'

'He died a few years ago while I was at sea. My elder brother now holds the title.'

'How sad. You missed the funeral?'

His face clouded and he paused before he answered. 'Yes.'

'Is your mother still alive?'

'Alas, my mother died many years before. She

was a lovely woman. I miss her greatly. You lost your parents young also, I believe?'

'I have no memories of my mother. She died when I was a babe.' Although Thea still missed her, wondering what her life and her character might have been like if she had grown up with a woman's guidance. Probably less wilful and impetuous.

'My father was a don at Cambridge. He taught mathematics and is still widely regarded in that field.' Which was probably why he never quite understood his daughter. Thea had no head for figures and the only thing they had had in common was a boisterous sense of humour and their twin fiery tempers. 'Did you go to Cambridge or Oxford?'

'No… I went abroad.'

'To study?'

'After a fashion. I'm not much of a scholar, I'm afraid. I certainly have no head for numbers.'

'Me either.' They had something in common. Something deathly dull and inconsequential in common. 'Aside from swimming scandalously naked with your dog, what do you enjoy?' Why had she said that? Instantly her cheeks heated while she wrestled Impetuous Thea back into her box.

He shot her a sideways glance and chuckled, the deep sound warming her in places that had no right being warmed. 'I thought we had drawn a veil over that. Or is the memory too awful for your tender sensibilities to forgive and forget?' He was flirting. Despite refusing to meet his eye she could hear it in his voice, but she was already blushing and doubtless he could see it. What had made her bring it up again? He would think she couldn't stop thinking about it, which was, of course, mortifyingly true. Aside from the memory of him naked, the wayward, wilful part of her nature was seriously considering swimming naked in the brook, too. It was ridiculously hot— even for July…

As if he could read her mind, he stared knowingly at her, the wretch. Better to acknowledge the discomfort head on and then brush it blithely aside. She was almost twenty-four, for goodness' sake. Ladies of that age were expected to be a bit more worldly, no matter how well bred and proper they were.

'I have forgotten it.' *Liar.* 'As much as one can forget such an outrageous anomaly so early in the day, especially as the day is nowhere near over yet and here you are again—being exactly where you shouldn't be and encroaching on my privacy. Thankfully, it was a brief encounter, so therefore unlikely to make a lasting impression on my *tender* sensibilities. I am hopeful it will be nought but a distant memory by tomorrow.' Gracious! Her true tartness had materialised out of nowhere when she had intended to be nothing but polite.

Clearly she needed a much stronger padlock on the box around Lord Gray.

'That is good to know. Nothing makes a man happier than knowing he is quickly forgettable. Especially when all his *credentials* have been laid bare for scrutiny. I shall sleep soundly tonight, secure in the knowledge the spectre of my bottom will not be encroaching on your dreams.'

It was funny that she could hear his smile. Funnier still that her own mouth was curving upwards, too, when this entire conversation was outrageous. Gloriously so. Not being immediately suspicious was liberating. 'So shall I. For they would hardly be dreams, Lord Gray. I fear if your bottom scandalously encroached, surely, they would be nightmares at the very least. When one is as decrepit as I, one needs one's beauty sleep.' She was flirting! When she never flirted any more in case it gave untrustworthy men the wrong impression. This man clearly brought out the worst in her and she hardly knew him.

'If you got any more sleep, you'd be dangerous.'

'Although I should warn you, I doubt Harriet and my uncle will allow me to forget the incident completely until they have fully had their fun at my expense...' Had he just paid her a compliment? Thea gave up staring off into the distance and risked flicking him a glance. He was sat staring cockily right back at her. Utterly gorgeous, the seams of his coat straining slightly against the muscles of his folded arms, those unusual blue-grey eyes twinkling with mischief. Her heart did a little stutter at the sight. That and his scandalously pretty comment, which the sensible part of her cautioned was probably best ignored. Reacting would only encourage him, making him think she was interested, and she certainly didn't want that. Just in case he was a bounder in wolf's clothing. 'Kindly repeat what you just said.' So much for ignorance and disinterest. Impetuous, easily seduced Thea was loose and running roughshod all over the terrace.

'I *said*, if you got any more sleep, you'd be dangerous. Obvious decrepitude aside, you are quite beautiful enough already, Miss Cranford. I'm not entirely sure I could cope with any more. I find myself already totally smitten with you.'

Internally she was sighing and was in grave danger of melting into a puddle at the man's feet. He thought her beautiful. Was already smitten... How lovely. Of course, outwardly, she hoped she looked unimpressed because she was far too sensible to be waylaid by flowery words any more— no matter how lovely Impetuous Thea thought they were to hear. 'Oh, my!' She fluttered her hand in front of her face and batted her eyelashes. 'What a swoon-worthy compliment! If only I hadn't seen you similarly flirting with my aunt a short while ago, I'd be tempted to be flattered.'

'There is a distinct difference. Your aunt flirted

with me first and it would have been rude not to respond in kind. That was merely social flirting, Miss Cranford, and therefore innocuous. My flirting with you was wholly unsolicited and wholly spontaneous. It was *genuine* flirting.' The arrogant grin suited him and Thea found herself enjoying it.

'Ah—I see.' She tapped her lip and attempted to look thoughtful, enjoying this unexpected sparring match with a man who met none of her strict criteria, but seemed to be able to pick the locks that bound the chains around the inner Thea's locked box. 'So if social flirting is innocuous, does that make *genuine* flirting noxious?'

'It makes it dangerous. Especially when both of us engage in it as we are now. It hints at intent.' He raised his dark eyebrow. 'At promise…'

Instinctively, she folded her own arms, mirroring his casual pose. 'I hardly think I am flirting, Lord Gray.'

'Gray will do just fine. And you are most definitely flirting, Miss Cranford. I'm afraid I recognise all of the signs.'

'Really? Pray enlighten me, for I confess I am at a loss.'

He shuffled closer on the bench and leaned in conspiratorially, smelling sinfully of sunshine and spicy cologne. 'To the unobservant, it would be difficult to tell, but there are subtle clues. Your insistence on reminding me of this morning, for example. Unconsciously, despite all my very proper clothes, your mind is scandalously picturing me naked.'

She scoffed, bristling, wondering if he really *could* read her mind. 'I most certainly am not! Ewwwgh!' She shuddered for effect. 'I can assure you my brain has far better things to think about than the unsavoury picture of you in the altogether, although even if I was, which I most definitely am *not*, a person's private thoughts hardly constitute flirting.'

'The coquettish side glances and pretty pink blushes which accompany them does.'

Thea turned her head and stared him dead in the eye. 'I'm a redhead and if I am a bit pink, then I have clearly been in the sun a tad too long, my lord.'

'A plausible denial, to be sure—but it doesn't fool me. And I thought we agreed you could call me Gray going forward, seeing as you've seen me in the altogether? But…your preoccupations with my impressive, manly nude body aside, there are other damning clues which only a true connoisseur in the subtle art of flirting would pick up. A moment ago, for instance, when you brought your finger to your lips… Why, it was obvious you were doing so to purposely draw my eyes there and set me wondering if they are as soft and inviting as they look.'

She had touched her lips quite innocently, or

so she had thought, but now they tingled. 'You are delusional.'

'Right now, we both know the position of your arms has only one true purpose.'

She didn't unfold them. 'To show you I am not a fool, nor suffer fools gladly?'

'To display your figure to its best effect.' She hastily uncrossed her arms and gathered the shawl tighter, irritated at the missish response when he reacted with a knowing chuckle. 'And…' The word came out in a sultry whisper as his head leaned closer still before he paused and failed to finish his sentence.

'And?'

'That was a test and, I'm sorry to tell you, you failed.'

'I did?'

'Indeed. Because *you* leaned closer, too, obviously eager to hear what I had to say despite my intimate, wholly inappropriate conversation and my close proximity to your unchaperoned person being most impertinent.'

'You *are* impertinent.'

'I am—but you'd like to kiss me regardless.'

She would—which came as a huge, unwelcome shock—but she most certainly wouldn't.

Ever.

On principle.

'Oh, Lord Gray, you are labouring under the most fanciful of misapprehensions.' With purposeful, indifferent, possibly flirtatious slowness, Thea stood and shook her head pityingly. 'Perhaps it is you who needs to be mindful of the sun's rays and ration them going forward, for today they have clearly addled your mind.'

Chapter Five

*'D*id you have to bring that dog?' Lord Fennimore glared at Trefor's rapidly wagging tail and grimaced.

'Miss Cranford was very taken with him. I reasoned his presence would only help our cause.'

'They won't let him in the house.'

'He will be perfectly content tied up outside for the duration of our visit. He loves to sleep in the sun.' Unbidden, images of Miss Cranford lying in the garden instantly sprung to mind and he found himself smiling. Granted, flirting with her yesterday might well have been foolhardy and counterproductive to their mission—undeniably his superior would castigate him for the misdemeanour if he knew and a truly sensible spy would have avoided it—but Gray had enjoyed it immensely. She was tart, sharp and tasty. A glorious, intelligent and feisty armful and he would not regret the overwhelming, yet too-brief indulgence in the slightest. In that moment, it had felt right and life was too short for regrets. 'Besides, as we are posing as country gentlemen, he gives us an air of the authentic. What says Suffolk more than two robust fellows striding across the fields with their faithful hound in tow?'

'We could have ridden instead. It would have been a darn sight quicker than constantly stopping and waiting for that dog to continually sniff the air.'

'Trefor is rusticating. Which is what *we* are supposed to be doing.'

They turned on to the Viscount's short drive, both lapsing into silence as they mentally prepared themselves for the task in hand. Again last night they had meticulously gone over their backstory. Lord Fennimore was still convinced the closer Gray stuck to the truth of his past, the more chance he had of manoeuvring himself into Gislingham's inner circle. With the Viscount's extensive web of criminal contacts, it would be simple to make enquiries and the truth would be swiftly and categorically confirmed. Lord Graham Chadwick was a ne'er-do-well of the first order and had been since birth. He had lost his twenty thousand-pound inheritance at the gaming tables in just three short months. He had been understandably disowned by his only brother and his father, the upright and blemish-free Marquess of Talysarn, and then disappeared off to sea when he had worn out his welcome and his line of credit in the capital. After that, nobody really knew what had happened to the lad…

Before the men had left for Suffolk, the necessary lies had been sprinkled among a few reliable government allies and in the browned pages of certain parish records. The errant Lord Gray had returned after a scandalous decade of adventuring and been taken under the wing of Lord Fennimore—a distant cousin of Gray's dead mother—in the hope of encouraging him to tread the path of the respectable going forward. To that end, and to keep him away from the seductive mischief of town, Lord Fennimore had rented a property deep in the countryside.

Until yesterday, Gray had been entirely satisfied with the story. Now, despite knowing the filtered, censored truth was perfect for their purpose, he wasn't so keen. Yesterday, Miss Cranford had asked about his past and, oddly ashamed, he had brushed over it. While no longer a wastrel, he had been. Once he had given up all hope of winning back Cecily, he had lived an aimless life doing whatever had pleased him. There had been no master plan, no commitments nor any responsibility. Once the pleasure in the place, the woman or the entertainment waned, he had moved on to seek diversion elsewhere. Whatever it took to make him forget the pain in his heart, he actively pursued it until the pain became an ache and eventually that ache became a scar. Bitter truths he had never admitted to anyone and never would. Better the world chastise him for being a wastrel than pity him for being a love-addled fool who hadn't quite passed muster.

But such a past would make him more appealing to the crooked Viscount. As old Fennimore had rightly pointed out when he had suggested, over the soup, that they tweak the truth a little to mask the fact he had been home and almost respectable for two whole years: birds of a feather always flock together. A confirmed reprobate stood a greater chance of becoming a friend than an upstanding, reformed character. However, the same foibles which would make him more appealing to Gislingham would make him significantly less appealing to Gislingham's lovely niece.

As much as it irrationally pained him, that couldn't be helped.

King, country and his promotion depended on it.

Gray secured his dog to a low fence near the dappled shade of a horse chestnut and the pair approached the front door, both supremely aware that this first meeting with the man would be crucial. His superior handed over their calling cards to an ancient butler who had made no effort to remove the buff apron he wore or to discard the polishing rag he held in his hand. Such a conscientiously informal greeting was a nice touch, suggesting there was nothing to hide behind this heavy oak door but an unpretentious country squire.

'Lord Cedric Fennimore and Lord Graham Chadwick—we have come to pay our respects to his lordship and Miss Cranford if they are at home.'

The butler did not attempt to suggest they might not be and cheerfully welcomed them to sit in a bright parlour while he informed his lordship of their presence. They waited less than five minutes before the old retainer reappeared and asked them to follow him. He led them up a flight of sweeping, creaking wooden stairs to a small sitting room stuffed with furniture unashamedly built for comfort over style and not at all what one would expect from a man who earned hundreds of thousands of pounds from illegal free trading.

Before they sat, Miss Cranford hurried in, smiling, looking stunning in turquoise and with her riotous Titian hair already escaping its pins. The sight was quite the highlight of his morning and, without thinking, Gray turned his gaze and unwaveringly drank her in. Her eyes flicked to his, dipped briefly, then focused solely on Lord Fennimore.

'My lords, how lovely of you to come. My uncle will be with you presently. He is just finishing off something in his study.' Unconsciously, her head gestured to the door opposite the one they had entered.

'His study is up here? On the first floor?' An interesting titbit Gray tucked away for future reference. At some point, he needed to go through Gislingham's desk and private papers; most probably in the dead of night after breaking in.

'He prefers these apartments to the larger rooms downstairs. They are more self-contained and easier to navigate now that his mobility is not what it was. Please… Sit.' She gestured to the furniture nearest the enormous bay window where the lace panels billowed softly in the breeze. 'Bertie is fetching tea.'

'Bertie?'

'My uncle's manservant. He sees to all his needs. We would all be quite lost without him.'

Lord Fennimore took one of the two large wing-backs while Miss Cranford perched on the sofa, the picture of a proper hostess who never blew raspberries or allowed her eyes to wander freely down his naked body. This was the Miss Theodora Cranford she wanted the world to see. He rather liked knowing that, with the right encouragement, she was a completely different Miss Cranford underneath. Because he simply needed to, Gray sat next to her. 'You look particularly lovely this morning, Miss Cranford.' And she smelled divine. Whatever perfume it was that she wore, it had now become his absolute favourite scent in the whole world. Reminiscent of the heady evening jasmine he had encountered in the Orient.

She ignored the compliment, but smiled politely as she refocused on his companion. 'We did not expect you this early, although the hour is a good one for Uncle Edward. He's an early bird by nature, as am I.'

As she was intent on ignoring him and his ridiculous need to flirt with her, he decided to resort to basic good manners to see if she would respond to that instead. 'Something we have in common—although I confess I would sleep longer if it were not for Trefor. He needs to get out early…to do dog things.'

That worked. 'You should have brought him. I adore dogs.'

He couldn't resist an I-told-you-so look at Lord Fennimore. 'Despite *Cedric's* forceful objections, I did. He's currently sat on the drive.'

'Then you must bring him in! Uncle Edward is a dog person, too. Left to us, we would have a house full, but my aunt loathes them. They make her sneeze.'

'Perhaps he is best left where he is, then? I should hate to cause her ladyship any discomfort.'

'And the dog is a menace,' added Lord Fennimore with barely disguised irritation. 'My young relative has been most neglectful of the animal's training.'

'Her ladyship has gone shopping in Ipswich and we do not expect her back until much later, so Trefor is welcome to visit. Besides, a little wildness is perfectly acceptable in a dog. It gives it character.'

Gray didn't argue. If his poorly behaved mutt would aid the transition from new acquaintances to friends quicker, he would shamelessly use him. He fetched the dog and did his best to wrangle him back towards the Viscount's private apartments without Trefor's blurred tail knocking anything over in its exuberance. By the time they reached the sitting room, the tea had arrived, along with a large bowl of water for the hound. A middle-aged servant stood pouring, but paused with the cup and pot held aloft as the dog barrelled towards him. He needn't have worried. The dog only had eyes for the deliciously smelling redhead. Like Gray, Trefor was irresistibly drawn to her.

'My uncle is finishing up his business for the morning. Something he insists on doing himself rather than employ a secretary.' Another interesting insight and not at all the norm. Most estate owners employed a legion of staff, from book-keepers to estate managers, but then most had nothing to hide. 'Bertie, this is Lord Gray.' Miss Cranford's eyes did not lift from the animal as he ran in giddy circles about her feet being thoroughly petted, almost as if she was purposefully avoiding his gaze at all cost. 'And this handsome rascal is Trefor.'

'*The* Trefor?' The servant was soft-spoken, but clearly amused. 'The one that almost drowned you?'

'The very same.'

'What do you mean he almost drowned you?' His superior's eyes darted between Gray and their hostess before skewering him alone.

'Trefor knocked her into the brook.'

'It was an accident,' said Miss Cranford graciously, oblivious of the way old Fennimore's eyes had begun to bulge at the revelation. 'And hardly poor Trefor's fault. My maid got all the mud out of my dress, so no real harm was done. Apart from to my hair, which was a disaster all yesterday.' Her eyes wandered to Gray's briefly and she unconsciously blinked rapidly, a sure sign she was not quite as composed in his presence as she wanted him to believe. 'I blame Lord Gray entirely for that shambles.' Was she rattled by the flirting? He certainly hoped so.

'I thought your hair looked lovely.'

'I thought it looked an absolute fright.' A deep, chuckling, slightly slurred voice came from the doorway. 'Had me laughing for hours.'

Viscount Gislingham was not at all what Gray had imagined. He was tall and broad, a full head of thick sandy hair, greying at the temples, and a face that was undoubtedly considered handsome in its prime—before the stroke which had apparently now frozen half of it. That aside, he was smartly turned out. The well-cut green coat covered a jaunty striped-silk waistcoat that was all the colours of the rainbow. He was also much older than his wife. A good twenty years older. He walked into the room, leaning heavily on a cane, his left leg dragging slightly.

'Don't get up, gentlemen, for then I shall feel the need to shake your hands immediately and as only one of them works properly, and I have a wonky leg which is little more than useless, I will doubtless fall over and embarrass us all. Let's save the hearty handshakes for the end of our visit. Besides, I've worked out which of you is which already. Harriet was very fulsome in her descriptions.' His head nodded to each of them in turn. 'Welcome, Lord Fennimore, and welcome, Lord Gray. I am glad Kirton House is peopled again. It has been empty and miserable far too long. The grounds have been neglected, I'm afraid—so feel free to do with them as you will. Anything would be an improvement on those acres of grass and daisies.'

The manservant took his weaker arm and manoeuvred his master to the vacant wing-back while his niece hovered nearby. 'Tea, Uncle?'

'Indeed. Two sugars, if you please.'

'Half a teaspoon and not a speck more. The physician has him under strict instructions to keep his weight down.' Gislingham rolled his eyes at his servant's determined admonishment, then huffed in a good-natured way at his guests.

'Once upon a time I was master of this house, now I'm scolded like a child. Between Thea and Bertie's conspiratorial nagging, I now have no vices left.' The Viscount settled himself before making a fuss of the bouncing Trefor at his knee. 'If that were not enough, my pride is further dented by my inability to climb down stairs. I can go up them well enough, but I have to suffer the indignity of having the footmen carry me down.'

'You could always move your bedchamber and study downstairs,' Lord Fennimore said reasonably, earning him a stunning smile from their intoxicatingly jasmine-smelling hostess.

'Exactly! I have said as much a thousand times, for there is plenty of space, but my uncle is stubborn. He absolutely refuses.'

Gray saw the Viscount exchange an odd look with his servant before his expression became shuttered. Hardened. 'We are not discussing that again, Thea. I like my privacy, always have and always will. I picked footmen with strong backs for the express purpose of transporting my knackered carcase down and reward them handsomely for the inconvenience.' As if the Viscount sensed Gray was watching, his serious expression swiftly evaporated and he was all easy charm again.

'I take it this is the handsome fellow responsible for sending you flying, Thea?' Clearly not a good judge of character, the dog lapped up the attention, his eyes half closing in ecstasy as Gislingham rubbed one of his floppy ears. 'And the other equally handsome fellow is responsible for rendering you speechless with his unabashed nudity?' He glanced up at Gray and grinned. 'I'd have paid good money to see my niece mute for once. I had thought such a miracle impossible. I'd shamelessly imitate you and stroll about buck naked, too, if I thought it would get me any peace, but the sight would likely send all the servants running for the hills before it silenced her and then who would carry me downstairs?'

'I was hardly mute, Uncle.'

'Harriet said your jaw dropped to the floor and you were stuttering and spluttering while glowing crimson like a beetroot.'

'Harriet exaggerates.' She carefully placed the cup within his reach, but out of the radius of Trefor's ferociously wagging tail, the apples of her cheeks a little pink again as she resolutely avoided glancing anywhere near Gray's side of the sofa. 'Once I had recovered from the shock of Lord Gray's abysmal lack of propriety, I gave him a thorough telling off. I would have said much more—but I ended up in the brook.'

The Viscount laughed and shared an amused look with his manservant before grinning lopsidedly at Gray. 'She told you off? I am impressed.

Thea is usually painfully, politely aloof at all times to everyone bar me and Harriet—and even then she tempers her words. It is most irritating because she used to be such an entertaining, stubborn and delightfully troublesome child. Blissfully cursed with a true redhead's quick temper. Age has softened the shrew in her and I miss it. You must provoke it, Lord Gray. I wonder why?'

'She professes to have forgiven me, has promised to draw a veil over it, yet continues to reprimand me regardless. I *have* apologised for the misdemeanour, my lord. Repeatedly.' Gray smiled at the older man, attempting to appear contrite despite the overwhelming temptation to spar and flirt with his niece again rather than doing the job he had come here to do.

'My Thea is a hard nut to crack. Far too picky. And shrewish. It's why she's still unmarried despite her lovely face and figure. I live in hope that someone will break through that tough outer shell and take her off my hands. But the young gentlemen hereabouts have proved themselves to be very lily-livered in the face of her icy indifference. It will take a great deal of perseverance on your part, Lord Gray, to chisel through it. I hope you are up to the challenge.'

'I'm sure Lord Gray has worked out already it's not worth his effort.' Her eyes met his properly for the first time since he had arrived and there was definite challenge in them, warning him not to play along with her uncle's jesting. 'When it comes to *unworthy* gentleman, no matter how handsome or penitent, I have skin as thick as an elephant's. In fact, I am positively pachydermatous.'

'She thinks herself clever, too. Worst thing I ever did, paying for her governesses. Some of those lacked perseverance, too, but it was fun to watch her run rings around them. She's a troublesome handful. It's what I've always enjoyed most about her. Never could predict quite what she was going to do.' He smiled indulgently at his niece, who quickly focused blandly on her teacup. Was it the reminder of her childhood wilfulness, her uncle's teasing or Gray's attempts at flirting which made her uncomfortable?

'I'm an irritatingly persistent fellow, my lord. Dogged, even. For the sake of your continued sanity I shall do my best to mine through to that soft kernel.'

The mobile half of the Viscount's face curved into a smile, one too friendly for a murdering cutthroat. 'I cannot tell you how relieved I am to hear it. Harriet said you showed promise.'

Gray's eyes wandered boldly to hers, then lingered. Despite the very long list of good reasons why he couldn't, there was a tantalising, fiery woman beneath her icy aloofness. One he irresponsibly wanted to know better.

'I wouldn't allow him anywhere near my niece

if I had one.' Lord Fennimore must have seen the heated look and decided now was the optimum time to drip in their story for maximum effect. Something they had agreed on, although it now suddenly left a bitter taste in Gray's mouth. 'Miss Cranford's assessment is quite correct. He is unworthy...although I am hopeful I can turn him into the gentleman he was born to be. Gray has always been very wild.' Once she learned exactly how wild, all his chances of pursuing the attraction for King, country or himself would be bludgeoned to death with the unpalatable truth.

'He was? Do tell.' Miss Cranford picked up her teacup and settled back, all ears.

'I'll spare you all the gory details, although it would be very easy for you to find them out...' Drip, drip. Fennimore was teasing his prey with bait. 'Suffice it to say that he had to leave these shores in disgrace a decade ago and has only recently dared to return. As the only family member who deigns to speak to him and out of the affection and respect I had for his dear mother—my cousin—I have taken it upon myself to rehabilitate him. To his credit, he has trod the path of respectability for over a month now...'

Chapter Six

'The light here is very poor.'

As it was blazing sunshine everywhere, Thea bit her tongue. Harriet had already dragged her to three locations, and made them set up her easel in the blistering heat twice before declaring the site unsuitable. The reflections on the brook were not shimmery enough, the vista from the highest point duller than usual and now it was the fault of the light. 'I doubt you will find a spot with more light.' Thea pointed up at the scorching yellow ball in the sky for emphasis.

'Which is exactly the problem. There is far too much light and it is washing out all the colours. We need some dappled shade. Perhaps we should head over there to those trees?' Trees which sat dangerously close to Kirton House and a certain handsome scoundrel Restrained Thea would be quite delighted never to see again. Not now that she knew her initial assessment of the man was quite correct and she never should have allowed herself the luxury of flirting with him.

That foolhardy bit of flirting had given Lord Gray ideas he had no right having. Not when he possessed none of the necessary attributes on her list, despite what anyone else had to say on the subject, including Impetuous Thea. Lord Gray was neither trustworthy nor respectable. He certainly wasn't the least bit proper. A complete rascal. A thrill-seeker. A man who made poor choices and lived for nought but fun. A man exiled from his family and shunned by society. Not that she held much stock in society, but their universal condemnation couldn't be wrong. You could only fool some of the people some of the time after all. Lord Gray was the sort of man who led people astray. Thea did not want or need the temptation of such a wholly unsuitable fellow, no matter how much her wilful side was drawn to him.

His poor cousin had his work cut out trying to turn him into something vaguely resembling respectable and, being a realist, Thea was highly sceptical of his chances in view of the overwhelming evidence to the contrary. His wildly outrageous flirting after such a short acquaintance said a great deal about his commitment to becoming respectable. The only attribute on her list the outrageously flirtatious Lord Gray happened to possess was being easy on the eye. Too easy on the eye.

'You paint. I'm going home.' Where she could

avoid any contact with the wastrel, Harriet's un-subtle meddling and her own embarrassing pre-occupation with the image of the man's bare buttocks.

'The walk back to the house is significantly longer than to those trees and you are already beginning to resemble a lobster. Are you certain you want to risk it?' Instinctively Thea's hands went to her cheeks and probed. The sensitive skin just under her eyes did feel warm. Harriet smiled with mock sympathy. 'Think of your complex-ion, darling, and don't be a spoilsport. I promise we shall bury ourselves into a secluded, shady nook where I can paint to my heart's content and you can read whatever nonsense you are currently reading without burning to a crisp. I shan't traipse you anywhere else. Promise.' Thea hesitated, and her friend spotted it. 'Unless it's a little too close to the abode of a certain handsome nude bather, in which case I completely…understand.'

'What is there to understand?'

'That his close proximity unnerves you and your inappropriate attraction to the man fright-ens you because he is not at all what you *think* you want.'

'I most certainly am neither unnerved nor frightened nor attracted! I couldn't give two figs whether I see the fellow or not.' And like a sap, she was already striding purposefully towards the dratted trees to prove it, despite that being the exact opposite thing to the one she wanted to do. 'I'm simply fed up trailing after you in the heat.'

'If you're sure, Thea, darling. I'd hate to think my choice of spot was the cause of any distress… Although I am intrigued to meet his cousin properly. All I managed was a brief how do you do.'

'Are you talking about Lord Fennimore?'

'Indeed I am. I thought he was very distinguished, with an attractive, confident manner about him. I like a confident man. *And* he's apparently a bachelor to boot. He definitely requires further scrutiny.' She gazed wistfully towards Kirton House, then shrugged at Thea's bemused expression. 'Don't look so surprised. If you think decent gentlemen the right side of forty are thin on the ground here in Suffolk, you should try being my age. They are either married or so dreadful nobody can bear their company. Like Colonel Purbeck, who completely dominated Lord Fennimore at the tea and I couldn't muster the enthusiasm to suffer his droning company—even for a handsome stranger. Not when it is inevitable I will collide with him naturally in the grounds one day. Not today, of course, seeing as we are avoiding his gorgeous younger relative at all costs.'

Because Harriet was speaking loudly, Thea slowed her pace. 'Keep your voice down or he'll hear us and then my day will be well and truly spoiled!' The last thing she wanted was that shameless flirt coming to his door to investigate. Not when she now knew she should have trusted those alarm bells and not been goaded by Harriet into getting to know him better—then outrageously goaded by him into flirting.

Although the flirting on the terrace had been fun at the time despite the fact her subsequent re-action to it was unnerving. His boldness and con-fidence had tempted her to be bolder herself and for once she forgot to be polite and instead, for a short while, had been her true self in front of him. The old, unburdened Thea who always did as she pleased and acted before thinking. The one who had exceedingly poor taste in men.

Yet she had still found herself looking forward to his potential visit the following day, despite there being no firm plans, and had spent far too long at her *toilette* in preparation, wondering if she should allow a little bit of Impetuous Thea out of her box again just for the thrill of it. Until she realised that was exactly the problem. Like the seductive soldier who had been the last man to thoroughly lead her astray with no thought to the consequences, Lord Gray was too tempting.

Yesterday she had initially kept her guard up each time he tried to flirt because there were witnesses—that had been hard because the parry-ing, teasing comments had been on the tip of her tongue the entire time, but she had promised her-self she would resist. A resolve which had hard-ened to granite once she had found out about his dreadful past. Her impeccable instincts had been correct all along and she should have heeded their warning rather than listen to her flighty inner self. He was as bad as Mr Hargreaves—if not worse.

However, despite his blatant unsuitability and her obvious lack of interest during tea, Uncle Edward had continued to make unsubtle hints that Lord Gray should court her right up until the second he had left. Because he was a thoroughly disgraceful scoundrel all the way through to his perfectly proportioned bones, Lord Gray had intimated that he fully intended to do so. A prospect as disagreeable as it was appealing—and that simply wouldn't do. Henceforth, he and his dangerously silver tongue would be avoided unless it was under the strict confines of a proper social occasion filled with a room full of people to act as chaperons. Aside from the fact she didn't trust him, Thea also did not trust the buried part of her which his face, body and mischievous, bold manner inappropriately responded to.

The part that kept whispering that she and Lord Gray were well matched.

Harriet paused, shielded her eyes from the sun and rather unsubtly stared at Kirton House. 'I don't think anyone is home. Look—the windows are all shut. Nobody shuts their windows here unless they are out. We should be perfectly safe walking past—not that I see what the problem is. I found Lord Gray positively charming and am quite happy to further the acquaintance with him, too.'

'It's far too hot to socialise. This afternoon all I want to do is read.' She waved her book for emphasis. 'Something I have been denied this last hour because of your dithering.' Thea ploughed on, somewhat relieved that Kirton House did indeed look deserted. The dust needed to settle, more internal locks and safeguards needed to be applied, before she was brave enough to weather another minute with him.

I'm an irritatingly persistent fellow.

Indeed he was—irritating in the extreme and so confident and cocky. His outrageous flirting on the terrace and her peculiar reaction to it were still too fresh in her mind. What sort of man mentioned kissing within a scant few hours of meeting a lady? Now she couldn't think about him without thinking about kissing him, which played havoc with her pulse. Clearly her body was as outraged as her sensibilities were. His utter cheek and overall lack of propriety were astounding, as was the way everyone dear to her seemed intent on matchmaking.

Matchmaking! With a man who had been so wicked he'd had to leave England in disgrace! They could matchmake all they wanted; nothing would convince her to be tempted by that smooth-talking scoundrel ever again.

I shall do my best to mine through to that soft kernel.

Where he would find she didn't have the feeble shell of the common or garden nut at all, but the tough, granite exterior of a castle. A castle whose battlements were protected by a hundred archers and fearsome-looking knights with vats of boiling oil which they would enjoy pouring on his annoying dark head the moment he had the audacity to attempt to breach the defences and find the real Thea locked in the dungeon beneath…

Dungeon? Since when had she thought about her life as a prison? Now there was an unsettling thought to add to the new and unnerving list of them.

'You're doing it again, you know. Talking to yourself.'

'I never said a word.'

'Maybe not out loud, but by the scrunched-up sourpuss expression and your nodding and shaking head, you were ranting inwardly to yourself. You really need to stop doing that, you know. It's very odd. If I stumbled across you and didn't know you to be a perfectly sane person by and large, I'd think you were a recently escaped inmate from Bedlam.'

Thea did not dignify the accusation with a response, lest it condemn her further, and instead plunged into the trees, ruminating on the idea that she felt trapped by the life she had created for herself. Dismissing it from her mind as humbug brought about by her own foolish lack of propriety with *him* on the terrace, she found the ideal spot—a small clearing around an enormous, ancient fallen trunk that was completely bathed in sunshine one end and sheltered by an umbrella of filigree leaves the other. It was also reassuringly surrounded by so many trees, nobody would see them if they happened to be striding arrogantly by. Not feeling particularly generous after being virtually forced into compliance, she left Harriet to wrestle with the easel and took herself to a patch of soft grass in the shade and dropped her bottom down. Resting her back against the gnarly old trunk, she opened her book decisively and decided to revel in one of life's simple and uncomplicated pleasures—a good, reassuring book.

It had taken months to track down a copy of *Pride and Prejudice* by the unnamed author of *Sense and Sensibility*. Having found none existed in Suffolk, she'd had to send to London for a copy. Already, just a few chapters in, she was backing the dashing Mr Wickham and saw a lot of herself in the feisty heroine Lizzie. A sensible young woman who didn't suffer fools or idle flattery gladly. Like Lizzie with the arrogant Mr Darcy, Thea would not waste another second thinking about *him*.

After five minutes of silence where she tried and failed to focus on the words, she sensed her friend watching her. She looked up to find Harriet holding up her paintbrush like a proper artist and measuring her. 'I hope you don't mind, Thea dear, but I'm going to paint you. The muse has struck and I simply must listen.'

'The *muse*?' Her eccentric companion always thoroughly embraced each new hobby with over-the-top enthusiasm before discarding it like an old newspaper. 'You have a muse now?'

'A most insistent one.' Harriet waved her arms about her expansively, undeterred by Thea's dubious expression. 'This charming little clearing, the aged wood, the emerald grass…the butterflies dancing on the hazy pollen-filled air combined with your vivid, Celtic hair… Don't you see it?'

'See what?'

'The charming whimsy, of course! Why, it is reminiscent of the mythical Scottish faerie stories I adored as a child. The tableau is perfect… simply divine… Take your shoes off, darling. Faeries don't wear shoes.'

'Will it give me some peace if I do?'

'Most assuredly. I'm itching to get started. The light is magnificent.'

'Hallelujah.'

Harriet grinned and began rooting around in the undergrowth, returning with a handful of cheerful dandelions, white Queen Anne's Lace and some tangled ivy. 'For your crown,' she explained with mock solemnity. 'Every faerie has to have a floral coronet.' Thea suffered having the foliage poked into her hair, but scowled when she felt a pin removed, causing a fat corkscrew to fall over her eyes, reminding her she was fundamentally just as wayward as her hard-to-tame hair. She reached up to stop Harriet's interfering hands and withdrew as hers was impatiently swatted away. 'Allow me a few curls to feed the muse. I can hardly paint a Celtic riot of hair without something riotous to go on.'

'One pin.'

'Three.' As they were already sailing through the air into the bushes, it was pointless arguing, so she glared so fiercely that her friend stepped back with her palms raised before she dared pull out one more. 'I have enough hair... Lounge against the trunk again, Thea. Try to look wistful and magical as you read.'

Harriet scurried back behind her easel and the peace for Thea to enjoy Mr Wickham in his smart regimentals descended at last—although for some unknown and worrying reason, now Lord Gray's mischievous, disgraceful dark head was sat on top of the broad shoulders of her fictional hero. And his shoulders were broader, much broader, and his buff breeches tighter. Despite the unwelcome encroachment on her reading pleasure, she stubbornly persevered until Wickham and Lord Gray were interchangeable, one and the same.

Distracting and enticing. And thoroughly naked once more.

It was most disconcerting.

Lord Fennimore shook his head and tucked his pocket watch back in his waistcoat while he watched Gray lead their mounts to the stable. 'Five hours on horseback! We must be missing something.' But it was highly unlikely they had. Shortly after dawn the King's Elite had set off en masse in search of water deep enough for smugglers to utilise that conveniently also ran directly to the sea. Every waterway which had seemed initially promising had tapered off inland, until eventually each group of agents had arrived at the prearranged meeting point in Leiston—the closest point on the Suffolk coast—with the same conclusion. Leiston *was* the closest significant body of water to Gislingham Hall. And it was two hours away.

Hardly the ideal distance between a committed, ruthless, prolific smuggler and the hundreds of barrels of illegal French brandy delivered daily on to English shores. 'Unless Gislingham is not our man at all. Which doesn't make sense, when we know he's involved.'

Their intelligence had been faultless thanks to the new Baroness of Penmor; so faultless that the French side of the operation was in tatters and several English traitors had already been charged before being ruthlessly murdered in gaol by The Boss's henchmen to ensure their silence.

If Gislingham was the mastermind of the whole operation, the geographic isolation of the Viscount's house combined with his obvious poor health had thrown a huge spoke in the wheels. The Boss relied on water and communication and ran a tight ship. While the Viscount clearly had all his marbles and only seemed to suffer from some physical disability, the set-up at the hall did not lend itself to the task.

Or perhaps it did. So well that nobody would ever suspect foul play. The odd and inconvenient location of his study, the loyal and constantly hovering manservant, that pointed, cold response to his niece when she reasonably suggested he would find life easier downstairs. *'I like my privacy, Thea.'* Fiercely liked it despite the obvious inconvenience it caused. The jovial, easy fellow had disappeared for a few seconds then, replaced by a calculated, stubborn man whose tone had brooked no argument. The odd look which passed between him and the manservant. There was something there. A dark secret. Gray was sure of it.

Another agent, posing as their groom, took the reins and led the horses away, leaving the pair of them to wander back to the house, stretching out their aching limbs. 'We were never going to find what we needed straight away.' Not when The Boss had run rings around them for two years. As much as Gray wanted a quick resolution, he knew it was also highly unlikely. Suffolk could well be their home for many months. A daunting prospect indeed when just a few days of Lord Fennimore was significantly trying his patience. 'This was always going to be a waiting game. Now that we have made the acquaintance we can build on it. Once his guard comes down we'll discover more. We've been here three days. I'll wager in three weeks Gislingham Hall will have given up more of its secrets. In three months...'

'Field work is so frustrating!'

'Which is why you don't usually do it, sir.' Although Gray didn't hold out any hope of the old man disappearing back to his desk in Mayfair any time soon. He wanted The Boss brought to justice more than any of them. Lord Fennimore had built the King's Elite from scratch and, despite his gruff exterior, felt every agent's death keenly. They had lost nineteen men in the last two years, nine of whom were slaughtered when they were ambushed at Penmor castle just seven weeks ago. Those losses were still raw. Many more had been injured, including Gray, the cracked bone and damaged muscles in his arm barely healed. This mission was intensely personal for both of them. 'If it's any consolation, I think Gislingham likes us.'

'He likes you well enough and seemed to like you all the more once I apprised him of some of your dubious past. That is a good sign.' The Viscount had found the younger Gray's exploits entertaining. Unlike his niece, who hadn't bothered trying to disguise her wholehearted disapproval.

'Not if you want me to seduce Miss Cranford at some point in the future.' Where had that come from? At no point had a seduction even been tabled, let alone sanctioned.

Old Fennimore's bushy eyebrows disappeared into his hair as he glared. 'I categorically forbid you to seduce Miss Cranford! Or his obviously willing wife for that matter. Both ladies must be our last resort. Especially now that we have made such a good impression on Gislingham. The man might find you amusing and might well see you as some sort of kindred spirit, which is excellent, but I can assure you that will soon stop the moment you make a play for one of his womenfolk.'

'I wasn't going to seduce Miss Cranford.' Which was a crying shame because he sincerely wanted to. He couldn't get her and her tart mouth out of his mind. 'I was merely pointing out that if you over-egg my scandalous past then it will put her off me for the future—should a seduction be required.' And Gray was an optimist at heart. If the need arose, he would happily seduce her, for King, country and himself. It might get his unusual, tenacious fascination with the woman out of his system where she had apparently taken root. 'Besides, it would be foolhardy to completely alienate a potentially fertile source of information.' Or have her hate him. That would be awful after their splendid flirting and after he had spent all last night and the one before dreaming about her. 'I can be very charming and very persuasive. Who knows more about the Viscount's comings and goings, save his wife, than his only niece? They are obviously devoted to one another.'

'That is a good point.' By the look on his face, one his superior had not considered. 'You are correct. The seeds are sown. Gislingham can make his own enquiries henceforth if he's a mind to, but I shall cease scaring off Miss Cranford. Just in case. We run the risk of over-gilding the lily and we can't afford to burn all our bridges so early in the game. Befriend the girl. Earn her confidence—but do not touch.'

Gray opened his mouth to speak, then promptly shut it. There was no point questioning why his curmudgeonly superior had agreed with him, as he would only take it back and spoil the victory. The important thing was he *had* agreed with him. A momentous occurrence in itself. He would take it as a step in the right direction and keep his sarcastic, disbelieving but incredibly witty retort to himself.

'It makes sense for you to be cordial to Miss Cranford and try to pick her brains, although after seeing her reaction to you, her uncle is right. You will have your work cut out. She was heartily un-impressed with you.'

That stung. Lord Fennimore's laughter stung more. 'No, she wasn't. I thought she enjoyed my flirting.'

'She loathed it, dear boy. Her face was an absolute picture of disgust.' He was still chuckling, totally unaware how much his words bothered Gray. 'But while it is vastly entertaining to watch, such things have a tendency to grate after a while. Avoid any and all flirting until you have improved her low opinion of you. From this point, until further notice, you are to be a complete gentleman around her and save the scoundrel for her uncle.'

Any and all flirting! That blow stung the most of all, despite him seeing the sense in it. For the sake of the mission, the promotion and his constant endeavour to be a better spy, Gray would reluctantly comply. Even if it royally spoiled his mood.

As they turned on to the path towards the house, he spotted a black head appearing and disappearing in the window. Trefor was bouncing up and down to get a better view of his master's arrival, pink tongue lolling, big ears flapping with excitement. Gray might well be a constant source of disappointment to his superior most of the time, his family all of the time, but at least Trefor was always pleased to see him.

'That dog is quite mad.'

'The poor thing has been cooped up inside for

hours. I'm going to take him for a walk. I could do with one myself.' The truth. His neck was aching and his spine and leg muscles were constricted. 'Five hours sat on the back of a horse has made me as stiff as a board.' And five hours of listening to Lord Fennimore was grinding on his nerves. There was only so much bluster a man could take before he bit back.

As soon as they opened the door, Trefor shot out like a bullet, his brown eyes pleading and expectant, the tantalising message in them clear. It was a beautiful summer's day. Too beautiful to waste it all on work, and Gray needed some space. Something that was blessedly plentiful here in the middle of nowhere. Living cheek by jowl with a staid perfectionist reminded him too much of living with his humourless father. It was a lot like wearing a collar too tight. Initially bearable, but so damned constricting soon after that you wanted to ruthlessly tug it off. They had done all the spying they could for one day and the balmy evening of freedom beckoned. Like his former home, this beautiful countryside was perfect to disappear in and roam around. 'Come on, boy!' He and his hound could explore the endless horizon for hours. Throw and catch sticks. Sniff the air. Enjoy. Breathe. Live in the moment...

'I'll come with you.' In one fell swoop, his lovely walk and dream of a pleasant evening was spoiled, too. Capital.

Chapter Seven

'Must he chase butterflies?'

Gray's fist tightened around the stick he was carrying, snapping it in two. 'He's a dog. They chase things.'

'Not if you trained him properly he wouldn't. A good hunting dog walks obediently next to his master, awaiting his command; he doesn't run off and chase insects or bark at sheep or spend an eternity sniffing one patch of grass.'

Oblivious to the litany of criticism, Trefor's black nose was now glued to the ground as he found the scent of something which took his fancy and followed it intently. He did that a lot and it was something Gray had often wondered if humans could exploit. In the same way packs of hunting dogs chased a fox or located whichever unfortunate bird their owner happened to shoot for fun rather than food, perhaps good sniffers like Trefor could be used to hunt down other things which the less sensitive human nose could not. Like barrels of illegal brandy, perhaps? Or gunpowder or criminals? The heady, intoxicating perfume favoured by beautiful redheads…

'Now what is he doing?'

'He's tracking something.' At speed, apparently. His wagging black tail disappeared into some bushes before popping out again as the dog found a better route to whatever it was he was seeking with great urgency. Because Gray couldn't be bothered to listen to Lord Fennimore any longer, or trust himself not to bark at the man for being such a moaning old windbag, he picked up his pace and jogged after the dog into the trees, then smiled when he saw what it was Trefor was clearly hunting.

Jasmine.

Miss Cranford, hair down and feet bare, was draped across the top of the trunk of an enormous felled oak, propped on one pale elbow reading while Lady Crudgington painted. They turned simultaneously at Trefor's delighted bark.

'Good day to you, ladies.'

In her scramble to get off the log quickly, her skirts caught momentarily on the stray nub of a branch, giving him a tantalising glimpse of knee before she pulled them back in place, looking mortified at being caught being less than proper once again.

'Lord Gray! How delightful!' Lady Crudgington was the only woman present who appeared happy to see him. Miss Cranford's smile was polite. Forced. But she was blushing again as she stuffed one foot in the slipper Trefor had not picked up in his mouth. She made a half-hearted attempt to salvage the other one from his jaws, then quickly stopped herself, attempting to stand with all the decorum of a genteel young lady regardless of the lack of one shoe and a head full of weeds. That, combined with the wild tendrils of hair which she was desperately trying to stuff back into her chignon, made her lack of an exuberant welcome understandable—and ripe for some sport. Correct appearances were important to her. Just as Lady Crudgington had said, Miss Cranford was a little too buttoned up.

'We have a habit of meeting when you least want us to, Miss Cranford. Fear not, I only saw half of one scandalously pretty bare leg—but I shan't tell a soul about your impropriety.' Because he knew it would vex her, he winked as he tapped the side of his nose and laughed as she tried to think of a suitable way to put him in his place in front of her friend. Already, he knew she was more polite in front of others and more her tart self when alone with him. He rather liked that.

'A true gentleman wouldn't have mentioned it.' Despite her snooty expression, one hand had already found its way to Trefor's ear as he danced at her feet in adoring circles, that slipper still tightly clenched in his mouth.

'But a true gentleman would have looked his fill, too, Miss Cranford. Be in no doubt of that. I am simply more honest than most and, in my defence, it was a very fine example of a leg.' At the sound of a twig cracking beneath Lord Fennimore's obstinate boot behind him in the trees, and mindful that he was under strict orders not to be flirting with her at all, he rapidly changed the subject to avoid the obligatory lecture. 'We were walking across the meadow, minding our own business, when Trefor scented you. After that there was no stopping him. The mutt seems to be irresistibly drawn to you, Miss Cranford.' Exactly like his master. He wouldn't mind being caressed by those elegant, pale hands either. 'I think he likes your perfume.'

To prove his love, Trefor threw himself on the ground and flipped over, his eyes rolling back in his head as she bent down to tickle his tummy. Gravity allowed the loose tendrils to escape again and they crackled copper in the sun's waning rays to torment him. He enjoyed the sight for a scant few seconds before his superior found them all in the clearing and he had to behave himself. 'And here is *Cedric* now.' Fortunately, too late to hear Gray's teasing banter with the young woman he had been expressly forbidden from wooing—the one frantically tugging wildflowers from her hair.

'I'm sure I speak for both of us when I say we apologise for interrupting whatever it was we interrupted.'

'You are not interrupting at all.' Lady Crudgington beamed at the old man, who blinked a little awkwardly, then miraculously smiled back. At least Gray assumed it was a smile. As he had never seen one and they had been bouncing around on horseback all day, it could just as easily be a spot of wind. 'We were just finishing up. I've been painting Thea as a faerie. Come and look, gentlemen—and give me your honest opinion.'

Dutifully they both stepped forward and gazed at the picture. The garish daub was barely comprehensible. He assumed the brown splodge was the tree trunk and the orange explosion in the middle to be Miss Cranford's hair, but aside from that it had neither shape nor form. 'What a rare talent you have, Lady Crudgington.' Gray's eyes sought and found Miss Cranford's, which had lifted. Hers were suddenly filled with mirth at his diplomatic choice of words. 'This work positively screams summer. Doesn't it, *Cedric*?'

'Er…yes. Summer and faeries.'

'Painting is Harriet's newest hobby,' said Miss Cranford, uncharacteristically deadpan. 'Would you believe that a sennight ago she had never before picked up a brush?'

'No! *Really?*' That she had used one at all came as a surprise when the paint appeared to be slapped on with the leafy end of a carrot. 'Then I am doubly impressed.' To stop the laugh escaping, Gray tapped his fingers to his lips, making sure his thumb wedged up his jawbone to prevent it bursting open, while imagining all sorts of sad things to conquer the urge.

'As...am... I.' Lord Fennimore's staccato response was almost his undoing, but he rallied manfully before Lady Crudgington put him out of his misery.

'You lie more convincingly than your cousin, Lord Gray, and heaven only knows I appreciate the sentiment, but we both know it's a travesty. Before you arrived, I attempted to soften the harshness of the lines with a wash, but applied too much and now it is ruined.'

'Not that it was much better before she applied the water.' Miss Cranford was giggling. It was a luscious, earthy, naughty sound that immediately conjured images of rumpled sheets and lazy, cosy mornings. Not at all the subdued and tempered laughter of a prim and proper miss—the sound travelled straight to his groin.

'True. Another shocking disaster in my quest to become a grand master. But it was worth all the wasted effort to watch you two handsome gentlemen attempt to spare my feelings so inarticulately. That was priceless.' Her hands went to her hips and she smiled. 'Now that you are here, you might as well make yourselves useful and help me carry my equipment back to the house. We have dallied long enough on our quest not to be bored senseless by Suffolk, but I promised Thea I would keep her company at one of Edward's dreadfully dull business dinners and we must head back to change.'

Lord Fennimore stepped forward and was soon press-ganged into putting away cakes of paint and folding the easel, leaving Gray with nothing better to do than retrieve Miss Cranford's slightly soggy shoe from his dog's mouth. He passed it to her and she sat on the trunk again to put it on. When she had finished, he held out his hand to help her up and she took it, and the impact that tiny, innocent touch had on his body was as unexpected as it was pleasant. He felt her everywhere, head to toe, the tips of his fingers tingling and itching to tug her into his arms and tangle in her hair.

If she felt it, too, she did a very good job of hiding it and showed no desire to continue holding it once she was upright again. If she had tugged her hand away quickly, he might have thought she was bothered, but she didn't. If anything, she disentangled herself absently while brushing the dust from her dress, then, retrieving her book from the tree trunk where she had discarded it, she hugged it to her body. 'Isn't the weather lovely?'

'Oh, dear. I have been relegated to small talk. That is not a very good sign.'

'I am trying to be polite, my lord.'

'No you're not. You are trying to minimise our connection to one of indifferent acquaintances when you are fully aware I am not the least bit indifferent to you and I suspect you are not the least bit indifferent to me.' Gray had dropped his voice to prevent his superior catching him doing exactly what he knew he shouldn't be—but being a good spy when she was so close and so beautiful it made his heart ache was practically impossible.

She glanced down at the book in her hands and made a great show of reading the gold-embossed lettering on the spine. 'I am not the slightest bit interested in flirting with you, my lord, so please desist.'

'Dear me… Icy politeness, too.' He stepped forward and looked around her. Lord Fennimore was distracted and going pink as he fought with the easel. 'What happened to the fiery, tart red-head I met on the terrace? The one who blows raspberries and gives as good as she gets.'

'You caught me at a bad moment, my lord, and I temporarily forgot myself.'

'I liked her. I should like to get to know *her* better.'

'If you are going to continue to flirt, I shall have to terminate this conversation, my lord.'

Aloofness. She did that very well when she had a mind to—but he had always enjoyed a challenge. 'All right, no flirting. But, I beg you, no small talk either.' Gray smiled and rapidly changed tack. 'A business dinner? That does sound dull.' It threw her and she blinked, but quickly rallied, clearly relieved the uncomfortable subject had been side-stepped.

'My uncle finds it difficult travelling into town to manage his affairs, so once a month his banker and solicitor travel down. They arrived this afternoon, so should be long done with most of the dull stuff, but sometimes the conversations continue over dinner.'

'Very dull, then?'

She smiled, her shoulders and spine relaxing a little. 'Yes, very. Unless you find talk of investments riveting.'

He yawned. 'Does your uncle have extensive investments?'

'Not extensive. He prefers to invest in what he knows.' She blinked as she regarded him, as if that was explanation enough. Or she was mindful that she had already said too much.

'Are you purposefully being cryptic or is it a secret? Something dark and mysterious, perhaps?' Was she involved? Complicit in her uncle's crimes? As soon as the thought popped into his head he dismissed it. His gut told him no and he trusted his instincts.

'Nothing so exciting, I'm afraid, else I wouldn't need Harriet to save me. Uncle Edward invests in imports and exports. Years ago, he lent money to a friend starting such a business and discovered he had a talent for it, too. Since then he has always dabbled.'

Imports and exports. Smuggled brandy in exchange for English guns? Too coincidental to ignore. 'I should imagine Lady Crudgington is a godsend at such events.'

'Indeed she is. Men of business are prone to be serious and, as Harriet rarely is, she is an excellent diversion.'

'Much like me. I pride myself on being an excellent diversion. As your new and most neighbourly neighbour, I'd be happy to come, too—to help alleviate some of your boredom. My dour cousin and I have no dinner plans for this evening.'

'You are very bold, sir, to invite yourself to dinner.'

'I am that, Miss Cranford. Bold and diverting and very, very hungry.'

'Is there no food at Kirton House?' That sparring twinkle in her eye was returning, telling him she was not as politely indifferent as she would have him believe, nor as buttoned-up as she wanted to be. It cheered him immensely despite the fact that a dedicated spy would stalwartly resist the overwhelming urge to flirt with her when the advancement of his career hung in the balance and they had one very dangerous criminal to catch. Perhaps he wasn't that dedicated? Or more likely, promotion or no promotion, the wild streak in him that always took advantage of the moment ran too deep to be tamed so easily.

He leaned closer, far closer than was necessary, and treated his nostrils to her unique, inviting scent. 'There is. But the company leaves a lot to be desired.' Her gaze followed his to where Lord Fennimore was glaring at his dog. 'Pity a poor neighbour and give him something lovely to stare at across the dinner table just this once. I'm sure your uncle won't mind extra guests and you would be bestowing an act of gratefully received charity on a very worthy recipient. Aside from Lord Grump Weasel over there, I don't know another soul in Suffolk. I get lonely…'

'Ah—I see. Because of absolutely nothing to do with me, I should pity you *and* suffer you again at dinner tonight?'

At that, Lady Crudgington turned around and beamed. It was too well timed, so very innocent, he would bet good money she had been shamelessly eavesdropping the whole time. 'Are Lord Gray and Lord Fennimore also joining us, Thea?' She seemed delighted at the prospect and he was quietly confident Gislingham's niece would be too polite to rescind the invitation in front of Lord Fennimore, who was also smiling, clearly impressed with his subordinate's canny opportunism while oblivious to the shameless flirting that had led to it. 'How positively splendid! And there I was trying to figure out a way to get to know our new neighbours better.' Lady Crudgington rammed the easel into Gray's chest unceremoniously and wound her arm possessively through his superior's arm. 'You must sit next to me tonight, Lord Fennimore. I have a million burning questions…'

Chapter Eight

Against her better judgement, the emerald silk she had been too reticent to wear had beckoned and, before she could think better of it, Impetuous Thea had put it on. Now, waiting for the arrival of their unwelcome dinner guests after a mind-shattering report of the current state of her ever-increasing finances with the solicitor, she was supremely conscious of the bold gown's low neckline and tightly fitting bodice. It was a gown which displayed her figure to the very best effect without the need for folding her arms at all. A gown that had sat in her wardrobe for almost a year for that very reason. She should have sent the dratted thing back and insisted the modiste attach some shielding trim the moment it had arrived last summer, because now she was purposefully wearing it. For him!

If the abundant display of cleavage wasn't enough, she also had butterflies in her stomach which simply refused to fly away no matter how much she tried to distract herself from thinking about them. 'Would you like more wine, Mr Rendell?' Being the perfect hostess gave her something to do.

'I'll have some.' Harriet held out her glass. 'And if you don't mind me saying, Thea darling, you look like you could do with some, too.' Her friend shared a conspiratorial look with her uncle before dropping her voice to a whisper. 'Might help calm those nerves.'

She didn't dignify such an outrageous—and entirely correct—assumption with a response and snatched the proffered glasses away to refill them. Despite thoroughly enjoying the odd tipple, Thea had purposely eschewed all alcohol thus far this evening because of him, too. The last thing she wanted was the heady wine lowering her inhibitions and releasing Impetuous Thea into the wild, when she clearly was in dire need of all of them if this inappropriate dress was any indication. With a little wine in her system, she was prone to be more vocal with her opinions and the suppressed rebellious and wilful aspects of her character came to the fore. Aspects which were only too ready to jump to the fore with him when no alcohol whatsoever was involved.

She was pouring when she heard him arrive in the hallway and found her hand quiver a little at the prospect. Good gracious, she *was* nervous.

Nervous and excited and decidedly off-kilter. To give it something to do other than flutter, she poured a third glass, gripped it with both hands and feigned nonchalance, her back to the door while she awaited the butler to announce him.

'Lord Fennimore and Lord Graham Chadwick, my lord.'

Despite the instant awareness, Thea turned slowly, the politest of indifferent smiles pasted on her face, just in time to watch him stride into the room looking quite something in his evening clothes. The deep red silk waistcoat and its matching fat ruby stickpin might have been a garish choice on someone else, someone less cocky and confident and intrinsically disgraceful, but he effortlessly carried it off.

'My Lord Gislingham.' He inclined his head towards her uncle, then turned his gaze to hers. She watched his eyes widen slightly, then heat, making absolutely no attempt to hide his pleasure at what he was seeing. She felt the warmth of it all the way through her shockingly inappropriate dress, straight through the gauzy linen shift she also never usually dared to wear, to the scandalously cut corset Harriet had bought for her last birthday—the one which maximised her décolleté in the most inappropriate way.

'Miss Cranford. I am delighted to see you.' Because of course, he could see rather a lot of her. Her tightly trussed bosoms were positively heaving beneath her chin now that he was here and those wolf-like eyes were gazing at her so intently. 'You look beautiful tonight.' He meant it. She could see it as plain as the perfectly straight nose on his handsome face and that knowledge did odd things to her pulse.

Her uncle inadvertently saved her from stuttering something inane and nonsensical in reply by immediately introducing him to Mr Rendell, the solicitor, and Mr Squires, his private banker. As Thea went to war to control her rampant nerves and flighty body, she took a big gulp of the wine in her glass before she became aware of Harriet grinning at her. Bravado had her feigning a yawn of boredom and sipping even more wine, before she sailed across the room to greet Lord Fennimore as if his cousin had ceased to exist.

It was then that Aunt Caro decided to grace them with her presence, making a beeline for the wickedly rugged and irritatingly confident Lord Gray and attaching herself to him for the rest of the pre-dinner drinks like a limpet. As she had previously excused herself from the dinner pleading disinterest, as she did nearly every social occasion which didn't involve her cronies, Thea could only assume that her aunt had had a rapid about-face the second she learned their flirtatious new neighbour had arrived. Husband and wife usually avoided each other like the plague and Aunt Caro had her own dining room down the hall. One that was never short of an irritating sycophant or three which she hoped might make her husband jealous.

However, Thea couldn't really judge her. Uncle Edward was no better a husband than Caro was a wife. Half the time he treated her with barely contained hostility, the rest of the time he pretended she didn't exist—as he clearly was determined to do tonight. Rudely, he did not even cast her a withering glance as she sailed into the room. They were an odd partnership, one Thea had long ago given up trying to understand but was determined never to replicate. Marry for love, Uncle Edward often cautioned. Settle for nothing but the deepest and all-encompassing kind. Hard to do when every man she knew came with a desire for a veritable mountain of coin.

The next two hours were painful. Not because the conversation was stilted, because it wasn't. Her uncle had always been a lively dinner companion, Harriet was her customary entertaining self and Lord Gray certainly held up his end. He was quite the raconteur, it turned out, delighting everyone with his outrageous stories of faraway places and exotic, colourful people. Even her aunt was on good form, no doubt because of their scintillating new guest, and the formal room was filled with lively debate and much laughter.

It was Thea's own conversation that was stilted

to the point of non-existence. No matter how much she racked her brains for a witty retort or an interesting sentence to contribute to the proceedings, nothing came, and to cover the lack of things coming out of her mouth she put far too much in it. Wine mostly, but there had been a second helping of trifle which her tight corset was now bitterly regretting. She was so stuffed it was a wonder the laces had not popped under the strain caused by her unladylike gluttony and her scandalously upward-thrusting bosoms.

Lord Gray did not seem similarly afflicted despite his second helpings and seemed vastly amused by her rigidly upright posture and pained expression. She had just spotted the wretch smiling behind his napkin when he caught her subtly trying to adjust a particularly jabbing stay when she had assumed nobody was looking. Except he was. Drat him.

Constantly.

To his credit, and no doubt just to vex her, he skilfully avoided Aunt Caro's blatant flirting without appearing the slightest bit rude or uncomfortable with it, which might have earned him points in his favour had he not persisted in locking eyes with Thea repeatedly and allowing her to see the mischievous passion for her dancing in them unabashed. He flirted with her, too. More than once, but so subtly and swiftly that if you blinked you'd miss it. None of the other guests appeared to notice, but she didn't miss it. How could she when he had positioned himself in the seat directly opposite hers? Her own fault for not sticking to the correct rules of etiquette and failing to label the place settings.

Twice, thanks to his excessively long legs, his booted foot had found her slipper. The first time she had withdrawn her foot like a frightened deer. The second, and she was going to blame the wine entirely for unleashing the wanton within, she had allowed it to linger next to hers until common sense returned and she kicked him hard in the shin. He covered the pain well, but he'd almost choked on a boiled potato in the process. It was Thea's lone successful moment in a meal devoid of any and she blamed his presence entirely for that, too.

'Shall we enjoy our port over a game of billiards?' Her uncle seemed buoyed by the excellent company. 'I'm rather good if I sit in a chair to pot and you'll forgive me certain liberties.'

'A splendid idea!' Lord Fennimore had already started to rise.

'Surely all the gentleman aren't going to abandon us for a silly game?' Aunt Caro's eyes were fixed on Lord Gray as she said this, but he didn't appear to notice.

'I'm only playing if there is money involved.' He stood, his big body unfolding from the chair and suddenly looming in front of Thea. Goodness, he was tall. She had noticed it before, of course, just as she had noticed practically every minute detail about his impressive physique, but never from this angle. He noticed her looking and, to hide it, she glugged more wine, hoping the glass would prevent her from seeing his cocksure look—but the glass magnified it and that, and the additional wine, made her head spin.

'Oh, there is always money involved, young man,' said her uncle with a heartening twinkle in his eye, 'and although I like you a great deal, do not think for a second I shan't enjoy relieving you of some of it. Once I've trounced you at billiards I shall give you a thorough drubbing at cards. I like to win, Lord Gray.'

That he did. Always had and, since his stroke, tiny victories in parlour games or on the stock market made him feel less redundant and more like his old self. She tried not to judge him for it, realising it must be a massive blow to one's self-esteem to not be as robust as before—but sometimes he went too far and outright cheated. He was a charming cheat, but shameless. Winning was now everything, by whatever means he deemed necessary. His poor sportsmanship the previous Christmas over a spirited game of Speculation had been so blatant and outrageous, Thea had almost allowed herself to lose her temper with him again before Bertie interceded and poured oil on very troubled waters. But she now actively avoided playing any sort of game with him just in case she succumbed and did lose it. That said, it wouldn't hurt for Lord Gray to be thoroughly drubbed. He was far too sure of himself.

'Challenge accepted, my lord. I hope you don't expect any leniency from me.'

'Leniency! By Jove, you'll be begging for mercy by midnight, dear boy. Mark my words.'

'Well, if you gentlemen are intent on making a night of it, I shall bid you a good one,' said Harriet, rising. 'I want to get up early to paint the sunrise.' The Judas wasn't fond of Aunt Caro's penchant for superficial gossip and her constant need for reassurance. Her aunt feared ageing above all else and discussed it at great length, while Harriet totally embraced it. She was sensibly abandoning ship while she still could. She caught the butler in a vice-like grip. 'Have my carriage brought around immediately.'

In a flurry of activity, the gentlemen and her friend left, leaving Thea sat with just her aunt at the big formal table. 'Shall I order some tea?' It was a half-hearted invitation. Her aunt was well meaning, but hard work. More so than usual with every passing year, although Thea had no idea why. Caro's maid had told Thea's maid it was because she was on the change and her courses were about to stop. This, apparently, made her more fragile. Something Harriet dismissed as pure self-indulgence, but then Harriet was made of sterner stuff than her poor aunt and she had had children. Both her sons were now grown and had flown the nest while poor Caro's womb had remained barren, largely because Uncle Edward had not set foot in his wife's bedchamber in years. Callous, self-serving, unfeeling witches, he was often prone to say when the port flowed freely, were not at all his type.

'Yes, dear, it has been ages since it's been just the two of us without your uncle dominating your time. I've missed our little chats. Let's take it in my sitting room.'

Splendid. Another hour of interminable torture beckoned. The idle gossip of a very bored woman who filled her days with visits and luncheons held minimal appeal, not when Thea's silly pulse would undoubtedly quicken at the prospect of *him* a few feet away down the hall. Stripped of his coat as gentlemen playing billiards were prone to do, those muscles in his arms and back would bunch as he gripped the cue, the fabric of his breeches pulled taut over his equally taut buttocks as he leaned over the table to take the shot…

Good gracious! Would she ever get the image of his naked body out of her mind?

With heavy feet and a slightly spinning head, Thea followed her aunt. Then the pair sat like bookends at either end of the uncomfortable damask sofa. Aunt Caro always favoured this room to receive her visitors, although heaven only knew why. Probably because her husband avoided it. It was west facing, which meant it caught the full heat of the sun from mid-afternoon through to evening, making it stuffy by the end of the day. The opulent Venetian chandelier was burning brightly, adding to the oppressive temperature, and all the windows were firmly shut because of Caro's hay fever. Like dogs, flowers made her sneeze so all the arrangements in the rooms she preferred to use were silk and needed constant dusting. Their bright, fake petals always depressed Thea because they reminded her too much of her poor aunt. Desperate to be as adored as all the other flowers, but lacking in something elusive and special as each day passed. Ground down by Uncle Edward's determined indifference.

'Lord Gray seems taken with you.'

'Is he? I hadn't noticed.' Now even her aunt was matchmaking! Inevitable, she supposed, but irritating. The one thing her aunt never did was attempt to foist her off on a man. Until today, it seemed.

'You would have to be blind not to notice, Thea, dear. He barely took his eyes off you all night.'

'I have no interest in Lord Gray.' But her skin warmed regardless, simply by thinking of him.

'I am pleased to hear it.' Thea had not been expecting that.

'Why?'

Her aunt frowned as she sipped her tea. 'While he is a charming dinner companion, exceedingly handsome and a delightful gentleman for any woman to play the flirt with, I have to confess I made some discreet enquiries into his background and was shocked by what I found.' Not shocked enough not to want to flirt with him herself, though, Thea thought ungraciously before she chided herself for the reaction. It was petty to criticise her aunt when she herself had severe doubts about Lord Gray and had still happily succumbed to flirting with the charming wretch.

'Lord Fennimore has already apprised us of his long tenure in the merchant navy after his family disowned him.' For some reason, she didn't want her aunt to have the satisfaction of putting her off the man. 'I had already decided he was a thoroughly bad sort within a few hours of meeting him, but Uncle Edward seems to like him.'

'Edward has always been attracted to naughty boys. He is too easily led astray.'

Pots and kettles. Both as bad as one another while Thea tried to navigate the murky chasm called their marriage. 'Uncle likes interesting company and, despite his dubious background, one cannot deny Lord Gray is interesting.' Thanks to the wine, perhaps more interesting presently than he had any rights being. Images of him in the brook *sans* his shirt kept dropping into her mind willy-nilly, as they had done all night. After her fourth glass of wine, and in the absence of any suitable conversation to delight their guests with, Thea had given up trying to ignore the errant thoughts and had decided to enjoy them for the duration of the meal, but made a mental note to limit herself to one glass at dinner going forward until her obsession waned.

'But under the circumstances, he shouldn't be *gambling* with the man.'

'I don't see any harm in it. Bertie will step in if Uncle Edward overtaxes himself.' They paused while the tea was brought in and Aunt Caro poured.

'I wasn't talking about your uncle's health, dearest, more our new neighbour's penchant for reckless wagers. When I said I had made discreet enquiries, I was thoroughly shocked by what I discovered over luncheon with Lady Horndon yesterday.' She picked up her cup and stared over it, quite pained. 'Lord Gray was disowned by his family *after* he lost his entire fortune at the gaming tables! And it was a sizeable fortune, be in no doubt. He remains, to this day, both shunned *and*, to the best of everyone's knowledge, penniless. I doubt the merchant navy is *that* lucrative. While I am reassured that you seem immune to his charms—and we both know heiresses do attract shameless fortune hunters—I hope he doesn't see your uncle as a means to an end either. Will Bertie have the wherewithal to step in if Lord Gray takes advantage of *him*, I wonder?'

Thea felt sick. So sick the trifle threatened to make a reappearance. Up until that moment, she had not considered Lord Gray as a fortune hunter when she normally considered every man in possession of a pulse as one as a matter of course. A shameless flirt, yes. A bad influence, definitely. But he didn't outwardly seem like a man who only saw her money. Not when those unusual silvery eyes darkened with blatant desire every single time their gazes locked...

What on earth was the matter with her? He had to be a vulture, too. It certainly explained his single-minded preoccupation with her instead of her attractive, flighty and easily seduced aunt. The unpalatable truth jarred, but couldn't be denied. She knew only too well that a fortune hunter could feign whatever emotion he so desired to part an unsuspecting heiress from her money. But attempting to seduce an heiress aside, was he truly such a man to stoop so low as to take advantage of an invalid? 'He wouldn't? Surely?'

'We barely know the man.' The truth. 'Yet he now has a seat at the table after a scandalously short acquaintance. And the gossip was bad enough to have made its way here to Suffolk where it had remained fixed in people's minds for a decade and could easily recall it when I happened to mention his name. All I know is he has lost a fortune, yet dresses like a man in possession of one.' Another good point. That beautifully tailored red silk waistcoat positively oozed class. 'Where does he get his money from?'

'Perhaps Lord Fennimore is subsidising him?' Thea wasn't entirely sure how she felt about that either. A man of Lord Gray's age should be supporting himself, not living off an elderly relative. Or anyone else for that matter.

'Perhaps…but did you see his ruby stickpin? Jewels of that size do not come cheap.' Something a dedicated shopper like Aunt Caro would know. Aside from idle gossip and a diary filled with luncheons, the only other thing that woman did was shop.

Chapter Nine

To say the Viscount swindled him out of ten pounds would be unfair because it hadn't been a swindling in the strictest sense. However, Gislingham's unlikely victory at billiards had certainly come about with the use of some foul means peppered among the fair, which he made no attempt to hide. The weaker arm and leg caused him to lean extensively on the table, where the sleeve of his shirt, his wrist and on one occasion his elbow nudged the balls in directions which favoured him, but hampered Gray. At worst, it had been a good-natured, unsubtle, comical and vastly entertaining bit of knavery. All done with a charming smile and a wink. He was either an out-and-out cheat or the cheating was a test to see if Gray was brave enough to call him on it. He hadn't, but despite being ten pounds lighter in the pocket, he'd left the table liking the man. A great deal more than he should.

Now Lord Fennimore was being treated to a dose of the same warped rules and the same boisterous camaraderie. If Gislingham hadn't been one of England's most wanted criminals, he was exactly the sort of fellow you would want for a friend. Funny. Loud. The sort of man who drags you into his outrageous antics and makes you very glad to be there. No wonder he was so good at what he did. The charmer and the murderer. He was a dangerous contradiction indeed. Not that Gray had learned anything remotely useful over dinner. Despite his niece's claims to the contrary, the Viscount and his cronies had let nothing slip over the dining table or the billiard table, despite old Fennimore's subtle questions.

To see his superior in the field was also interesting. He must have been a canny spy in his day, for already he and the cheating Viscount were as thick as thieves, backslapping and laughing like old friends. While Lord Fennimore was keeping him occupied, Gray decided it was probably a good time to visit the retiring room via a meandering poke around the ground floor.

Fortunately, this late, much of the house was quiet and dark. One lone footman sat snoozing near the front door and somebody was in the kitchen in case they were summoned to feed or water the guests. Everyone else appeared to have turned in for the night aside from Gislingham's quiet manservant, who had been downstairs several times to check on his master and encourage him, unsuccessfully, to get some sleep before reluctantly leaving with a reminder that he would be back soon. That made venturing up to their host's private apartments nigh on impossible.

Instead, he methodically worked his way around the downstairs rooms, consigning their position and layout to memory as he went. Like the dining room, each room he entered was formal and dressed to impress. Persian rugs, ormolu clocks, bold damask sofas which looked pretty but were not really made for men to sit on, huge urns stuffed full of silk flowers and peacock feathers. This was very much the public face of country aristocracy who were conscious of their place in the social pecking order and keen to make the right sort of impression. Form and fashion over function, like his father's house in Wales. Nothing at all like the informality of the Viscount's private sitting room. Another contradiction.

There was a neat, feminine study with a dainty mahogany escritoire near the window. It was unlocked so, like a good spy, he carefully rifled through it, but found nothing but notepaper, quills and inks. On the opposite wall, illuminated by the moonlight, was a flattering portrait of the Viscountess from her youth, hair down and smiling winsomely in a garden. As there were no other family pictures anywhere to be seen, he came to the conclusion this room was hers, although it had the air of a space rarely used.

The next room seemed to have no purpose other than to be a place to house a harp. By the looks of it, it had never been played. Another small parlour looked to be a receiving room of some sort. A third room served as a second library, although why they needed another when the one down the hall was twice the size he had no idea. Perhaps they were big on reading here at Gislingham House? As Miss Cranford had said, there were plenty of places downstairs to accommodate the Viscount's lack of mobility, all more convenient than the rooms he favoured out of the way.

Curious. Although significantly less private.

Across from the dining room was the drawing room they had gathered in before dinner. He already knew that room well. The door was ajar and one lamp glowed softly on the mantel. He would have walked straight past it had the lace at the French windows not been billowing slightly. Either a servant had forgotten to lock them, or someone was in the garden. He had a very clear idea of which someone he hoped it would be. Like a man lured to the rocks by the sirens, he soon found himself peeking out of the French doors and he wasn't disappointed.

Miss Cranford was stood at the stone balustrade on the terrace, staring out at the stars, the moon casting her in an ethereal silhouette. A few tendrils of her heavy hair had, typically, broken free and caught on the breeze. The same breeze moulded the fabric of her gown to one side of her body. The exact same gown which had haunted his thoughts since he had first seen her in it earlier and which had fair taken his breath away for most of the evening. More·than once he had allowed himself to imagine what it would be like to peel her slowly out of it. Unpin her heavy hair and let it fall over the pert breasts that had taunted him as he had tried to be a good guest and failed to be a better spy.

In no hurry to stop staring, he lounged against the frame and looked his fill. She sensed him. Her head whipped around, her lush mouth momentarily slack. 'Lord Gray!'

'We've been over this. It's just Gray… Thea.'

'It is Miss Cranford, my lord, as well you know. And I shall remain Miss Cranford to you till the end of time.'

'As you wish.' Although he fully intended to always call her Thea from this moment on. It felt right on his tongue. 'I thought you had long gone to bed.'

'I wasn't tired.' Without thinking, Thea put her hands to her hair and began to tuck the errant strands back in their proper place. She did that a lot, he realised, as if she was embarrassed by her hair. Although why a woman with such exquisite tresses would be embarrassed by them was a mystery to him. 'After the stuffiness of the drawing room and the big meal, I needed some fresh air.'

'Too much trifle does that to a person. How many bowls did you have? Three?'

'Two. And a gentleman wouldn't mention such a thing.'

'I suppose a gentleman wouldn't mention all the wine you drank either, so I won't. But we both know you drank far more than you usually do because my presence opposite rattled you and now you cannot sleep for exactly that same reason.'

Her lovely eyes widened and blinked twice. 'I was not the least bit rattled.'

'Liar. Of course you were. You scarcely said boo to a goose all evening. It was most unlike you. You are still rattled. Admit it.'

Stop flirting with her, you fool. Think of the mission. Your promotion. Lord Fennimore's specific instruction! Your heart...

'I believe I would know if I was rattled or not, my lord, and can assure you I wasn't then nor am I now. Let me say it plainly, seeing as you seem to be having some trouble understanding—disgraceful scoundrels are not my cup of tea.'

'That's a shame. Because tart and fiery redheads are exactly mine—and, for the record, I *was* rattled. Every time I see you I'm rattled. I'm rattled now. Can't you tell?'

This was madness.

He was going out of his way to seduce her—
willingly and for his own selfish reasons rather
than all the lofty, patriotic reasons he was supposed to be upholding. This was not the time to
live wholly in the moment! What the blazes was
wrong with him? What was it about this woman
that drew him? Lust, yes, but he desired more than
a single night of passion. He wanted to know her.
Talk to her. Understand her. Knowing full well
she was the sort of woman it would take more
than one night of passion to tire of.

'Are you a chancer, Lord Gray?'

'I suppose that depends on your definition. Do
I take chances—yes. If opportunity knocks, who
am I to turn it away?'

'But what if the opportunity presented encouraged dishonesty?'

Her suddenly fierce expression bothered him.
'I am not a criminal, Thea, if that is what you are
suggesting.'

'But would you take advantage, sir?'

'I would hope not…'

'Hardly a reassuring answer when I know
about your dubious past.' Oh, dear. Bad news
certainly did travel fast. In this case, in less than
twenty-four hours. Which meant the family had
been digging. That was good for the mission, even
if it felt depressingly bad right now. 'I know you
squandered an entire fortune at the gaming tables
and ran up huge debts all over London!'

He folded his arms, instantly defensive, but didn't deny it. There was no point denying the sorry truth. 'My dubious past is exactly that. The past. It has no bearing on who I am now. People can change.' And in the main he had, and for some peculiar reason he wanted her to know it. With age had come some wisdom to see his desperate, immature quest for more riches all those years ago would not have made a single jot of difference even if he had miraculously won more than he had ultimately lost. Cecily hadn't only wanted his brother's larger fortune—she had wanted his title as well. Now she was a viscountess and the mother of Gray's two nephews and niece. Children he had never seen, that were never meant to be his, borne of a woman who had loved his brother's superior prospects far more than she had ever claimed to have loved Gray. It had taken losing everything—his heart, his fortune and all his self-esteem—to finally grow up and see life through a crystal-clear lens.

Now, he had the ability to err on the side of caution if he felt the situation warranted it. Granted, he still had some of the same tendencies of the young man he had been. The love of spontaneity. Adventure. The zestful, joyful, reckless lure of the dream. The heady, reckless heat of the moment.

'A leopard doesn't change its spots.'

'Well, actually, having had the good fortune to witness some leopards in India first hand, I can tell you categorically that they can. New-born leopards have big black patches that slowly develop into smaller spots.'

'You are being pedantic.'

'Hardly, I'm merely...'

'Are you still in debt?'

'No.' More truth, but money meant nothing to him any longer. It had been the root of his downfall and his heartbreak. Money turned goodness into bad. Twisted, manipulated and destroyed things. He had enough to get by, but was considerably richer in other ways. Ways an uppity young lady who had grown up in cossetted luxury in this quiet corner of England couldn't possibly understand.

'Not even to your cousin Lord Fennimore?'

'I owe him a debt of gratitude for seeing past the reckless youth I was and giving me a second chance.' Another completely honest answer. Despite everything, his superior had believed him capable of more else he never would have enlisted Gray into the King's Elite. Lord Fennimore handpicked every agent and hadn't picked a duff one yet in all his twenty years in charge.

'And you owe him nothing else? The clothes on your back, perchance? That expensive ruby sat in your cravat.' Her finger flicked it and he caught her hand, annoyed that she thought so little of him despite knowing her opinion was probably justified based on what he allowed the world to know.

'This ruby is all I have left of my mother. Left to me in her will, if you must know, and more precious to me than anything else I own. She wore it as a pendant. Never took it off. It is the one thing I never gambled away. Even when those creditors were banging on my door, baying for my blood, I refused to part with it—knowing it would likely clear a huge chunk of my debt if I did. And as for the clothes on my back, I earned them in the same way I earned everything since that reckless summer when I lost it all. Through hard work.'

'Do you consider thrashing my sick uncle at the gaming tables hard work?'

Gray felt instantly queasy at the accusation. As low as he had fallen all those years ago, he had never stooped that low. Ever. He had trod a solitary path of destruction till the bitter end. 'I am insulted that you would think I would take advantage of your uncle—especially as he just relieved me of ten pounds and did so through flagrant cheating. What made you think such a thing?'

She tugged her hand away and folded her arms. 'Because it's all a little too convenient, don't you think? Your supposed interest in me—an unmarried heiress—combined with your sudden desire to socialise with my wealthy invalid uncle.'

It was a little too convenient, that was the problem, and while he knew he had to brazen it out, lying to her didn't sit right. Under different circumstances, with a different sort of man from him, her suspicions would be wholly justified. 'Until this moment I didn't know you were an heiress.' The honest truth. 'And frankly, neither do I care. We met by chance. I was in the brook. Throwing a stick at my dog, if you recall, and while I will admit to intentionally furthering our acquaintance since, I did not do so because of your dowry and nor did I do it to ingratiate myself with your invalid uncle.' King and country aside, this persistent need to seek her out and flirt with her was not something a good spy would do. He was selfishly jeopardising everything because he couldn't seem to control himself around her. A very worrying prospect indeed when he had promised himself he would never be that drawn to a woman again.

Say goodnight and go back inside! Thea is off limits.

'Then why did you do it?'

He raked a hand through his hair and, in the absence of the desire to do his job properly and leave her well alone, decided to continue to stick to as much of the truth as he dare. 'Because we are neighbours. Because I felt awful that you stumbled across me naked in the brook and wished to make amends.' *Stop there!* 'Because I am irresistibly drawn to you and, despite your obviously poor opinion of me, I would like to get to know you better. I have no expectations beyond that Thea. None.' Good grief, what was he doing?

Why was he actively pursuing her, almost courting her, when that wasn't who he was at all?

'I certainly have no interest in your uncle's money, your money or—Heaven forbid—marrying for money. I am quite content being a solitary scoundrel and make no apology for that. Nor have I attempted to cover that up. A true chancer would have covered his tracks well, not displayed all his shortcomings to the world. I haven't lied, Thea. I took the twenty thousand pounds, left to me in good faith by my grandfather, the day I turned twenty-one and lost the lot in the hells in a matter of months. Then I went to sea and travelled the world, during which time I like to think I grew up a great deal. Being the worst gambler ever born doesn't make me a confidence trickster, nor the sort of scum who preys on the vulnerable. Although your uncle is hardly vulnerable. He has a mind as sharp as a tack and you insult us both by insinuating otherwise.'

She stared deeply into his eyes, searching for the truth, then dipped her head, her hands disappearing behind her back. 'Uncle Edward is nobody's fool... I jump to conclusions. I apologise for suggesting you might take advantage.' Her eyes flicked to his again defiantly. 'Although you might have just said that when I asked directly.'

'You didn't ask me that directly. As *I* recall, you asked me if I was the sort of fellow who would take advantage and I said that depends...'

'On what?'

'On the situation.' He wanted to kiss her. Badly. Kiss away all her nagging doubts about him and make them both feel better.

Don't do it!

He couldn't kiss her. Wouldn't kiss her. She already had her suspicions and he was under strict instructions to befriend her.

Avoid any and all flirting!

And deep down he knew that kissing her would be dangerous to him personally. Something about Thea tempted his dormant, embittered heart to stir. He had to protect it at all costs. 'Some situations demand I take advantage...' Some devil inside of him had apparently taken control of his body, his voice and his mind. He had lost the ability to think straight, simply because she was there.

Against his woefully absent better judgement, he reached behind her and took her hand. She stared at her palm wrapped in his larger one, a little bemused—but didn't pull it away. 'Would I take advantage of an invalid—even one who just crowed like a cockerel for relieving me of my money after he shamelessly cheated at billiards? No. Of course I wouldn't.'

'Uncle Edward is a shameless cheat.' Her voice wavered slightly as she blinked at where they were joined. 'I hope you called him on it. Nobody ever does because he can be so charming...' He was still holding her hand, his thumb moving in lazy circles over the sensitive centre of her palm. As she tried to change the subject, she also tried to gently disentangle it. He wasn't going to let her get away with that again either. Not when this foolhardy discussion was nowhere near done and he felt as if invisible cords were wrapping themselves around them, pulling them closer together. From nowhere, the self-destructive, needy part of his soul that had led him headlong into heartbreak with Cecily had apparently fully possessed him.

'Would I take advantage of the darkness and the pale moonlight? This empty, quiet garden? The close proximity of a beautiful woman who likes me far more than she wants to, who is as rattled as I am and is desperately fighting the attraction?' He could feel his jaded, stitched-together heart beating faster in his chest, urging him on, controlling him in the heat of this all-consuming moment against all his head's sensible objections. *'Absolutely.'* Gray leaned closer, the air crackling expectantly between them, his fingers finally giving in to the temptation to touch one of the loose tendrils framing her lovely face as he slowly inhaled her intoxicating perfume. 'I would be a fool not to.'

'I don't like you.' But her voice was breathy and she made no attempt to step away, her eyes dropping to his mouth before attempting to fix indifferently on his face—but failing. She was being lured into the fire, too, attempting resistance as he was, but failing. Whatever strange, magnetic force existed between them, it was too strong to fight. Worse, he didn't want to.

'Liar.' It came out as a whisper a second before his lips touched hers and she proved his point by sighing against them and kissing him back.

What should have been a simple kiss wasn't. He'd kissed many women since Cecily, yet none, including the woman who had so mercilessly bludgeoned his young heart to a pulp, had ever felt like this one.

All the usual sensations were there—the quickening pulse, the building lust and need, the delicious sensation of skin touching skin, the understandable and natural urge to deepen the kiss and taste the woman beneath—yet woven among those familiar sensations were new ones. A sense of rightness and belonging. The strange feeling in his chest, dangerously in the exact vicinity of his hardened heart, which should have terrified him but didn't. The peculiar sense of relief that he had found her and she had found him. Because out of nowhere, this unplanned and unexpected kiss was significant. Monumental. Meant to be.

Meant to be!

Not again…

Never again!

Shaken, it was Gray who pulled away first and removed his hand from where it had embedded itself in her curls. Most of the pins were now gone—he must have removed them, but had no memory of it—and all that molten copper shot with silver in the moonlight hung to her waist, where his other hand had made itself at home in the perfect curve at the base of her spine above her hip. Her arms had snaked beneath his coat and looped around his back. He could feel the heat of her palms on his shoulder blades and the soft press of her breasts flattened against his chest.

They were both breathing heavily. Both a little stunned at the intensity and power of just that one once-in-a-lifetime kiss to pull them out of the conscious world and send them into another, sensual plane where time and place no longer mattered.

Where the past apparently no longer mattered either.

'That was…enlightening.' He sucked in a calming breath and blew it out slowly. Although enlightening was entirely the word, he was more confused than enlightened. Torn between the half of him that was now immune to anything beyond the carnal and the old Gray who romanticised physical displays of affection and had willingly given all of his heart unconditionally once before. That long-forgotten need had inexplicably re-awoken. Almost as if his shattered heart was suddenly now miraculously whole and ready to give itself completely again.

That didn't make any sense.

She was staring up at him, swollen lips parted,

arms still clamping him to her. Of its own accord his head bent again and her eyes fluttered closed, until he remembered his heart knew he couldn't kiss her again tonight—or ever. For his own sanity. Last time he had allowed himself to feel, it had taken years for the wretched pain of loss to lessen. He had been an empty, broken husk cast adrift in the world. Only recently he had found himself again. Found purpose. Dared to look a little towards the future rather than living entirely in the moment. He couldn't—wouldn't—lose sight of that again. Gray was all done with being lost and he had finally found his place.

Reluctantly, he let go of her and stepped back. 'Apparently, there is still enough of the gentleman in me to remember the number of glasses of wine you drank over dinner. More's the pity.'

The sensual spell broken, she blinked and her eyes dropped to the floor. 'Yes…that was a mistake. Brought about by too much…' Her fingers gently touched her lips and she sighed, then stiffened. 'If you will excuse me, my lord… I am not myself. The wine has…er…never mind… Goodnight.' Then she picked up her skirts and practically sprinted inside.

Needing the distance, Gray made no attempt to go after her. It *had* been a mistake. A big one— for both himself and the mission. What had he been thinking? He took himself to the bench and sat heavily, trying to analyse exactly why he felt peculiar and why he had kissed her when every sensible thought in his head had screamed at him not to. Yet all he could listen to was his heart. An organ he had believed was now immune to those sort of feelings.

What was it about Thea that drew him? Why, when he had staunchly avoided thinking about it for almost a decade, was this place and that woman churning up all the things in his past he would prefer never to revisit? Was it another strange symptom of turning thirty? Like his new-found ambition, was he suddenly looking for more in his life? Had his broken, wary heart really finally mended and now sought someone else to adore as it had Cecily, or was all this uncharacteristic introspection and behaviour symptomatic of the new weight on his normally weightless shoulders? Dredging up his past to sabotage his future?

Yes!

That had to be it. With his record of failing, and his legendary ability to disappoint, he was subconsciously destroying this new dream before Lord Fennimore callously did it for him. It was always much easier to orchestrate your own downfall, on your terms, than have another tell you, yet again, that you didn't quite measure up—despite all your best attempts to convince them otherwise. The countryside, the comfortable, gentrified house, the gentleman's clothes, the rules and restrictions of this provincial society reminded him too much of the home of his youth. Fond memories of bygone days with his mother, with his childhood sweetheart before his world caved in and he lost himself in grief. He was obviously transferring his father's, his brother's and then Cecily's disappointment of the younger Gray on to the man he was now, muddying the water with nonsense from that miserable, wretched, god-awful time and making it real once again.

But he wasn't that green, unworldly, naïve boy any longer. He was a grown man hardened by life and enriched by its many experiences. He no longer needed to keep sabotaging his own destiny and he certainly did not have any desire to tread life's future path with his hand holding another's when for ten carefree years he had competently walked it all alone. He could do this. He'd earned that promotion and, by Jove, he wanted it! The ghosts of his past could go to hell. He would not do them the courtesy of failing, nor allow them anywhere near his foolish heart.

Decisively he stood and stalked back into the house. As it was when he had left it, it was as silent as a tomb aside from the boisterous male laughter still coming from the billiards room down the hall. That was where his mission and his future lay. The awful past and the boy who wore his heart on his sleeve were dead and buried. He had mourned them both enough before he had set his gaze staunchly forward.

He walked purposefully until he saw the staircase. The single lamp that had been burning on the landing had died. Because he was a man who knew exactly when to take advantage and needed to be a much better, more focused spy, Gray turned and gripped the banister, then hastily withdrew when he saw a shadow grow on the panelling.

'Lord Gray? Are you lost?' Bertie appeared above him, his face bland while his eyes narrowed slightly with suspicion as he came down the stairs to meet him.

'Not at all, my dear fellow. I've been out on the terrace, lamenting the new hole in my purse. I am still not entirely sure how I lost to his lordship... But enough melancholy for things past.' Truer words were never spoken. 'It's time I fetched my cousin and headed home to my bed.'

'Yes, my lord. It is rather late. And contrary to whatever he says, his lordship does need his sleep, too. I shall accompany you, if you don't mind, and shamelessly use you to force him to listen to reason.' Like a sentry, the manservant walked next to him through the hallway. 'I suppose he cheated?'

'Very subtly.'

'Then that *is* a first.' The servant smiled. 'My lord and master has the most competitive nature. Always has had, but it's worse now—since his stroke. He takes shocking advantage nowadays. He can be quite ruthless at times.'

Chapter Ten

Like the biggest of cowards, she avoided him for a week. He and Lord Fennimore had certainly been keeping her uncle entertained during that time. They had gone shooting, played cards twice and dined with him once again. She had obviously been invited to the latter, but had foisted herself on Aunt Caro and suffered Mr Hargreaves for the evening instead. The closest they had got was when she had spotted him twice walking his dog in the distance and she had hidden. It was pathetic. She was pathetic! All because Gray had kissed her senseless and, in so doing, had forced her to dream about the dratted, splendid kiss every single night since.

And it had been splendid. Nothing at all like the kisses of the army officer who had led her astray all those years ago, which were perfectly pleasant but nowhere near as thrilling. Or the one lamentable slip under the mistletoe the Christmas

before last, when the wassail was clearly off and
she had stupidly allowed Colonel Purbeck's ambi-
tious nephew liberties she had instantly regretted.
Like his uncle, the younger Purbeck, although significantly more handsome and interesting, made
far too much spit. That unfortunate but blessedly
brief interlude had been a moist affair which had
quite put her off kissing for ever.

Until Gray… Heavens, that man knew how to
do it! Thea still hadn't forgiven him for her outrageous and wanton reaction or herself for actively
allowing it to happen while doing absolutely nothing to stop it. Blaming the wine was cowardly.
Not when the worst of it had left her system by
the time he had happened upon her on the terrace and when Sensible Thea hadn't been bothered to make any effort to talk Impetuous Thea
out of the folly. In fact, quietly and only to herself,
she was prepared to admit in that one moment
she wouldn't have listened anyway regardless of
which Thea was in charge of her mind. In that
moment, she had wanted him to kiss her. If she
wasn't very careful in the future, the shameful
truth was she probably would let him kiss her
again. In a heartbeat.

Obviously, and despite all her concerted efforts in the last few years to the contrary, the
scary truth was she still had appalling taste in
men. Chancers, ne'er-do-wells and fortune hunters still held far too much appeal, although she

was still not certain quite which category Gray fell into. Definitely the first two, but the jury was still out on the latter.

'Order me three cakes of the Prussian green, one Dutch pink, an Ackermann's yellow and four of the Azure blues.' The poor shop assistant was struggling to write down all the things on Harriet's order because she was rattling them off so fast. 'And get me one of every kind of brush they do.' As this was the second time in a month they had made the pilgrimage to Ipswich to buy more paint, he probably thought her friend was in the process of painting an entire battleship. She did go through it at an alarming rate.

'I'm hungry. You promised me luncheon.'

'Patience, Thea. I haven't even started looking at paper and charcoal yet.' Which would effectively kill another hour.

'I'm putting my foot down.' To prove her point, she did. The loud thud on the shop floor raised a few eyebrows and made Restrained Thea wince. 'I need to eat and the charcoal and paper you really don't need can wait. I've suffered the milliner's, the haberdasher's and now the never-ending paint purchasing, when lord only knows you have enough art supplies at home to last a lifetime. Frankly, I'm rapidly losing patience.'

'She's always crotchety when she's hungry,' said Harriet in an aside to the shop assistant, 'and she is hungry most of the time. Who knows where she puts all the food she devours. By rights, she should be as fat as a house. I'll be two minutes, darling. Promise.'

Which meant twenty at least. 'I'll wait by the door.' Where Thea had every intention of tapping her foot and generally looking impatient in the hope it chivvied her friend along. She didn't hold out much hope.

She had been stood there belligerently for a full five minutes when she saw him through the window. Or at least she assumed it was him. The same dark head, the same ridiculously broad shoulders. The same stupid, instantaneous effect on her silly pulse. Only his clothes weren't right. The Gray who had just ridden past the shop was dressed nothing like a gentleman.

She took herself to the corner of the window and peered through the piles of fancy goods displayed there and scanned the busy street. She picked him out almost immediately, sat hatless atop his enormous horse, deep in what looked to be a very serious conversation. That in itself was off, when her irritating new neighbour was always mischievous and didn't appear to have a serious bone in his irritatingly perfect and manly body.

Next to him, similarly dressed in dusty commoner's clothes, were Lord Fennimore and three other men who she had never seen before in her life. Two more dusty strangers rode up and pulled alongside. One passed a note to Lord Fennimore, who read it quickly, then passed it along. Gray frowned and, if she wasn't mistaken, it seemed whatever grave news was in that missive prompted her naked bather to begin issuing terse instructions to his companions. Instructions for what?

Intrigued and desperately trying to convince herself it was more his suspect behaviour than her overwhelming desire to see him better, Thea checked Harriet was fully engrossed in her purchase. If her friend caught wind of their presence, she would insist on saying hello and the thought of that after her scandalous reaction to his kiss was horrifying. If she never had to say hello to him again, it would be too soon. But that natural reluctance did not mean she wasn't curious to see if her instincts were correct.

He was up to no good.

Because he was a chancer and a ne'er-do-well—and very probably a fortune hunter, too. Tangible proof would stop those silly butterflies flapping whenever he was around and perhaps she would also stop picturing his bare buttocks and tasting his lips while she slept.

Satisfied the shop assistant would keep Harriet busy for a little while longer, she ventured silently out of the door and surreptitiously picked her way along the street, keeping her back close to the shop fronts in case she needed to escape. Feeling like a government spy on a secret mission, she darted behind a flower stall opposite the very inn they were due to dine in, to watch and attempt to listen to him incognito.

The random snippets of conversation which floated her way over the hubbub of the busy street made no sense. 'Another shipment arrived last night... Excise Men have turned a blind eye... We need more...six thousand pounds.'

Six thousand pounds! Excise Men and shipments! Suddenly the dusty, unobtrusive clothes and the five strangers made her feel uneasy. What was he involved in? She had accused him of being a chancer and now that appeared to be the tip of the iceberg. Either that or her rampant imagination was running away with her again.

But she had heard it with her own ears. Damning things. Why would the Excise Men need to turn a blind eye to shipments if everything was above board and legal? She hadn't imagined those words, but hadn't heard the whole sentence. She was about to risk edging a little closer to hear more when Harriet's hand appeared out of nowhere, grabbed her arm with more force than was required and tugged her into plain view as she waved, oblivious of her complete lack of decorum or Thea's reluctance.

'Yoo-hoo! Lord Fennimore! Lord Gray! Fancy seeing you here?'

Both men turned, obviously startled, but both covered it quickly and smiled. The man she was avoiding quickly leaned to speak to one of the other men and within seconds their five strange companions rode off while their new neighbours dismounted.

Practically dragged at speed towards them by her purposeful friend, Thea pasted on her best I-have-no-recollection-whatsoever-of-spying-or-of-an-illicit-midnight-kiss expression and stubbornly refused to blush. He would not see that his presence bothered her, nor would she ever let on the annoyingly invigorating effect he had on her heart.

'Ladies, what a pleasure!' It was Lord Fennimore who attempted a smile while his usually bold, flirtatious companion merely nodded. There was no mischief in his silver-blue eyes today either and inexplicably she missed that. 'I see you have been shopping.' Solicitously he took the package Harriet was carrying. 'Can we escort you back to your carriage?'

'You may escort us to the inn where we are having luncheon—and, if you've a mind to, why not join us?' Harriet had already woven her arm possessively through Lord Fennimore's, blithely ignoring his slightly bewildered expression, and was determinedly leading the way. It left Thea to trail behind with the only person in the world she'd wished never to see again. Silently she willed them to turn down her friend's off-the-cuff invitation.

'I am afraid business precludes us from enjoy-

ing the pleasure of your invitation, Lady Crudgington.' It was the first time Gray had spoken and,
despite saying what she had vehemently willed
him to, she experienced the deflated sense of disappointment at his polite refusal. 'We have already eaten and have an appointment.'

'Really? What sort?' It was none of her business, but Thea wanted to know. To let him see
she had noticed his peculiar apparel, she allowed
her eyes to fix on the scruffy coat. 'If you will
forgive me for being blunt, my lord, you are not
dressed for *serious* business.'

His eyes held hers unwaveringly. There was
none of his usual warmth in them and she found
she missed that, too. This was a very different
Gray from the man who had kissed her so thoroughly on the terrace. 'My cousin and I have been
thinking about breeding horses. We both have a
nose for good horse flesh and have been looking
for suitable animals since we arrived in Suffolk.
It is quite staggering how much more expensive
a decent stud is if you are wearing a fine coat.'

'Indeed it is,' said Lord Fennimore, turning
around. 'And while we are still relatively unknown here so far away from London, we thought
it best to capitalise on that anonymity. Two mid-
dling, hard-working farmers can negotiate significantly better deals than two lords in polished
Hessians.'

'Very prudent,' said Harriet, staring up at him

adoringly. 'What a clever man you are, Cedric…
I can call you Cedric, can't I?'

The older man blushed and stammered. 'Why…
yes. Of course.'

'Splendid. And you must call me Harriet.' Her
friend brazenly squeezed his arm again, running
her other hand over his bicep. 'How strong you
are, Cedric. It is such a pleasure to meet a gentleman who hasn't allowed the years to soften him.
So many gentlemen of *our* age allow themselves
to run to fat. Tell me, do you enjoy a good ride?'

'I do.'

'So do I! We must ride together one morning.
An invigorating gallop across the dewy, dawn-
kissed fields to get the juices pumping. Wouldn't
that be lovely?'

'Er…yes…'

Thea allowed her gaze to flick to her silent
companion's at the same moment his turned to
her and there it was, that glorious, warm, amused,
dancing light of mischief. Fleeting because he
quickly snuffed it and stared at the inn.

'Saturday, perhaps? I shall call on you at, say…
seven?' Harriet was shameless in her pursuit and
poor Lord Fennimore could do nothing but nod
while his expression suggested he wanted to run.
Very fast down the high street. As if his breeches
were on fire. 'Thea and Gray can come, if they've
a mind to.'

'I am helping my uncle then as you well know.'

The truth, but she'd have lied shamelessly to get herself out of any prolonged and enforced contact with *him*. 'Dear Bertie is going away for a week at least and therefore I shall be needed constantly.' A big, fat lie. Uncle Edward would rather die than have her attend to his personal needs while Bertie enjoyed his annual visit with his family, but at some point during the mornings she would help him with his correspondence. As usual. Thea's days were all depressingly much the same.

'Then it'll be just us, then, Cedric,' said Harriet coquettishly. 'How exciting.' The older man simply blinked and offered a peculiar cross between a grimace and a smile before he was practically dragged onwards.

They reached the door to the inn and the blessed escape from the awkward cloud that hung between Thea and Gray. The package exchanged hands again and while Lord Fennimore bowed politely, his cousin simply inclined his head and refused to meet her eye. If she had to use an adjective to describe his behaviour, then only one sprung to mind: shifty. Thea had caught him up to no good and he knew it. 'Good day, gentlemen.'

'Good day, ladies. Enjoy your luncheon.'

Harriet couldn't resist one last attempt. 'Cedric—can I trouble you to assist me in getting these packages to the carriage?' They all knew full well that the servants would do that, but Lord Fennimore smiled, then hesitated, then to Thea's utter horror, and his disgraceful cousin's if the sudden hard set of his jaw was any indication, he grabbed every package. 'It would be my pleasure. Gray and Miss Cranford can wait here and mind the horses.'

Before Harriet disappeared, she looked back, her traitorous lips silently mouthing one word. *Leap.*

Gray found himself reluctantly stood all alone opposite the siren who had haunted his thoughts and his dreams for the past week. The very woman who tempted him heart and soul as no woman had since Cecily and whose magnetic draw frankly terrified him. He could feel the pull of it now despite vehemently trying to suppress it. After the ill-advised, earth-shattering kiss that had apparently confused the hell out of him, he had promised himself he'd keep a safe distance from the vixen. Something he had managed with a great deal of difficulty when her uncle was his mission. But thanks to his now encyclopaedic knowledge of her schedule, manage it he had.

Thus far. Although he knew such avoidance was unsustainable. He needed a better line of defence long term. Women who tugged at his heartstrings were strictly off limits.

For ever.

That was the mantra he silently repeated in his head over and over as he tried and failed not to be sucked in by her toxic allure, with her dangerously less than a foot away, blatantly staring, those dark eyes slightly narrowed with either hostility or suspicion. Or outright indignation after he had passionately kissed her, stalwartly avoided her and was now doing his damnedest to forget about it. Like a coward, he stared at the ground, hoping she was in no mood to converse with him either, only to watch her foot tapping impatiently.

'Horses, you say?' So much for that ploy. What had possessed him to resurrect his old dream as an excuse? Granted, he had more than enough knowledge to be able to blag his way around the lie, but that dream churned up the past again and reminded him of the blindly hopeful young man he was. The foolish one who had paid an awful price for daring to dream.

'Yes. We want to purchase one stud and at least four mares.' The blasted sultry jasmine scent was like opium. He wanted to lose himself in the smell. Bury his nose in the perfect alabaster spot just behind her ear that he had tasted all too briefly and now desperately wished that he hadn't. 'Cedric hopes that breeding horses will keep me out of mischief.' Now he was grateful for his scandalous past and would ruthlessly use it to hammer a huge wedge between them—for his own safety. 'It might work.'

'Might?'

'A leopard doesn't change its spots.'

'Yet only last week you said a leopard could.' Damn her excellent recall.

'Technically it does, yes. But it is still a wild animal and, as such, must be approached with caution.' Or not at all. Preferably not at all. Inexplicably, he could feel the heat of her body this close to his, the gentle tug of the invisible cords which pulled them together, and immediately took a step backwards in the hope it would make his own body less aware of her. It didn't work. Already his heart was pumping, his cravat too tight and his eyes kept drifting to her lips. The vixen had bewitched him and whatever spell she had cast was too strong to completely ignore.

'I thought you didn't know a single soul in Suffolk?' One of her hands found its way to her hip and forced him to recall in exact detail how perfectly his own hands had fitted in the cradle of that curve. Fortunately, her hostile glare went some way to taking his thoughts away from the carnal. 'In which case, who were your companions?'

'Staff. Grooms. His stable master. Cedric brought them from his house in Mayfair.' Gray was thinking on his feet and hoping he would have the opportunity to brief his superior on his mounting tower of lies before it all came tumbling around his ears. 'We need people we trust to see to the horses once we purchase them.'

'Interesting.'

'How so?' It was apparent she was studying his reactions carefully, something as disconcerting as it was worrying. It was obvious she was suddenly suspicious, more so than when she had accused him of being a chancer, which meant something had caused her hackles to rise. Had she heard him talking to his men? Because he had learned from one of his Invisibles that she had no fixed plans for the day, it hadn't occurred to him they would collide with her an hour's ride away in Ipswich. A foolish assumption when this was the largest town anywhere near in the vast ocean of unspoiled countryside and probably the only place ladies like her could shop. He and Lord Fennimore needed to be more careful because Gislingham's sceptical niece was nobody's fool.

Damn and blast, she was as sharp as a tack, which was part of the problem. Since Cecily, he had avoided dalliances with exceedingly clever women despite having a penchant for them. Clever women fired his blood as well as his loins. Clever women were dangerous. Losing them hurt. He would never risk that pain again.

'It doesn't suit you—the horse-breeding. It seems too sedate a pastime to hold your interest. A man who once blithely took root at the gaming tables and then sailed the seven seas strikes me as one who would seek something more adventurous to occupy his time. Something more thrilling and dangerous?'

'Is that how you see me? Thrilling and dangerous? I *like* that.' The flirting had leaked out of its own accord before good sense could stop it. Worryingly, she kept having that effect on him. The timely arrival of the afternoon post gave him a moment to steel himself, but as the noise created an excellent diversion she took the opportunity to lean close and hiss in hushed tones, her warm breath torturing his ear and giving his primed body all manner of wholly inappropriate ideas he really could not afford to indulge.

'I have found no reason to reappraise my initial assessment of you, my lord. *You* are a chancer and a ne'er-do-well. A man with scant regard for the proper rules of society. I suspect you are a scoundrel to boot. A deceitful, lying, self-serving scoundrel of the first order! Am I correct?'

He found himself leaning closer, too, so that his mouth was scant inches from her crackling hair. Those invisible strings pulling again and he was apparently powerless to fight them.

'Are you still miffed about that kiss? I knew it rattled you.' Hell—it had rattled him. Petrified him, truth be told. Because it had meant something. Something he had never expected to be seduced by again. Her lush mouth opened to speak, then promptly closed. The delicate, outraged blush which stained her cheeks made him smile as his eyes shamelessly feasted on her lips. 'I knew it.' And against his better judgement he needed to touch her again. One last time. To test the waters and see if what he suspected was true. His hand had made its way to her arm, the backs of his fingers grazing the filmy fabric of her sleeve. He couldn't seem to stop himself, any more than he could stop wanting to kiss her again or revel in the heady feelings of excitement and rightness welling in his chest.

He needed to, though.

Ruthlessly crush this moment in his fist because she was dangerous. Both to his mission and his heart.

Yet his index finger had finally found her wrist and softly traced along the outer edge of her hand, down her little finger. Her own hand tangled and closed around his.

Did she feel it, too? That inexplicable connection, that need to be close.

She ruthlessly snatched it away, stared at her palm before her fingers closed tightly around it in front of her heart. 'Why, you insufferable—'

'What are you two whispering about?' Lady Crudgington appeared from nowhere, arm cosily wrapped in his scowling superior's, her expression intrigued. 'Are you two *flirting*?'

'We most certainly are not!' Thea gripped her reticule tightly with both hands and poked her pretty nose in the air. 'Well—*I* am categorically not! Lord Gray is a law unto himself. Normal rules of decorum do not appear to apply to him.'

A comment which earned him a blood-curdling glare from Fennimore, but also saved him from himself and those lethal, invisible cords. For the first time in his tenure in the King's Elite, Gray was supremely grateful for the comforting, familiar protection of the old man's hearty disapproval. It made secret, whispered, unsanctioned, highly dangerous conversation impossible henceforth. Or at least he hoped it would—seeing as he apparently couldn't control it all himself.

Chapter Eleven

There was something not quite right about Lord Gray. Thea felt it in her bones. Granted, she always felt her ludicrous suspicions in her bones, but this time it was different. She had decided that after hours of tossing and turning as sleep eluded her and her mind circled around the words she had heard.

Shipments.

Excise Men.

Turning blind eyes.

It all pointed to something illegal—like smuggling. A topic which was particularly pertinent at the moment. The London papers were rife with terrifying stories of bloodthirsty cut-throats and traitors, all lured by the easy riches of free trading, and had been for months. Even in this quiet corner of rural Suffolk, the news had caused a stir. It was all anyone could talk about yesterday at the inn as Thea had choked down her luncheon, and it was a little too coincidental that she had over-heard Gray talking about shipments on exactly the same day as a veritable battalion of Excise Men were crawling over the port of Ipswich, searching every boat with a fine-toothed comb.

His behaviour had been decidedly odd, too. He had looked uncomfortable. Guarded. The charming flirt had been missing for nearly all of their brief interaction, until he used it ruthlessly to prevent her from asking questions. It galled that, like a dolt, she had fallen for it. His touch had made her momentarily forget about his shady-looking companions and his unbelievable assertions that he was going to breed horses. That gentle, posses-sive brush of his fingers down her arm and bare hand had made her silly body want and her lips hungry for his kiss again. She had felt that touch everywhere, in places that shocked her, and the illicit memory could still conjure those same feel-ings of desire instantaneously even now.

Why was that, when she knew in her bones he was not at all who he pretended to be and not at all trustworthy? He was a gambler. A fortune hunter. Very probably a smuggler if his reference to the Excise Men was anything to go on and he had the charming, practised air of a skilled philan-derer, too. She didn't want to be drawn to him or feel how he made her body hum with excitement. And she certainly didn't want to like him, spar or spend time with him. Or pathetically hope that all her suspicions about him were wrong so that they could continue from precisely where they had left off on the terrace after he had kissed her—and she had wantonly and greedily kissed him right back. Clearly Impetuous Thea was predisposed to be hopelessly attracted to scoundrels no matter how hard she tried not to be.

Horses!

There had been no sign of such an endeavour at Kirton House thus far. Of that she was in no doubt. She might well have been avoiding the scoundrel for the last week—but she had found her feet taking her within viewing distance of the house on more than one occasion and had, to her great shame, watched it quite intently for several minutes as she slowly strolled or rode past on the off-chance she might catch a glimpse of him.

At least today she was watching the house for quite different reasons. Today, Thea was on a mission. A dawn mission to ascertain exactly what was what and decide if her suspicions about the man were well founded. Thea knew horses. One couldn't grow up in the countryside without a rudimentary knowledge of what such an endeavour would entail and she had significantly more than a rudimentary knowledge. Uncle Edward's stable was the envy of the county. If her new neighbour was intent on breeding them, there would be signs. An exercise area. The stables would need to be readied for the stud and the brood mares.

There would be hay. Lots and lots of hay. And those *grooms* would be busy. Although perhaps not this early in the morning. After a night of never-ending insomnia, she had flung herself out of bed as the sun had begun to rise and left the house as the clock struck five. By her calculations, she had a good half an hour to spy before the servants rose at six.

After checking the coast was clear, she risked leaving the dense bank of trees that shrouded the brook from the house and attempted to look nonchalant as she walked, clutching the basket she had brought by way of a disguise for all she was worth. If spotted, she reasoned she needed a good excuse to be out and as one of the local farmer's wives was on the cusp of giving birth, the hastily wrapped bread, cheese and fruit cake she had grabbed from the pantry would look like the perfect, helpful gift from a thoughtful neighbour. All perfectly plausible.

She heard a bark and froze. Then in a panic dropped to the floor, hoping the patchy carpet of wild flowers would be enough to hide her. The dog barked again and didn't stop, causing Thea to scramble on her hands and knees back to the cover of the trees, her eyes never leaving the house.

Thea had barely made it when to her horror the front door opened and the man himself, complete with bouncing hound, emerged into daylight. Dressed in just his shirt and breeches, he didn't appear ready to be seen outside, but her eyes drank in the sight regardless as he stretched and flexed his arms. Magnificent arms aside, he wore those breeches well, too. Even from this distance, how well couldn't be denied. Drat him.

He grinned down at his dog and ruffled Trefor's black ears, then he appeared to prise something out of his mouth. She watched, fascinated, as he threw it, marvelling at how far those strong, muscled arms beneath that gloriously flimsy white linen could send it. The dog bounded after it, tail wagging, picked it up and began to run back to his master. But then he stopped, sat and pointed his nose skywards, sniffing the air.

What had possessed her to throw herself guiltily on the ground rather than shoot him a withering glare as she marched past? When she had every right to be striding across her uncle's land no matter what time of day it happened to be! Now there was every chance he would find her if his dog was this curious.

Suddenly feeling very exposed and stupid crouched among the leaves, she held her breath for a full ten seconds, but it was too late. As if he sensed her, Trefor's eyes locked with hers and he began to race towards the trees at speed. He barrelled through the undergrowth with what appeared to be a leather cricket ball in his mouth. He took one look at Thea and then deliriously nuzzled his head against her shoulder while his tail whizzed from side to side.

'Trefor!' At Gray's shout from behind the screen of trees, the animal froze momentarily before continuing his worship of Thea. 'Come on, boy! How can we play catch if you've run off with the ball?' There was a pause, as if he had stopped walking and was listening, then he spoke again. 'Fetch the ball, Trefor! Fetch the ball!'

Realising he had no idea she was here and was probably content to walk on by, she felt no compunction to apprise him of her presence—or allow his dog to. With minimal movement, she prised the soggy ball out of Trefor's jaws and tossed it in the direction of both the trees and his master. Immediately, the animal bounded after it, rummaged and then proudly held it aloft in his mouth as Gray called him again.

'Come on, Trefor! Do you want me to throw it again or not? Fetch the damn ball!'

Bizarrely, Thea got the distinct impression the dog knew exactly what his master was saying, because he dithered for a moment as if torn. Then he decided to bring the dratted thing back to her, dropping it in her lap and then eyeing it expectantly as if it was the only thing in the world that truly mattered. She tossed the surprisingly heavy ball again as if it were something offensive and whispered to the dog, 'Go! Shoo!' Her arms gesticulated wildly, but silently, in the direction of the man she very definitely did not want to see while she mimicked his instructions in a whisper. 'Fetch the ball, Trefor. Fetch it for *Gray*!'

Fetch was clearly the magic word because the dog was off like a shot, another thing Thea was determined to mimic. She scrabbled to stand, simultaneously snatching up her basket, before darting to the bank of trees in the opposite direction and escape. She hadn't moved two yards before the dog followed. He did a quick circle of her legs before dropping the dreaded ball at her feet again. It clipped her toe and made her wince, but self-preservation made her bite back the instinctual cry of pain.

Fearing imminent discovery, she grabbed it and threw it again, though this time she put all her weight behind it. The ball flew beyond the canopy to the meadow beyond. There was a dull thud, then a yelp, and Thea realised she had managed to hit *him* in her panic.

Good heavens, what disaster!

To compound her misery and despite her spirited throw, the dog had stubbornly chosen to stay put at her feet and helpfully decided to bark in case his master was left in any doubt of her location. 'Shh!' A command which apparently made him bark louder as he proceeded to follow, then hamper her hasty dash for freedom. Inevitably, and to her complete mortification, the shambles continued.

'Were you attempting to kill me or simply knock me out?' He emerged through the branches, rubbing his temple, typically handsome and wind-swept—the wretch.

'If I had been attempting either I would have succeeded, believe me. I dare say it's no less than you deserve.'

'For kissing you?'

And just like that she felt the power of that kiss all over again. 'For being a scoundrel! I am on to you, Lord Gray.'

'On to me?' While his face was expression-less, his wolf-like eyes were amused. 'I see you are still obsessed with my being a chancer and…' He snapped his fingers as if searching for the right word. 'What was it again? A ne'er-do-well?' He stopped dead and stood on the bank a few feet away from her, his hands on his hips as he glanced around, taking in the basket, her dishevelled appearance and then smiling knowingly as his eyes finally rested on the brook. 'In view of your apparent vehement dislike of me, this is in an interesting venue to choose this morning. The original scene of the crime…'

Foolishly, she allowed her gaze to follow his to the water and immediately pictured him in it. Naked. Shameless. Then the splendid kissing sprang to mind and, to her mortification, a fero-cious blush began to creep up her neck. 'Crime is an *interesting* choice of word!' Before he mentioned how naked he had been that fateful morning, Thea decided to vent her suspicions openly to detract him from the blush. People went red with anger, too, although perhaps not in quite the same way. 'Especially when one is a criminal, Lord Gray!'

'It's just Gray—and what the blazes are you talking about?'

'Horse-breeding indeed? Do I strike you as daft, *Lord* Gray? Kirton House is not ready for horses and I heard you yesterday! Excise Men turning a blind eye to shipments! Six thousand pounds of ill-gotten gains! You are worse than a ne'er-do-well. It wouldn't surprise me if you were a smuggler!'

He was silent for the longest time before he threw his dark head back and roared with laughter. 'A smuggler! That is priceless. I believe Lady Crudgington's assessment of you is spot on. Your imagination is as vivid as your hair, Thea!'

'I know what I heard. I have excellent ears.'

'I know. I nibbled one of them. Sensitive, too. You moaned, if I recall, the second my lips found it.'

'Stop it!'

'You're the one who brought up your ears.' Those unusual silvery eyes were dancing as he slowly edged towards her. 'Now I can't stop thinking about them.' Nor could she stop her stupid ears tingling with the memory. She had moaned when his lips had found them. Moaned loudly and writhed shamelessly against him. That was mortifying.

'And stop right there!' Thea held her hand outstretched, palm out in warning. 'I will not allow your incessant flirting to succeed in scaring me off or distracting me from saying what you do not want to hear this time! I heard you. Clear as crystal. Discussing an illegal shipment with Lord Fennimore and all those strange men— illegal shipments worth six thousand pounds.'

'That's right. I was.' He folded his arms across his chest and stared at her levelly. 'It was all anyone could talk about at that inn in Ipswich. Although surely you must have seen the Excise Men yourself swarming along the river that day, too? They were very hard to miss and the subject of much speculation from the locals. By all accounts, the free traders sailed it all into the city as bold as brass only that morning. Although I dare say you can read a better summary in the newspaper if you've a mind to? Even in the wilds of Suffolk smuggling is big news. Especially nowadays. After that big trial in the capital a few weeks ago...'

Chapter Twelve

Gray watched her mouth open as if to speak, hesitate, then clamp shut as his convincing lie marinated. Thank the lord he had had the wherewithal to link her accusation to the smuggling trial. A trial which had been all over the London scandal sheets since they had first arrested Viscount Penhurst two short months before. His arrest on charges of high treason, subsequent conviction and sentence of execution had been all anyone could talk about—as only a story about English peers complicit in a plot to restore the hated Napoleon to power could. Penhurst's brutal murder in Newgate alongside another convicted and titled traitor just a few weeks later by the very criminal gang they had diligently smuggled for had created widespread fear and panic.

As it should have. If those smugglers had been able to get into Newgate, there was no telling what they were capable of. The whole country was obsessed with unmasking The Boss—not just the King's Elite. For good measure, and to compound her indecision, he decided to drip in a little bit more.

'Rumour has it, it is the exact same gang of cut-throats that lynched that fellow in Newgate! Who'd have thought they would turn up here— unless here is where the criminal mastermind of it all lives?' He watched her carefully, looking for clues, and saw only shock at the suggestion. 'Perhaps this particular corner of Suffolk is not so sleepy after all?'

A delightful crease appeared between her eyes. 'Perhaps...' Then she shook her head and refused to meet his eyes. Several seconds ticked by during which she chewed on her lush bottom lip to torture him. 'I suppose I owe you an apology for jumping to conclusions?' Although she didn't look convinced. Gray had introduced doubt, but not conviction. He made a mental note to set the Invisibles the task of making the house look like a suitable place to breed horses as soon as possible, mindful the suspicious minx might well check.

'Well, if you are going to jump to conclusions, the very least you can do is make them outrageous. I have little time for lily-livered conclusions. Choose a course and commit to it wholeheartedly. That's always been my motto. Besides, no harm was done. Part of me is supremely flattered you think me that exciting—another part feels duty-bound to respond to your gracious apology with one of my own.' Best to get it over with. Old Fennimore would only nag him incessantly until he'd fixed things and it wasn't her fault Gray couldn't control his emotions around her.

He'd made a hash of things yesterday. First with his stand-offish belligerence brought about by sheer panic and then with his uncontrollable flirting, brought about by lord only knew what. His emotions around her were uncontrollable, when he prided himself on his control, and his normally reliable ability to rise above panic had saved the day on several occasions—particularly now that he was a government spy. Yesterday both attributes had deserted him and he had behaved exactly how he'd felt—terrified of the strange spell she held him under and yet a slave to it at the same time.

Neither would help the mission and, as his superior had vociferously pointed out in loud, clipped tones after the incident at the inn, he was supposed to be befriending Thea and ingratiating himself into her family circle, not making her want to kill him or insulting her with his inappropriate urges. Hiding and avoiding her was a pathetic way of dealing with the situation and after only a week already proving problematic, seeing as they had now collided twice in quick succession despite his best efforts not to.

He was now under strict orders to smooth

things over, pour oil on troubled waters and behave like a gentleman going forward. Something
he had promised to do at his earliest convenience.
That promotion hung in the balance, dangling like
a carrot again. If he didn't make things right, that
carrot would soon turn into a hard stick for his
permanently disappointed superior to beat him
with. For once, he needed to seriously consider
the consequences before he allowed temptation
to lure him to live in the moment. A depressing
thought when every moment with her crackled
with promise as well as danger.

After the unexpected and hostile exchange
with the woman who seemed destined to be an
itch he couldn't and wouldn't dare scratch, the
King's Elite hadn't left Ipswich till after dark last
night and had discovered nothing new. A slap in
the face when they had learned too late from the
Excise Men that The Boss had had the audacity to dock not one, but three ships just outside
of Leiston the night before. Hundreds of barrels
of brandy had then been offloaded into carts and
smaller boats and at least a quarter of those had
sailed brazenly up the River Orwell into Ipswich
to be sold at almost the exact hour they had arrived in the place. To know that his associates
were there, bold as brass right under their noses
while they had been oblivious, galled him. Constantly thinking about her, and that kiss, when

he was determined to be a better spy had galled him more.

'I'm sorry about my flirting yesterday…and for stealing that kiss last week. It's hardly a surprise you think me a scoundrel when I keep behaving like one. I really have no excuse other than to say you seem to bring out the worst in me and I've always had a tendency to act on impulse rather than think things through—as my indelibly stained reputation will undoubtedly attest.'

'I bring out the worst in you!' She didn't appear convinced of his sincerity either. 'That rather shifts the blame for your behaviour on to me, when I have done nothing to encourage it and repeatedly tried, and failed, to discourage it.' She hadn't always discouraged him. She had gazed at him with desire in her lovely eyes, held his hand, wound her arms around him and thoroughly kissed him back. Things a gentleman wouldn't mention.

'You are absolutely correct and once more all I can do is apologise and strive to do better in the future.'

'Again, another lacklustre statement. *Striving* to do better is nowhere as reassuring as a definitive promise to do better. It gives you a certain amount of leeway.'

He sighed and smiled. 'All right—no leeway, I will behave myself henceforth.'

'Thank you.'

'And I shall limit my flirting to only the social kind rather than the real.'

Her auburn brows came together in a frown. 'Now you are being pedantic and changing the parameters of your apology.'

'I'm a shameless flirt by nature and know for a fact I cannot swear I will *never* flirt with you again. I am only human, Thea, and you are the single most beautiful woman I have ever laid eyes on. You are a huge temptation, make no bones about it, but I shall alleviate a great many of your concerns by being upfront about my intentions—something which I know bothers you. What with you being an heiress and all.' And him in fear of what remained of his heart. 'I should like to state, for the record, that any social flirting I send in your direction is harmless because I have too much respect for you to shamelessly seduce you for sport and can't trust myself not to attempt to seduce you if I risk kissing you again. But as I have no desire to court you under any circumstances, stolen kisses are now strictly out of bounds.' He drew a cross on his heart with his finger. 'I am still a gentleman underneath it all and know that courting a proper young lady like yourself should only be done if the gentleman has designs on marriage, which I certainly don't.'

His completely honest response obviously surprised her as much as it did him, because the previously furrowed eyebrows raised, one disappearing under a heavy spiral of shimmering copper which refused to remain behind the ear she repeatedly attempted to curl it behind. That curl appeared shockingly lonely all on its own and his fingers itched to release every spiral from her coiffure and then arrange them artfully over her naked shoulders and breasts like Titian would undoubtedly do if he had the great fortune to have her as his model. More unchecked, unwise, unwelcome thoughts to cloud his judgement and bring about his downfall. Those invisible cords threatening to control his every movement like a marionette if he allowed them.

'I'm not altogether sure what you want me to say to that.'

'Nothing at all.' Definitely nothing at all. If she confessed to having a similar attraction to him, then no amount of sensible reasoning would be able to stop him from kissing her again until they were both a tangled, breathless heap on the secluded river bank. 'I am simply laying all my cards flat on the table and proposing a cautious truce.'

'A cautious truce?' She had given up trying to tame the curl and stood completely baffled instead. 'And I suppose I am expected to believe that on the back of it a leopard *can* change its spots? This sounds like a cunning ploy.'

'Nothing so devious or so premeditated. I am being honest. Frank. Expressing my limitations and desires plainly, for both our sakes. Because we both know you thoroughly kissed me back and that horrifies you as much as my partiality to you frightens me.' She blushed prettily, but he carried on before she could deny it. 'I can't say I blame you. I am a shameless flirt. A scandal. A tiny bit of a rogue. I am certainly not marriage material nor the sort of suitor a woman like you deserves, so we both have a vested interest in nipping this unwelcome attraction firmly in the bud. Hence the cautious truce. From this moment on I propose we give each other as much space as possible to prevent unwanted temptation. If social engagements throw us together—which they inevitably will—we can indulge in a bit of harmless flirting and nothing more. We must be casual, platonic acquaintances. Polite neighbours. We'll pass the time and chat if we meet, but never purposefully seek each other out or dally too long in each other's presence. A clear line has been drawn.' He swiped the air with his hand decisively and watched her blink in either affront or disbelief.

'Don't get me wrong. If I was in a mind to court a woman, you would be exactly the type I would choose. I have always admired intelligent, quick-witted females, especially those that come wrapped in such enticing packages, and something inexplicable about you calls to me and perhaps on a far deeper level than I care to admit. But, alas, my courting days are done and as I have no desire to dabble with the institution of matrimony again—even for a woman as tempting as you—I need to keep you at arm's length. For my own sake. And you have a reputation to preserve, so cannot go around kissing disgraceful gentlemen senseless. We cannot trust ourselves to be alone together. Well, I certainly cannot trust myself to be alone with you, so shan't be. Gracious—who knew complete transparency would be so cathartic?'

Aside from following Lord Fennimore's orders, verbalising his frustrations made him feel oddly relieved. Telling the truth was like lancing a boil and doubtless would result in them feeling better now that they both knew exactly the lay of the land.

'You have been married?' Why had he let that slip?

'No. Almost. Once.' More honesty which his mouth felt compelled to share in the spirit of the moment and against the express wishes of the cautionary voice in his head. Gray never discussed that part of his past. Not even with his friends. 'Poor Trefor is patiently waiting for some exercise and I did promise him some vigorous ball throws. Why don't I escort you back to Gislingham Hall, in a politely platonic and casually neighbourly way, and while on route we can both speculate as to what is happening between your friend Harriet and my grumpy cousin Cedric. Local gossip is perfectly acceptable between neighbours.'

He didn't dare attempt to offer her his arm, knowing that if she took it he'd want more. She nodded slowly after a moment of thought and they began to walk side by side.

'What happened between you and the lady?'

'It wasn't meant to be.'

'Ah, she broke your heart, Lord Gray.' It was a statement, not a question, which meant his expression must have given him away at some point. He hoped he hadn't appeared completely devastated and, in case he had, became flippant.

'Into smithereens, *Miss Cranford*.' He put emphasis on the formality, hoping it would remind her of their new boundaries.

She was silent for an age, staring down at Trefor as he danced backwards and forwards between them, waiting for the forthcoming doses of affection he always believed were his due. Eventually, she succumbed and leaned down to pet him as they walked. 'Then you have my sympathy, Gray. I know a little of what it feels like to be disappointed by another.'

'You do?' The idea that some blaggard had misused her or broken her heart immediately raised his ire. He wanted to punch the faceless man for having the audacity to hurt her and had to stop his fist clenching at his side. 'Are you nursing a broken heart, too?'

'No.' She stared off into the distance wistfully before flicking her gaze back to his. 'My heart has remained blessedly untrampled, but experiences have made me jaded. When one is an heiress…'

'One becomes the target of every fortune hunter in England?' Aspects of her character suddenly fell into place and he felt for her. He had never considered how difficult it must be if the shoe was on the other foot. Fate had cursed him with an inadequate fortune which had led to his love not being enough for Cecily. Thea had been cursed with the opposite. 'Then you also have my sympathy in return. It must be hard to not know whether a gentleman's interest in you is nought but financial. Money always brings out the worst in people.' As it had in Cecily. Money and a title. 'With the clarity which only comes with hindsight, I am strangely glad I lost all mine. I've found life much simpler without the burden of it.'

She paused in tickling his shameless dog's belly to look at him, although this time with openness rather than her customary guardedness or suspicion. 'It *is* a burden. One that seems to get heavier with each passing year. Nobody else seems to appreciate that irony. Especially my uncle. He has made it his mission to reinvest the enormous sum he gifted me, believing it gives me independence and freedom, when the opposite is in fact the case.'

An interesting confession that gave him an insight into her situation. 'I should imagine it makes you very suspicious of people. Men in particular.'

'Every would-be suitor has fallen foul of those suspicions. Sadly, all justifiably, although perhaps not quite to the outrageous extent my vivid imagination suggests.' She smiled then, the beautiful smile that took his breath away and made him question his solemn pledge to keep her at arm's length until he could leave her and those invisible cords behind. 'Hence you were immediately found to be guilty of smuggling when there are a thousand other more likely explanations for yesterday.'

As that was uncomfortably too close to the truth, Gray decided it was prudent to subtly change the subject. 'There is no need to apologise. I did behave like a buffoon.' He waved it all away as if it was of no matter and decided it was time to be that better spy he kept promising himself he would be. But it wasn't the mission that brought on the change, it was his wavering resolve. Having her companionably next to him, talking about personal things, was making him like her all the more. 'You gave your uncle control over your fortune?'

'Not at all. I abdicated all responsibility for it, and gladly, the same day I celebrated my majority, yet he still persists in educating me on the topic in the hope I will take over. That banker and solicitor you met are also my banker and solicitor. Their report this time took over an hour to deliver and I was forced to listen to it. My uncle then asked my opinion as to whether I wanted to speculate in coal mining or keep persevering with the shipping in light of the excellent return on my investment.'

'You invest in shipping?' Surely that was a damning titbit, one he needed to thoroughly investigate, but Gislingham Hall already loomed in front of them. 'What sort of shipping?'

She hesitated at the edge of the gardens, her eyes gazing towards the house rather than him. 'I am apparently the proud partner in a fleet of merchant ships which sail backwards and forwards to the Orient. Transporting silks, spices and other luxury items which are in high demand... See, I do listen, I just can't bring myself to want to care. Although there are benefits.' She gestured to the bold printed fabric of her frock. Then frowned at the twin dusty patches marring the fabric at her knees.

As he was determined to be a gentleman, Gray politely did not ask how they came to be there. 'That also explains the jasmine. Whenever I encounter you, the unique scent of your perfume sends me right back to that distant continent.' A lie. It drove him mad with lust. 'Perhaps I crewed one of your ships? Wouldn't that be a coincidence?' Not quite as coincidental as one of those ships taking a detour to France to pick up illegal brandy before it sailed back home. 'Name some of them.'

'I have no idea, although probably should. The written reports I get are very detailed. My uncle insists upon that, but my eyes glaze over before I've read a full page and I find it all so daunting I take them away from every meeting and then pretend I've read them.'

'If you don't read them, what do you do with them?' Because he now urgently needed to read those reports. 'I assume your uncle would become suspicious if you burned them.'

'They are shoved in a trunk in my dressing room. A travesty I suspect my uncle knows, because he has an uncanny knack of knowing everything that goes on under his roof, but he is an eternal optimist and believes one day I will miraculously take an interest in those ever-increasing figures. I cannot see that day coming any time soon, although I suppose one day I will have to. When…' Her face clouded briefly. 'When he is no longer around to take care of things.' Gray wanted to pull her into his arms and simply hold her, more so when she smiled bravely and bent to pet his dog rather than let him see that sadness. Another unsettling insight into her character he did not need. He clasped his hands behind his back to stop from acting on the impulse. 'Thank you for escorting me home, Trefor.' Her dark eyes shyly lifted to meet his. 'To my great surprise, it has been a pleasure. Although I do think the lines between casual acquaintances and friends have become blurred. We have certainly shared far more with each other than polite neighbours normally do.'

'Our cautious truce is in its infancy, so we will forgive it a little leeway. Once we've both learned the parameters, no doubt it will become easier, especially as we have vowed never to be alone together again.' Even as he said it, Gray didn't believe it. He had enjoyed talking to her openly and the cosy intimacy that created perhaps even more than he had enjoyed kissing her. He bowed politely, resetting the boundaries. 'Good day, *Miss Cranford*.' But his feet felt lighter and the day seemed much brighter all the way home regardless.

Chapter Thirteen

'Don't you look ravishing?' Mr Hargreaves used the fact that Thea's hands were occupied to run his fingers over her sleeve. The brief, bold touch did not make her skin tingle as Gray's had done, nor did it elicit any of the peculiar, needy feeling his had either. As usual, the unsolicited flirtations of her unwelcome and determined would-be suitor made her cringe. 'Once this game is done, I would be delighted to take you on a turn around the garden.' He had glued himself to her side at the start of the croquet match, intent on charming her—or so he claimed—and had succeeded in being a thorough pest for the duration.

'I am quite familiar with my own garden, Mr Hargreaves. And if you don't mind me saying, you are becoming quite over-familiar with my person.' She glared at the spot just below her elbow where his hand remained. 'Kindly keep your hands to yourself.'

'How long are you going to play the coquette, Thea? I've made my intentions quite clear. I hold you in the highest affection. Real, genuine, heart-felt affection.' He gave her a heated look which was nowhere near as incendiary as the ones he frequently gave her aunt when he thought nobody was watching. 'I am desirous of a proper court-ship, not this flirtatious toing and froing, and while I enjoy the chase—' his hand had found its way to the small of her back '—I am ready to offer you my heart.'

Heart! As if he had one! Insufferable man! He had a very warped view of things if he assumed her increasing hostility was flirting. She shrugged off his distasteful touch and stomped forward, letting her disgusted expression convey how ab-horrent she found him. And he had the bare-faced nerve to call her a *coquette*. Unbelievable. 'I have a mallet, Mr Hargreaves, one I am not averse to using.' To prove that, she lined it up in front of the ball, imagined it was his thick head and gave it a spirited whack. It rolled through the hoop, knock-ing his ball sideways in the process. 'Oh, dear! It will take you a few turns to recover, I'm afraid.'

By which time Thea fully intended to be done with the silly game and striding purposefully back towards the house. She had had about as much of her aunt's friends today as she could tolerate. Thanks to Aunt Caro, the lawn was currently stuffed with the dullest and most sycophantic individuals in Suffolk. Her uncle had pleaded fatigue long before the interminable, impromptu garden party had started and Harriet had miraculously disappeared to the retiring room a few minutes after Colonel Purbeck and his surfeit of flying spit had arrived and was yet to reappear. Knowing Harriet, she was likely to already be in her own parlour, sipping tea and congratulating herself on her hasty exit.

If Thea whipped around this course speedily, she could escape for a full hour before the next round of afternoon tea was served. Aside from the fact that the heat was making her rebellious hair twirl vertical and her pale skin glow beetroot in places, an illicit, quiet, hour reading was suddenly very appealing. Although, in truth, an hour watching paint dry would be more appealing than spending another minute in the company of Mr Hargreaves. The vulture was making a great show of examining his stray ball from every angle as he lined up his shot. Then he hit it with such precision, it rolled softly next to hers.

'You cannot get rid of me that easily, dearest Thea. I came here today with the express intention of talking to you about our future and I will not be deterred from that.'

'It's Miss Cranford to you. I never have and never will give you leave to call me by my first name, *Mr* Hargreaves.' Sudden awareness of another vexing male cut through her irritation, and, of its own accord, her head turned in time to see *him* stride on to the lawn looking his usual rugged, confident and handsome self. As if realising she was watching him, Gray turned and their eyes locked. He paused mid-step, seemed to take a deep breath, then inclined his head politely in accordance with their declared truce, before striding on towards the hostess with his cousin.

It had been a brief and altogether mundane exchange, exactly as he had promised, yet just that had the most unnerving effect on her body. Her pulse had quickened. Her nerve-endings had suddenly jumped to attention and her skin heated further, although this new warmth had nothing whatsoever to do with the glorious weather and everything to do with the disgraceful scoundrel who had kissed her senseless in this same garden only a week ago and thoroughly charmed her yesterday with his confession. Where she should be relieved he had no intentions of either seducing her or wooing her, Thea couldn't seem to feel anything other than intense disappointment at the prospect.

And more curious about the wretch than she had ever been. Who was the woman who had broken his heart? He must have loved her very deeply for the rejection to have such a lasting effect. Strangely, that made her envious. To have such a handsome, entertaining and exciting man head over heels for you must be the most wonderful feeling. One she hoped she would experience, but sincerely doubted she ever would. The burden of her fortune had made the plight of true love nigh on impossible, when most men desired great wealth far more than they desired true love.

Apart from Gray. He seemed to be genuinely sympathetic to her situation, almost as if he had first-hand knowledge of exactly how money brought out the worst in people. Another thing she had pondered over incessantly since yesterday. What had happened in his past to shape him? How irreparably had his heart been broken? Did he really mean never to attempt to kiss her again when, by his own admission, he thought her the single most beautiful woman he had ever seen? Her heart had done a little sigh at that heady compliment, because she had seen the truth of it swirling in his unusual, expressive eyes. Instead of wanting to adhere to the terms of the truce, she now had so many burning questions and desperately wanted to learn more. He had become a conundrum. An intriguing, alluring, attractive conundrum...

'It is your turn.' Mr Hargreaves's grating voice dragged her guiltily back to the present.

'I concede. I have a headache.' Thea tossed her mallet aside and rudely headed in the direction of the kitchen, purely because the kitchen was situated at the opposite end of the lawn to Lord Gray. Perhaps he would stop occupying so much of her brain if she couldn't see him.

'Then allow me to escort you back.'

'No, thank you.'

'I insist.' His fingers touched her elbow and she tugged it away as if burned. 'For I suspect this sudden headache has more to do with your reluctance to discuss the next steps of our relationship...' Thea had had enough.

'Are you quite stupid, Mr Hargreaves? Or is your desire to acquire my fortune so strong you will stop at nothing to get it?' Gray was right. Who knew complete honesty would feel so cathartic? 'Let me say it plainly, for the record and to avoid any more misunderstanding henceforth, I claimed a headache because I have no desire to entertain you—as a potential suitor or even a croquet partner, Mr Hargreaves. Kindly leave me alone. Preferably indefinitely.'

Thea marched across the lawn feeling pleased with herself. For once, she had allowed Impetuous Thea to take over because she had known Impetuous Thea wouldn't mince her words. She sincerely hoped the thick-skinned cretin would finally get the message, but no sooner had she rounded the tall, clipped topiary hedge that hid the kitchen and outbuildings from the house than her unwanted companion grabbed her elbow again and spun her towards him. 'I am in love with you, Thea!'

'Really? Does my aunt know? For I am quite certain she will not be impressed to learn that her lover's heart is engaged elsewhere.' Clearly, Impetuous Thea was not done.

'I don't know what you mean!' The outrage was constructed. Too constructed and for once she wanted to call a spade a spade and let the rebellious part of her do what the sensible, polite side of her never had.

'I *know*, Mr Hargreaves. I have *known* from the outset. Is it not bad enough that you have made my uncle a cuckold, but that now you intend to hurt my poor aunt as well?' Caro was a broken, barren bird trapped in a loveless marriage to a man who loathed her. A woman whose entire sense of self-worth was inextricably attached to her own waning attractiveness. With every new wrinkle, Thea watched a little piece of her aunt die. 'Your rejection will devastate her.'

She watched, fascinated, as he digested this. For a moment, she was convinced he was going to attempt to perpetuate the lie and deny the affair. But he surprised her.

'The heart wants what the heart wants. I do not love her. If you give me a single grain of hope, Thea, then I shall end things with her today.' His fingers closed painfully around her upper arm and refused to budge as she tugged. 'This very moment… It's you I want. It is you I have always wanted!'

'It looks as if I've arrived just in time.' Seeing as the nauseating Mr Hargreaves appeared about to thrust his unwanted attentions on to her and

Thea was poised to knee the fellow hard in the unmentionables, Gray thought it was prudent to emerge from the shrubbery. Not because the fellow didn't deserve a swift kick in the jewels, because he did, and not because he didn't think Thea could stand up for herself either. She was more than capable if the acid-tongued stream of comments coming out of her tart mouth were anything to go by, but Gray had stepped in simply because he couldn't bear the thought of her being manhandled by that scoundrel—or any other—under *any* circumstances.

He was going to determinedly think of his rescue as merely the noble act of a gentleman and steadfastly ignore the surging possessive anger which had made him follow the pair of them in the first place, despite promising himself, and her, he would maintain a polite distance and ration all contact with her going forward. Regardless of their wholly necessary truce, those powerful strings had pulled him once again and now here he was. And he was glad of it.

The jealous anger was still churning inside his gut, now combined with vengeful fury that she had been accosted. He hid both behind a bland, cold expression. Inside, he wanted to kill Hargreaves. Tear the blighter limb from limb. Pummel his deceitful, conniving, vile face with his fist until it was nought but a bloody smudge at the end of his arm.

'Lord Gray!' It was obvious she was relieved to see him, although in view of what he had just witnessed, she would doubtless have been equally as thrilled to see anyone, truce or not. 'Yes—timely, indeed. I am exceedingly glad to see you.'

'I am sure you are. Allow me to escort you back to the *safety* of the lawn.' He held out his arm as he glared at the brute and felt a fresh surge of possessiveness as she gratefully took it. He'd deal with Hargreaves later. That snake would never dare bother her again.

'Thea has a headache. I was merely escorting her back to lie down.'

As Gray locked his free palm securely over hers in the crook of his elbow, his eyes narrowed at the liar menacingly. 'I'm certain the only pain she was suffering was you, Hargreaves.' The idiot had the cheek to look affronted, which gave Gray the perfect excuse to indulge his roiling temper. 'Touch her again and I'll break your nose.' Along with both arms and legs.

'How dare you threaten—' Hargreaves didn't get to finish the sentence. Like a cobra, Gray's fist grabbed him by the cravat.

'How dare you manhandle a lady!' He lifted the other man so that he had to stagger backwards on tiptoe as he pushed him against the wall. 'How dare you ignore her rebuttals! When a lady *says* no, that means *no*! She is entirely correct in her assessment of you. You are a fortune-hunting weasel. A deceitful, conniving, self-serving vulture.' He twisted the frothy knot tighter, enjoying the way the toad's eyes bulged beneath the pressure. 'Apologise… Apologise for being…!'

'I'm sorry, Thea…'

'You do not deserve to call her by her first name!'

'I'm sorry, M-M-Miss Cranford!'

'Swear you will never come within ten feet of her again!'

'I s-s-swear it! Please let me go!'

'Are you satisfied with his apology, Thea?' He turned to her and felt some of his anger dissipate, almost as if he could hear her thoughts telling him that the idiot wasn't worth the effort.

'It will do.'

Hargreaves coughed and spluttered as Gray dropped him—'Get out of my sight!'—then ran like the pathetic excuse for a man he was towards the gardens.

'Thank you.' He felt her hand against his arm. That single, gentle touch shouldn't have felt so significant, yet it did. Slowly, he turned to face her and she was smiling. 'Although a part of me is annoyed I didn't get to finish what I started. I was going to kick him.'

'I know. I saw. Perhaps I saved him, too?'

'Would you really have broken his nose?'

'Into a million pieces. Then I'd have put all those pieces in a pestle and mortar and ground them to paste.' He had meant to be ironic, but to his own ears the reply was too forceful. 'The man is a menace.'

'The man is a pest. Calling him a menace gives him far more credit than he deserves and I am used to rebuffing unwanted advances from men of his ilk. Although granted, he is perhaps the most nauseating one so far.'

'You shouldn't have to put up with nonsense like that.'

'What? Men shamelessly flirting with me? At least he didn't kiss me.' The dig stung and she saw it, then smiled kindly. 'A poorly timed and unfair joke, Gray. I realise I had a significant hand in that kiss, too, and likening you to the irksome Mr Hargreaves is unfair. The man makes my flesh crawl.' Did that mean he didn't? Probably best not to pursue that line of conversation, especially as he could still feel the warmth of her hand on his arm through several layers of clothing and all over his body.

'You should tell your uncle what he did. He'll put a stop to him ever setting foot here again— regardless of what your aunt wants.'

'You heard everything again, didn't you?' Her expression was pained.

'Yes. But I had worked it out for myself well beforehand. It doesn't take a genius to see what is plainer than the annoyingly intact nose on Hargreaves's face.'

Her hand slipped from his sleeve and she sighed. 'I had hoped it wasn't common knowledge.'

'It isn't. Perhaps I am a little more perceptive than most guests.'

'Or more likely, they are all far too polite to gossip about us within earshot.'

'You can trust me to keep your counsel. I'm good at keeping secrets.' Never a truer word was spoken and once again his mission and his conscience were misaligned. 'Does your uncle know of his wife's infidelities?'

Her gaze flicked to his briefly and she shook her head, bemused. 'Indeed, you are perceptive. For I am sure there has been more than Mr Hargreaves. He is just one of a line spanning many years. But to answer your question, who knows? Like our guests, I have always been too polite to ask my uncle or confront my aunt. My uncle never utters her name in my presence unless he has imbibed too much after dinner. Then he calls her a cold, callous, self-serving and unfeeling witch. He hates her, when he never hates anyone, and I have no idea why. But it is deep-rooted and heartfelt. And if my aunt mentions him, it is also to criticise. Theirs is an odd relationship. One I am not entirely sure I understand, but alas there is fault on both sides so I try not to judge. He despises her and treats her with disdain; she disrespects her vows and fills her life with people who treat her better than he does. Yet neither seems inclined to separate as so many other unhappy couples do all the time. Uncle Edward cannot bear the sight of Caro and has more than enough money to set her up in her own household—but doesn't. Nor, to my knowledge, has she ever asked him to. I have never understood what exactly it is that holds them together—but I've never really thought it's my place to say.'

'Marriage can be a fraught institution.' His close brush with it had been—well, before it had even started. 'Whether the couple marry for love or for other reasons.'

'Is this another of our casual, platonic conversations, Gray?' The wry smile was mischievous. 'Only it feels a tad too personal for two people who are actively avoiding each other. At least I was avoiding you—as per the terms of our agreement, of course.'

'I was avoiding you, too, until that buffoon followed you across the lawn. Then my ingrained, long-forgotten gentlemanly manners kicked in and I came to rescue you. Now that I am assured you are safe from further inconvenience, as per the terms of our agreement, I shall bid you good day, Miss Cranford.'

Chapter Fourteen

'It's Thea. And I am curious. Seeing as you know so much about my situation, surely it's only fair you tell me a little bit about yours?' She watched him pause mid-step before warily turning around. At the last moment, he pasted his customary cocky expression on his face and that made her more intrigued. Whatever was in his past was something he was reluctant to talk about. She felt that in her bones.

'Further questions surely fall outside the parameters of our truce, as we dally longer than necessary.'

He was right, but suddenly the truce was as restricting as the silly corset Harriet had bought her. She wanted to know more. Oddly wanted to spend more time with him. 'Yet you have asked more than your fair share, nonetheless. You have already teased out the shocking state of my aunt and uncle's marriage, my fear of my finances and my abhorrence of unworthy, greedy men like Mr Hargreaves. I am merely seeking reciprocal knowledge in kind. For the sake of balance. It strikes me, we might have something fundamental in common. I am jaded and wary of romantic attachments to men because too many than I care to count have grievously disappointed me by being fortune hunters. You are jaded and wary of romantic attachments with women because one of them has grievously disappointed you because…? *It wasn't meant to be* really tells me nothing at all.'

Beneath the seemingly relaxed posture, those impressive shoulders stiffened and his spine became straighter, yet despite his obvious reluctance to talk, he stared her straight in the eye. 'I was young, foolish and caught up in the romance of it all. The sickness passed.'

'She broke your heart. To smithereens. Your own words, Gray, not mine. Who was she and what happened?'

The hand on his left side closed into a fist as he gazed heavenwards, then he raked that same hand impatiently through his hair and gazed at her levelly as if he had made an unpleasant decision to take vile medicine and was determined to get it over with. 'Her name was Cecily. Her father's estate bordered ours. We grew up together.' The staccato sentences were matter of fact. Almost clinical in their delivery. 'Her mother and mine were great friends. Cecily and I were inseparable.'

His childhood sweetheart then. 'You loved her.'

He sidestepped her comment. 'We made plans and promises. Far too many of them with hindsight and, like a fool, I believed them to be as real for her as they were for me. But, alas, I was mistaken. When my father brokered the suggestion behind my back that she marry my older brother, Cecily was given the choice by her father. Me or him. She chose him.'

'Because of the title?'

'No doubt. And the promise of the greater fortune, although I wasn't destined to be poor. My maternal grandfather had left me a generous bequest that had been held in trust until I became of age, but that paled into insignificance against the stately grounds of Talysarn and all the riches which would come with it.' His fingers went to play with his cuffs. A tiny, nervous gesture for a man who usually exuded confidence. 'My father told me the news in his customary cold and dictatorial way, expecting me to stand aside and accept the decision made by two peers based on what suited them, not me. As I'm sure you would expect, I exploded and immediately rode like a man possessed directly to her house to rescue her, assuming she would be as distraught by the outrage as I was, but she wasn't. She wasn't even particularly apologetic either. Circumstances change, she said, and she would be a fool to turn down such an advantageous offer. Needless to say, her

life then went one way and mine quite another.'
He shrugged as if it was of no matter, when Thea
knew it was and her heart wept for him. He had
suffered a triple betrayal. His father, brother and
sweetheart had all simultaneously stabbed him
in the back. 'At the time, I thought myself devastated. Now I am merely philosophical about the
experience.' He was lying. She knew it because
his unwavering silver gaze faltered and for a moment he refused to meet her eye.

'How old were you?'

'Two weeks shy of twenty-one. So you see, it
really was a very long time ago.' Coincidentally,
around the same time as he would have taken
control of all those funds left in trust. Without
thinking, Thea found her palm smoothing down
his arm in sympathy as several pieces of the puzzle fell firmly into place. 'And, with hindsight,
much too young to have been seriously considering marriage.'

'Oh, Gray—that must have been quite a year.'
Aspects of his character now made sense. Of
course he would prefer to live in the moment
when all those longed-for plans of his youth had
been crushed in the worst possible way. 'To lose
your love, all those hopes and dreams and your
fortune in one fell swoop.'

She felt the muscles bunch under his coat. Then
heard him exhale slowly before they relaxed.
'Clearly I am not the only one of us who is per-

ceptive. Yes, like a fool I thought Cecily would reconsider if my riches superseded my brother's, when I should have thanked her for her shallowness and moved on without a backward glance. Any woman who puts money and social status above love isn't really the sort any man should give his heart to.' Or vice versa. Another thing they had in common.

'And then they banished you.' It beggared belief. To be left reeling and floundering at such a young age. So vulnerable and alone. Thea instantly hated his awful family and the loathsome Cecily. If she ever met the witch, she would receive the full extent of Impetuous Thea's acid tongue and worse. Much worse.

'I was never banished. Disowned—yes. My father could not stand the scandal. But I left. Ran as far away from them all as I could get. I didn't want or need the reminders. Of all the skewed decisions I made that fateful year, it is the one that turned out to be for the best. Bizarrely, it made me. I grew up. Learned things about myself I never would have learned any other way and it allowed me to get the perspective I couldn't find here in England.' His eyes flicked to her before wandering to fix on something in the distance. 'But despite what you are obviously thinking in that overly suspicious brain of yours, I *am* over it. I would never have come back otherwise. Now, can we dispense with all this heartfelt honesty? By my reckoning we are now even and thus never need to discuss anything beyond the superficial and polite ever again. We really do need to work harder on this truce of ours, else it will collapse before it has had a fighting chance to get going.'

Thea didn't call him on it, suspecting he was partially over what happened yet intrinsically scarred by it at the same time. It was the easy, confident, charming Gray smiling at her now, although he was different and always would be. She understood there was a deeper, more sensitive human being under all that swagger. A complicated man of many layers who had lived a much harder life than she could possibly imagine. A man who had been a scandal, weathered it and emerged as someone she could respect. A man she was coming to like a great deal. Yet another thing which surprised her, when it had been an age since any man had piqued her interest enough for her to care about them on any level. 'Now I see we have a great deal in common. One way or another, money has changed us both and not necessarily for the better.'

His warm palm softly captured her hand where it still rested on his arm—it was a friendly gesture, not the least bit flirtatious, but to her surprise she wanted it to be. She certainly felt his touch everywhere. 'Things happen for a reason, Miss Cranford. Every trial and tribulation leads us to the path we were meant to take.' He was coincidentally leading her back up the path to the lawn and the rest of the guests. Back to the safe haven where their cosy intimacy had no place and temptation was well out of reach. However gentlemanly he was attempting to be, she knew it was himself he was ultimately protecting. She bothered him. Their fledgling relationship bothered him. His feelings towards her scared him. Feelings he would rather deny than articulate; run from rather than pursue.

'It's Thea. And I suspect our truce has unexpectedly made our path veer in a very different direction from the one for which it was intended, for I am convinced we were never destined to be polite, indifferent acquaintances, Gray. I am coming to believe we were meant to be friends.' Or more. Not only Impetuous Thea hoped they would be more.

His step faltered again and he glared in mock affront. 'Fate can be such a cruel mistress.'

'There you are!' Gray dropped the leather satchel on the kitchen table at the exact moment Lord Fennimore burst through the door, tugging ineffectually at the thoroughly ruined cloth at his neck with one hand while clutching a fresh cravat in the other. 'Where the hell have you been? And what the hell have you been doing at such an ungodly hour?'

'My job, sir.' Without being asked, Gray briskly

removed the hopelessly knotted disaster from his superior's collar and then set about tying the new one. Not one of the King's Elite could tie a damn cravat to save their lives and whenever they were on a mission they had to forgo servants. Spare beds were always better occupied by agents, so Gray often found himself acting as a valet. 'I took advantage of the prolonged absence of Gislingham's constantly hovering manservant and broke into his private apartments before *dear Bertie* comes back.' An idea which had come to him after hours of staring at the ceiling thanks to a certain redhead he couldn't seem to forget or avoid.

Were they friends now? If they were, he was supremely uncomfortable with the concept. As much as he found her surprisingly easy to talk to, the level of honesty he confided in her bothered him. She had made him talk about Cecily, for goodness' sake, for the first time in almost a decade and without that much pushing. The words had come, jagged and dry like rocks in his throat, then once they had, more tumbled out. It was unnerving. More unnerving was how much lighter he felt as a result of it all. Lighter and worryingly hopeful, and unfortunately, those niggling hopes all seemed to involve her in some way. He didn't want to be Thea's casual acquaintance. Friend. He wanted to kiss her again. Take her to bed. Make plans. Blasted plans, for pity's sake! No wonder he couldn't sleep!

'Good God, man! You might have told me! Were you seen?'

'Of course I wasn't seen. But with eagle-eyed Bertie away all week, it was too good an opportunity to miss. I found Gislingham's study, picked the lock on his desk and borrowed a few of the papers concealed in a strong box within it. I was careful to take only a tiny, random sample and hopefully I'll be able to return them before his sentry returns and our dastardly Viscount will be none the wiser.'

'What did you find?'

'Hard to say. It was too dark to read them properly and I didn't dare risk a light. Stocks and bonds mostly. Some accounts, I believe, and some private correspondence.' Most particularly, a thick stash of letters tied with ribbon had sat in that dusty strong box, kept quite separate and secure from the plethora of everyday correspondence in the unlocked drawers. 'I'm hoping there is enough to give us a flavour of what he's up to and perhaps throw up a name or two to investigate. Something tangible which will stop the blighter continually running rings around us.'

So Gray had hauled himself out of bed, determined to do something practical with the insomnia, even if that something took him within feet of the siren tucked up in her own bed asleep. Not that he had ventured up to her floor at all, despite knowing there was potential evidence about nefarious shipping investments stuffed at the bottom of her trunk. There was foolhardy and then there was madness. A sturdy plaster ceiling, wood and bricks had served as a necessary barrier. One that blocked out any hint of alluring jasmine in the air. But still he had felt her and the pull of those damned invisible cords, and that alone had tortured him.

He stepped back to assess his work and tweaked the folds of the cravat. 'Where are you off to at this ungodly hour?'

'Riding. With Harriet…' Lord Fennimore's suddenly jerky movements and sheepish tone were not like him. He looked hilariously awkward. Gray bit his lip to stop the bark of laughter escaping. 'You should come, too.'

'You want me to come riding with you and Lady Crudgington? I doubt the lady in question will be pleased to see me—not when she seems very taken with you, sir.'

'She's bound to bring a chaperon of her own and a thoughtful gentleman brings another to show that he would expect the proper proprieties to be adhered to!'

'You want *me* to chaperon *you*?' The laughter escaped then and earned him a glare. 'How… quaint.'

'That is the correct way of doing things, young man, and therefore that is exactly the way this shall be done! I shall use the opportunity to pick her ladyship's brains about Gislingham and you will ride at a respectful distance behind!' He marched out, slamming the door behind him.

Wearily, Gray set about fixing himself some coffee to prepare himself for the ordeal and sat drinking it while watching his dog eat breakfast, trying not to hope that Thea would be the other chaperon. Because he couldn't afford to indulge that whim. Not when the blasted woman had already crawled under his skin and made a home there. Friends! Not while he still had the remaining shrivelled, battered remnants of his heart. Those bludgeoned pieces had taken many years to heal and wouldn't survive another pummelling. Thea was just too tempting. Tempting enough to make him want to dismiss his painful past out of hand and plunge headlong into...what? Nowhere he was in a hurry to go to again. To take his mind off the unthinkable and frankly irrational thoughts it kept dwelling on, he decided to do something practical.

By the time Lord Fennimore was back, snapping orders and generally complaining about Trefor, Gray had relaid the fire, hauled in a day's worth of logs and made two rounds of toast and slathered them in butter. The pair of them ate in silence, as was the old curmudgeon's way, but he could see the man was also nervous and found himself intrigued at the idea. The unflappable head of the King's Elite, a man who loathed point-less socialising, most people as a matter of course and had always been content with his crusty old bachelor ways, was in a total flap over a woman. Life certainly liked to throw up surprises.

If nothing else, following the pair of them would be hugely entertaining and, while Gray had never been a letter writer, because he didn't really have a soul to write one to any more, he fully intended to fire off a brace of letters to his friends and comrades Warriner, Leatham, Flint and even Hadleigh, regaling them with the un-heard-of, miraculous phenomenon as soon as it was over. Lord Fennimore was nervous because he was courting! He couldn't resist a little dig to test the theory.

'You are not wearing *that* coat, are you?'

'What's wrong with it?'

'Black? Perhaps a little staid for a vivacious woman like Lady Crudgington? If you're intent on wooing her—*only* for King and country, of course—it sends out the wrong message. Black is for funerals and formal dinners, not invigorating gallops across the dewy, dawn-kissed fields…'

Biting the inside of his cheek, he enjoyed watching the old man stare down at his attire and dither.

'Yes…you might be right. What should I wear? The green?'

'Green will complement your eyes.' Eyes that

instantly narrowed at the sight of his uncontrol-lably twitching lips.

'Get your fun elsewhere, Gray! This is busi-ness. Pure and simple. If the lady has an interest in me, I'd be a fool not to take advantage! She is detached enough from Gislingham not to offend him and close enough to be useful. That is exactly what being a good spy is all about, rather than alienating the villain's closest living relative with your crass and improper and unwelcome seduc-tions. Choose your opportunities wisely! Some-thing I despair of you ever learning. Go sort out the horses! She will be here promptly at seven!' He stomped off indignantly, but came back to the stable with a face like thunder, wearing the green coat and smelling uncharacteristically of expen-sive cologne.

To say the next twenty minutes were tense would be an understatement. Lady Crudgington was late and his superior began to behave like a man jilted at the altar until she appeared on her pony, unrepentant, much closer to half past the hour, with the woman who had haunted his dreams smilingly trotting alongside on one of the biggest horses he had ever seen.

His heart gave a tiny stutter at the sight of her. The fitted blue riding habit perfectly both high-lighted her alluring, womanly curves and made her glorious hair pop in the hazy, early morning sunshine. On top of those untameable curls was a ridiculous little hat set at a jaunty angle, designed more for fashion than to cover the head. She looked delightful. Frivolous, saucy and dangerously confident. Damn her!

Like Thea, Gray kept a polite distance as old Fennimore greeted Harriet and had to turn his back when he heard him mutter something cringing about propriety and being glad they both had had the foresight to bring chaperons.

'You are *so* thoughtful, Cedric.' Although as he'd suspected, the lady seemed vastly amused at the prospect. 'But such nonsense is entirely unnecessary. One of the benefits of both age and widowhood is that propriety can be ignored. Something I try to do at every opportunity. Don't you? Thea is here out of coincidence and nothing more. She's off to the village to collect the post and called upon me as she had forgotten about *our* engagement. We shall be heading in a quite different direction, Cedric, I can assure you. I have a much more exciting route planned for us—but as Lord Gray is now set to ride, too, he might as well accompany Thea and leave us in peace, don't you think?'

By the stunned look on his face and the lack of words coming out of his mouth, Lord Fennimore had not expected that, but there was nothing he could do about it without appearing foolish, prudish and curmudgeonly. Harriet pointed a finger at

Gray and winked, clearly enjoying leaving both men floundering on the back foot with her outrageous suggestion. 'Don't do anything I wouldn't do, young man. Which, granted, gives you quite a bit of scope.' She nudged her pony forward with a grin as wide as it was naughty. 'Come along, Cedric! Let's see if you're man enough to keep up with me!'

Gray watched them leave while he considered his options. Riding all alone with the minx who continued to cause him insomnia was the last thing he should be considering. He could plead something more pressing to do and excuse himself, which in view of the current speed of his pulse was tempting, or he could accompany her. Something the devil-may-care, adventurous part of his nature was egging him on to do, but which scared the hell out of the rest of him. That route was unchartered and unpredictable territory, as well as a whole heap of temptation, yet there was no denying it was also the most prudent as far as his mission was concerned. If Lord Fennimore really did intend to use his morning gallop to probe Lady Crudgington for information, he should probably use this unexpected opportunity to do the same. Surely he could fight his urges on horseback? As long as he didn't allow his eyes to linger on that very tight riding habit.

'I can read your expression, Gray. If you'd

rather not ride to the village with me, then I really do not mind.'

'Up until thirty minutes ago, I was fast asleep and had no idea I was riding anywhere, but, seeing as I was dragged up and am dressed for it now, I might as well.' Her huge horse was dancing around on the spot although she controlled it effortlessly. The smattering of white hairs on his chestnut muzzle were testament to his advanced age. 'He's skittish for a hunter.'

'He always has been. Uncle Edward has a stable full of younger and more temperate horses, but Archimedes was my father's and I am the only person who ever rides him. He would be miffed if I chose another.' She smoothed a hand down his mane to calm him, then stared quizzically at the three Invisibles clearing and levelling the pasture close by. Because they had the appropriate audience, his men were working up quite a sweat.

'My new exercise yard. The sand will be delivered later this week, so the ground needs to be prepared, then the posts for the fences dug. The stables are already in reasonable shape, so they'll do well enough in the short term.' Especially as his men had much better things to be doing with their day than prepping for horses that would never come. They were irked enough at the charade he was having them act out now. But it was better to be safe than sorry—although if he said so himself, it was the perfect place for an exercise yard. It caught enough of the early morning sun to be bright and airy, but was shaded by the house and the parallel copse of trees in the afternoon when the sun was at its hottest. And it was close enough to the brook to ensure a ready supply of cool, fresh water.

Why had he put that much thought into giving credence to a lie? And why did the fact it was just a lie suddenly depress him when he looked at her? Gray grabbed his reins and heaved himself on to his own saddle. He was barely seated when his poorly behaved mutt flew like a cannonball into the yard, barking.

Archimedes reared slightly, but again she controlled him as Trefor panted and wagged his tail far too close to the animal's busy hooves, his devoted brown eyes locked on Thea adoringly. 'I'm so sorry. I shut him in the house, but he has a talent for escaping.' He called to one of his men, 'Take the dog indoors!'

'Oh, let him come with us.' Thea bent down to pat Trefor's bouncing head. The contact made him jealous. Of his blasted dog, for pity's sake! 'Archimedes was merely a little surprised. He's fine now and I'm sure your delightful dog would enjoy a run to the village with us.' True to her word, the old horse indeed seemed to have settled and was now simply glaring down at the dog in warning as they slowly ambled forward. As she was a few feet ahead, that meant he got to stare at the delectable peach that was her bottom. Capital!

Gray set his jaw and prayed for strength, channelling all his lusty frustration into hating the talented seamstress who had created that seductive confection, reminding himself yet again that he really did need to work harder at being a better spy in the hope that would make his errant thoughts purer. Unsurprisingly, none of those things worked.

Chapter Fifteen

Coming here had been a mistake. Too forthright. A little bit needy. Impulsive, and probably made her shallow, selfish motives totally obvious. It was also completely out of character when she usually actively avoided all men. The wariness had given way to curiosity. He intrigued her. More than any man ever had before. The shameful truth was Thea had only offered to collect the post as a pathetic excuse to see him again—knowing full well he wanted to maintain a respectable distance. But after yesterday, and after thinking about him for most of the night, it had seemed a plausible enough reason to happen to be riding past at the time. She certainly hadn't expected to do more than say a passing hello, exchange a few pleasantries, then be on her merry way, content that she had at least seen him. Then quietly sigh and swoon in private all the way home, just as she had all night. She hoped all that swooning was borne out of knowing him better and liking what she learned and not solely because he had declared himself off limits. But in her head alongside all the new regard she had for him, Gray had become forbidden fruit. Something she had a proven penchant for.

Casually meeting him was hardly throwing herself at him, but she had not factored in Harriet's matchmaking, nor Gray's ingrained sense of decency, and now the poor man felt beholden to accompany her and clearly did not want to. *'Something inexplicable about you calls to me and perhaps on a far deeper level than I care to admit.'* Words which still sang to her soul. That made her increasingly believe he was exactly what he claimed to be. Neither a fortune hunter nor a true scoundrel, but a man who saw past her fortune to the woman beneath. Gray was drawn to Thea. It was that simple and that glorious.

'Was it me, or was your cousin a tad nervous this morning?' She purposefully kept her conversation bright and friendly, hoping he wouldn't realise she had only come here for him when he had made it plain he would prefer to have little to do with her. But he had called her beautiful. Beautiful and tempting and exactly the sort of woman he would choose to court if he had a mind to. Those were not the words of a man who disliked you. In fact, if anything they said quite the opposite. He was avoiding her *because* he liked her. To protect himself. Because he couldn't trust himself to resist her. And to spare his heart. Yet instead of respecting his wishes, she was flagrantly going against them, claiming they were now friends when her body and mind clearly yearned for so much more. Was she here because she wanted to tempt him? To her shame and bubbling excitement, the answer was a definitive yes. She certainly wanted to tempt him to reconsider.

'Nervous? I've never seen him in such a state. He changed his coat twice, ruined goodness knows how many neckcloths and doused himself in cologne. It was one of the funniest things I've seen in a long time. Lady Crudgington has a most peculiar effect on him.'

'They were flirting yesterday on the lawn. Didn't you see? I was surprised Harriet had returned until I saw Lord Fennimore. She loathes Aunt Caro's friends and finds most of our neighbours boring, but she is very taken with him so she went against the grain and came back.' She was babbling. A sure sign of her guilty conscience. 'Decent gentlemen of a certain age are thin on the ground, or so she says, and she approves of the way he wears his breeches.'

Images of Gray *sans* breeches suddenly swamped her mind and she felt a fraud for pretending to be his friend again, although he felt like a friend. A charming, handsome, intriguing, wholly male friend whose kisses were lethal. Was she wrong to indulge in a bit of harmless selfishness? When there was clearly a mutual attraction and regard between them? It wasn't as if she intended to stomp all over him and force her will. Not even Impetuous Thea was capable of that! No—merely a little gentle prodding. Perhaps if they spent a little more time together, both of them would lower their defences and nature would take its course. That sounded much better. She would leave it to fate and hope that this time it would look upon her kindly.

'His breeches? Good Lord.' His shocked expression was comical. 'Although I suppose he is in excellent shape for a man his age.' He was riding so close to her that she could reach out and touch him if she had a mind to. She did, but neither Thea was brave enough. 'I am convinced he is taken with her, too. I have seen him smile now on two separate occasions in her presence. It should also be noted, those are the only *two* occasions I have ever witnessed him smile.'

They speculated on the unlikely romance between Lord Fennimore and Lady Crudgington for the first half a mile of the short ride to the village, almost as if both of them knew it was a much safer topic than anything else, when their last conversations had been so intensely personal and significant. Once that was exhausted, an odd tension settled between them. Of things unsaid, or maybe that was just her take on the silence or her own guilt for orchestrating the entire meeting in the first place. Rather than let it hang, it was Gray who blessedly broke it. 'Why are you collecting the post rather than leaving it to a servant?'

'My uncle is expecting a letter, one he has been quietly fretting about, so I offered to collect it and, knowing Harriet would leave your poor cousin waiting longer than necessary for her to turn up, I decided to kill two birds with one stone and chivvy her along.' That did sound a more plausible excuse than forgetting Harriet and Lord Fennimore had a prior engagement, when it had been mentioned repeatedly in his presence yesterday at her aunt's interminable garden party. 'She has a dismissive relationship with clocks by and large and time keeping has never been her forte. As it was, even with my interference, she was significantly past fashionably late. Making the poor man suffer too long from Harriet's tenuous grasp of time seemed unnecessarily cruel.'

'Cruel—but entertaining. It made me glad he had woken me. That, and his request for me to be the chaperon. I've never been asked to be a chaperon before and never thought I would. It is those odd and wholly unexpected moments that make life so entertaining. I am the last person to ensure the correct proprieties are adhered to.' His eyes flicked to hers, the flirtatious challenge in them instantly reminding her of exactly how many odd and wholly unexpected times he alone had tempted Impetuous Thea to stray. Except, right this second, it wasn't exactly Impetuous Thea who controlled things, nor was it Sensible Thea. It was an odd amalgamation of the two which felt reassuringly like her old self. The Thea not jaded by fortune hunters, who never checked her temper or pithy comments in case they caused her poor uncle to keel over. The Thea who embraced life and enjoyed a little risk. Thrived on it. Hence her spur-of-the-moment decision to accompany Harriet and take a chance on a man she would never have considered anywhere near suitable only a few days ago.

Before she wrestled Impetuous Thea back in her box, she stopped at the end of the meadow as the village came in sight and decided to ignore all the guilt and simply enjoy the moment. She was tired of being too buttoned up and suspicious. She was young, the sun was shining and the day felt much brighter than any had in a long time. She might not be ready to leap off the precipice, but she was certainly prepared to edge a little towards it. 'This land is Colonel Purbeck's. If you don't mind, I'd prefer we skirt around the edges rather than cross it directly.' Crossing it directly would also take half the time, when she was inclined to linger. 'If he sees us, we'll have to call on him and…well…'

'The droning man spits when he talks.'

'Precisely.' She loved that he already knew her

so well he could finish her sentences. She also loved the knowing smile she had only seen him use on her. The one that did odd things to her insides and made her forget all the reasons why she was supposed to be wary and suspicious. He didn't behave like a fortune hunter. Nor did his past indicate that he'd attempt to be one. He had a healthy disrespect for money. And a committed aversion to marriage. One he had been completely honest about lest she not know exactly where she stood, yet she was stood here despite it. 'Although he will be wounded when he learns Harriet prefers your cousin to him. Colonel Purbeck is also very taken with—' The gunshot came out of nowhere, startling them both. As Trefor barked repeatedly in warning, Archimedes simultaneously reared, throwing Thea helplessly from his back.

She landed with a dull thud on the grass, winded but otherwise intact, and managed to roll away a split second before one of his massive hooves hit her. Swiftly, she scrambled backwards and well out of his way, blinking and hearing only the sound of her rapidly beating heart.

Her old hunter was in a blind panic. One that needed to be quickly controlled for all their sakes. Before she could pull herself to her feet, Gray slid off his horse, patting his horse's flank to send it out of the way before he stepped bravely into the fray.

'Trefor! Back!' He pointed to where Thea now

stood and the animal listened, instantly pressing his body against her legs as if protecting her for his master. After checking that she was all right, Gray motioned for her to stay put while he dealt with the frightened horse, something which worried her because Archimedes truly was skittish to the point of being outright temperamental. Especially around strange people.

'Easy, boy.' He kept his voice level and even, his palms up as he edged forward. It was obvious, despite her accusation to the contrary only a few scant days ago, Gray knew horses. 'Easy… Shh.' The erratic jumping was lopsided. Her big horse was hanging one leg at the rear. Not only was he panicked, he was injured and it was all her fault. She should have been paying closer attention. She never should have been here in the first place. 'Good boy… Easy.' He caught the trailing rein in his fist and wound it quickly around his hand to steady him, his other hand reaching out to stay the horse's head. 'Shh… It's all right.' Gray rested his forehead against his muzzle and dropped his voice to a whisper, breathing slowly to encourage the animal to do the same, a soothing technique she had never seen anyone use before.

At first Archimedes fought him, then he slowly, miraculously, calmed. 'Thea—take the reins.' He waited for her to grab the slack before he risked unwinding his hand from the leather. 'He's hurt himself. The right fetlock. Hold him still while I check his leg.'

'He's lame!' Once again, she had been self-indulgent in her pursuit of the forbidden and fate was punishing her. Yet she had wilfully ignored the nagging voice of doubt in her head. 'Is it broken?' Thea couldn't hide the fear or the threatening tears from her voice as she stared on impotently. Archimedes was all she had left of her father. A broken leg would mean the old horse would need to be destroyed. She couldn't bear yet another thing she loved leaving her because of her own reckless selfishness. Gray gently probed the swollen muscle, then risked manipulating the joint. The horse flinched and so did she.

'I don't think so. But he's sprained it badly. He doesn't want to put any weight on it. Probably turned it as he reared.' He didn't need to mention that bad sprains could also be dangerous. Especially on a horse as old as hers. What had she done? This was all her fault. 'Let's get him back to the hall so I can check him over properly.'

Tentacles of panic wrapped around her organs that she tried to ignore. Panic was a selfish emotion and her innocent horse deserved better. 'Our stables has a big cart. Certainly big enough for Archimedes. Shall I fetch it?'

'Yes! And plenty of ropes and strong-backed grooms. The less he aggravates the injury now, the greater the chance is of it recovering.'

Grateful to have something to do rather than consider the bitter ramifications of her actions, she pulled up the skirts of the ridiculous riding habit she had worn solely for him and made no attempt to look ladylike as she heaved herself astride Gray's horse and then nudged the animal to a gallop.

The next two hours passed by in a blur, most of which was spent with Thea pacing and wringing her hands as Gray took charge. He coaxed Archimedes into the cart, secured him and rode in it with him for the entire painfully slow journey back to ensure her horse wasn't jolted. Then he took over her uncle's stables after the stable master suggested shooting the poor thing there and then, instead issuing rapid and succinct orders to the staff about the way he wanted the treatment to proceed.

Her horse's damaged leg was bathed in ice, then loosely wrapped in a poultice. Most ingeniously of all, he had lashed ropes over the ceiling beams tied to a hammock affair beneath Archimedes's stomach to support his weight and prevent him moving around. By the time it was all done, the sweet old boy was as comfortable and content in his stall as could be expected and well enough to munch on the carrots she had brought him by way of an apology—as if she could apologise for being so careless with his well-being. Now, alone in the garden, she sensed Gray come alongside her. One glance proved his expression was grave.

'Will he recover?'

'It's hard to say at this stage. The next few days will be crucial, but we'll have a better idea once the swelling starts to go down in a day or two. Then we can strap him up. Hopefully his lameness is temporary—as it so often is.'

'And what if the swelling doesn't…?' He silenced her by gently placing his index finger on her lips.

'Don't think like that, Thea. Don't think too far ahead. It serves no purpose. There are too many variables and all of them out of our control. He is calm and the fact that he is eating tells me that the pain is not unbearable. That is a huge positive and I find it's much more beneficial to focus on the positives than indulge in the what ifs. I will personally check on him daily and ensure that every possible thing can be done to see your horse back on all four of his feet again. Let's take this a day at a time.'

She nodded, too choked to say anything, and powerless to stop the tears she had been stalwartly holding back from falling. The guilt and shame was eating her from the inside and had been for hours. How many times did someone she loved have to get hurt because of her inability to control her own selfish desires? Thanks to her stubborn selfishness, her father was dead and her uncle nearly so. Because of her selfish desire to spend more illicit time with Gray, Archimedes was put in danger. Impetuous Thea was a menace.

'Don't cry, Thea.' He looked extremely ill at ease with her uncontrolled and noisy bout of emotion, but she couldn't seem to stop. 'Please don't cry.'

'Th-this is all my f-fault. I should never have taken him out this morning. It was a selfish thing to do.'

'Selfish? Of course it wasn't.' His thumb gently brushed one tear away. 'It was the fault of the blithering idiot who fired that gun.'

'You d-don't understand…' How could she explain it, when she knew to any rational person it would sound like nonsense? He wrapped his strong arms around her and she wept against his chest, grateful he was there and wishing he wasn't. 'I could have p-prevented this.'

She was apparently inconsolable, which affected him just as much as her horse's injury clearly affected her. In the absence of any clue as to how to make her stop crying, all Gray could do was hold her tight. A huge mistake. The second he took her in his arms, it played havoc with his emotions.

There was something unsettling about holding this indomitable woman when she was so distraught and he was powerless to stop it. For some reason she was intent on blaming herself for what happened and no amount of reasoning with her appeared to be able to change that. As in all things, there was nothing quiet and sedate about the way she expressed her grief. Each shuddering sob seemed to have the power to hurt his heart, while the front of his shirt was now completely soaked through.

A few minutes previously, Viscount Gislingham had appeared at the French doors, taken one horrified look at the dreadful state of Thea and retreated, stunned, back inside, shaking his head, leaving Gray to bear the brunt of his niece's breakdown all alone. The only weapons he had in his poorly stocked arsenal were the unwavering support of his arms as he held her and the odd platitude mumbled near her ear. The whole experience left him wrung out like an old dish rag and riddled with guilt that he couldn't do any more. But he wanted to. He'd move heaven and earth to ease her pain.

'It will be all right, Thea—I promise.' What was he saying? He was in no position to promise. Gray really had no idea if his common-sense treatments would work. His knowledge was rusty. He'd had no real cause to use it in the last decade and had long ago given up keeping up with the new ideas of the equine world. Although he was sure he'd read or heard mention of some fellow suspending a horse from the ceiling before and if a cooling poultice worked on a human sprain, it stood to reason it might work on other animals. The truth was, he might well have made no difference to poor Archimedes's situation whatsoever. He kissed the top of her head and buried his nose in her curls. She finally tilted her face up to look at him, her eyes so sad. 'I'll make this right, Thea. You can trust me.' He saw hope kindle then. Hope and belief in him that was both humbling and made him feel ten feet tall. Of its own accord, his head began to lower, intent on kissing away all her pain…

'Oh, my dear! Oh, my dear!' The Viscountess suddenly burst through the French doors, still wearing her bonnet and travelling clothes. 'I have just heard what happened. Poor Archimedes! And poor you!' The older woman rushed over and began to fuss around Thea, dragging her out of his arms and back towards the house, leaving Gray no choice but to impotently follow, ridiculously aggrieved to have been usurped in Thea's moment of need. 'I am sure he will recover, dearest. I know how much you love him.'

Back in the parlour, as a pale Thea quietly wept against her aunt's shoulder, Gislingham tapped Gray on the arm and gestured beyond the door, then limped out. Gray was glad to escape. Not because of Thea's tears—but because he wanted to be the only one who consoled her. Worrying and dangerous ground indeed. 'What happened?'

Gray told him every detail and watched the man bristle. 'Blasted Purbeck! The fool shoots off his gun at all hours with scant regard for his neighbours. We've had words about it before. A few years ago, back before this happened.' He pointed to his ravaged body. 'He came within a hair's breadth of killing me! He was shooting pheasants or grouse or something well out of season, and his bullet went clean through my hat. It took every ounce of my restraint not to punch the blighter on the nose. Now poor Thea's horse is injured! And for what? All so the idiot can brag to whichever lamentable soul he has forced to dine with him that he is so manly he killed the dinner himself! I've never understood it. The sight of blood has always made me queasy and I couldn't eat a thing I'd watched choke on its dying breath.'

But sleep soundly knowing men have been murdered at your word? Gray bit back the angry, incredulous retort and tried to push his understandable prejudices to one side. Not for King and country this time, but for Thea. His friend… The friend his arms still longed to hold. The same friend who was currently making his heart ache in a way that did not feel at all like simple friendship. If anything, it felt alarmingly like…affection. Perhaps more than that. A knot of emotion formed in his throat. Fear and realisation. He was in too deep—but knew he couldn't back away and that had precious little to do with his mission and everything to do with her.

'Tell me plain, young man, so I can prepare. Does the nag stand a fighting chance or are we merely prolonging the inevitable?'

'I think it's just a sprain. Perhaps a bad one. But if I'm right he might recover.' Seeing her so distraught, he'd nurse the beast day and night for a month if he had to. Whatever it took to make her smile again. What was that about?

'I hope you are right.' The Viscount clumsily lowered himself on to an ottoman by the wall, suddenly looking old and frail. 'Archimedes was her father's horse. Her last link to him bar me. I can only assume that is part of the reason she is so upset. She lost her father young. A carriage accident. Such a tragedy. Maybe this has churned that all up?' There was a chance. Her grief was that raw. 'She had nightmares for months afterwards and thoroughly blamed herself.'

'Why?'

'They argued that day. Something which was a frequent occurrence because they were both as headstrong as each other, but which always quickly blew over. He'd lay down the law, she'd rebel and then he'd despair of her wilful nature when she refused to comply. But once they had both cooled off, they would both apologise. My brother and my niece both had twin fiery tempers that matched their fiery hair. Tempers that burned hot instantly, then cooled just as quickly. Except that day, he stormed out in anger and they never got to make it up. She used to dwell on that a great deal, no matter how much I tried to tell her my brother wouldn't have cared. He adored his daughter and, like me, royally spoiled her rotten. But she forgot that in the midst of her grief. I suppose it's easier to focus on the negatives than remember the positives. To lose Archimedes through tragedy…well, that would be a bitter blow indeed.'

As Gray digested that, he realised it was entirely plausible. Those fragile links to the past mattered. He doubted he'd ever set foot in Wales again for exactly that reason. Wales, his mother, Cecily and the hornet's nest his life had quickly turned into were all inextricably linked to that place.

The butler approached on silent feet and coughed politely. 'The post has finally arrived, my lord. Did you want it now?' On the silver salver in his hand was one letter. A letter written in the same, elegant, sloping hands as the ones tied with ribbon locked in the Viscount's desk.

The older man glanced at it and sighed in relief. 'Put it in my study, thank you. I shall read it later.' Just as Gray would read the few he had pilfered from that same study a few hours ago at his earliest possible convenience. In an hour or three. Once he was sure Thea was all right.

Chapter Sixteen

~~~~~~~~

They were love letters. Beautifully written. Poignant and filled with all the angst and longing of a love that wasn't allowed to be, yet managed to survive regardless. The earliest ones were over twenty years old and intimate. The author of the letters described her joy at Gislingham's tenderness alongside the emotional fulfilment the intimacy had created.

> *I suspected you were the one. Now I know it.*
> *I refuse to feel guilty for loving you.*

A few years on and the situation appeared hopeless.

> *I know you are married and that I must be*
> *part of your past, but I think of you every*
> *single day and what we might have had and*
> *curse fate for introducing us to each other*
> *too late to change things.*

In his haste to grab a decent sample, Gray had missed a decade's worth of the doomed story of the star-crossed lovers, but the next letter had a wholly different tone. Chatty and filled with gossip. Family stories about her mother, her brother and her new nephew.

Such an adorable cherub with eyes almost as dark as your Thea's.

This was a relationship where everything was shared. Almost as if out of their initial passion, they had found a way to be friends. Yet the final paragraph discussed a stolen weekend by the sea where they had been free to be solely with one another.

You are my everything. Tonight I shall lie on my pillow and blow you a thousand kisses. Make sure you catch them.

By the date, he was sure Gislingham had remarried by that time. All their intelligence suggested he had walked Caroline down the aisle within a year of his first wife's death. Had he and his true love not reconnected before then? Was she also married? It seemed a great shame that these two people were clearly meant to be together, but, like ships passing in the night, never came quite close enough. He wished he had taken more of the letters to know the full picture, but was also glad he hadn't. The Gislingham on the page was too likeable. Too much like the old man who had fretted about his niece yesterday and who loved to laugh.

The accounts Gray had taken from the Viscount's desk were also surprising and thankfully thorough enough that Gray had no cause to break into Thea's bedchamber. Her fortune was quite staggering and diligently managed. She did have stocks in ships—but a totally legitimate fleet. You couldn't work hand in glove with the Excise Men and not know which companies were above board and which worked hard to appear to be. These were owned by Quakers and, famously, not only diligently paid all their levies and tariffs, but also eschewed transporting any items which had links with slavery. She also had shares in a successful pottery, several banks and a publishing house. None of which seemed even slightly dubious.

More curious were Gislingham's private investments. He had a similar portfolio to Thea, but a quarter of its size. He was a wealthy man to be sure, but the majority of his money-making efforts—on paper, at least—appeared to be on her behalf. Almost as if he really was securing her future after he was gone, but was perfectly content to live comfortably within his means himself.

Completely incongruous with the man Gray suspected Gislingham to be—and more like the devoted, loving man in these letters. Unless those accounts were all the clever ruse of a genius who had known that someone would one day come looking and had constructed a legitimate façade which he hid behind. The Boss wouldn't be stupid enough to keep any evidence of his criminal dealings at home. But were these love letters faked, too? He glanced back down at the one in his hand and cast it aside. The private emotions spilling on to every neatly written page made him feel ashamed to read them. Voyeuristic, even. Perhaps because he knew what it felt like to love deeply and then to lose it.

Unlike the Viscount's, every heartfelt letter he had sent to Cecily before her marriage had been returned unopened. Something he was glad of now. She had ripped his young heart from his chest and trampled it. That was enough. She didn't need to know exactly how much her betrayal had hurt him or how much he had wanted her back. The same day she married his brother in Wales, Gray had stepped on a merchant ship in Bristol bound for the Orient, strangely embracing the weeks of horrendous seasickness because it numbed the pain in his heart. Then he had banished her from his thoughts until he had arrived here in Suffolk, knowing the mere memory of her face, her voice and their shared childhood would stir it all up afresh.

Except it *was* different. Time had taken the sting out of the memories. He had to concentrate hard to conjure an image of Cecily. That face he had adored was hazy and blurred. He couldn't hear her voice any more. Didn't feel that sharp pain in his ribs when he pondered what might have been, because for some reason it no longer mattered—because she no longer mattered.

Why that was, he wasn't inclined to examine—suffice it to say that it was an entirely different woman who consumed his thoughts now. And as he approached the stables at Gislingham Hall, he felt his blood fizz with excitement at the prospect of seeing her. Another thing best not examined. He was here for Archimedes and to catch The Boss. Those were the only two tangibles he would focus on in a swirling sea of variables and he would cling to both like a piece of driftwood in a storm.

The big horse was munching hay, apparently quite content to have the ceiling bear most of his weight and not the least bit bothered by the peculiar harness supporting his belly. Without asking permission from the stable hands, he made a huge fuss of the brute, then crouched down to unwrap the poultice from his fetlock. Last night, to give his mind something else to do rather than worry about how badly Thea had taken the injury, Gray had visited the stable again late and reapplied a fresh one. Now the joint was still swollen, but less so. He was able to run his hands over all of it without Archimedes flinching once. A very encouraging sign.

Seeing as his unlikely treatment appeared to be working, Gray repeated it, bathing the leg in ice, then wrapping it in another cooling poultice, then took himself off to report the progress to Thea.

'She's gone off to lick her wounds.' The Viscount had insisted Gray eat breakfast with him in his private sitting room. 'Came down this morning apologising for carrying on, checked on Archimedes and I haven't seen her since. She does that, does Thea. She's one to mull by nature. Ponders everything far too long and then pretends to everyone she is fine and dandy, when we all know she isn't. She's always been the same. I never quite know what's going on inside her head.'

'Was she the same when her father died?'

'Worse. Bottled it all up inside. It took more than a year to see smatterings of the old Thea return.' He chewed thoughtfully on his bacon. 'Heartbreaking.'

'What happened?' Because all the King's Elite intelligence had focused on Gislingham's past, Thea's was a grey area. He watched the older man slump a little in his chair at the memory, then felt guilty for dragging it up. 'It's really none of my business. I'm sorry.'

'No… You of all people should probably know.' What did that mean? 'They were staying here.

They always came down from Cambridge to rusticate here over the summer. It's a short journey back and my brother would sometimes return to attend to whatever business he had to attend to. They'd argued. I told you that. Over something nonsensical, as was their wont, and he'd stomped out, muttering about being cursed with the most wilful daughter any man had ever been cursed with while she haired up the stairs like a banshee and slammed her bedchamber door. An hour later, the constable came. The brake on his gig had failed as he'd tried to avoid something in the road. I can't say I know exactly what happened that dreadful morning, suffice it to say his gig overturned and his neck was broken.'

Thea watched her feet swish backwards and forwards in the water, feeling both stupid and guilty. The logical, adult half of her brain knew that what had happened to Archimedes was a fluke. Out of anyone's control and just one of those awful things that happened from time to time when you least expected it. But Impetuous Thea's brain still remembered the crushing guilt she had felt as a child at angering her papa so that he had driven away for the last time in a temper. A memory which might have been forgotten, had her uncle not had his stroke within an hour of another blazing row brought about by her wilful, re-

bellious nature and selfish intention to do exactly
what she wanted—regardless of what he wanted.

Somewhere along the line, those two tragically similar events had become intertwined and
she had promised herself never to behave like
that again, just in case they were linked and she
was entirely to blame. It was nonsensical, yet
she couldn't shake it. She had always shouldered
much of the blame for both her father's untimely
death and her uncle's stroke—and always would.
Carried both events around in her heart daily
while trying, and ultimately failing, to behave
better than that wilful girl she had been. Digging
her heels in, shouting and slamming doors were
largely a thing of the past.

But as Gray had warned her, leopards didn't
change their spots. As much as she tried to curb
Impetuous Thea, sometimes it was just too hard.
Yesterday, she had allowed herself to be tempted
again by forbidden fruit and it had ended in tragedy. Or at least near tragedy. Another similarity,
which in her distressed state had petrified her and
rendered her senseless for a good hour.

Then common sense and reality had prevailed
and she was heartily ashamed of herself. It was
one thing to think nonsense in the private confines of one's own head. It was quite another to
allow the world to see it. Thea had worried her
poor uncle when he didn't need the stress, dominated all of poor Aunt Caro's afternoon with

her wailing and probably sent Gray running for the hills.

Lord only knew what the poor man had thought. One minute she had been shamelessly pursuing him and the next she was a snivelling, grizzling mess against his chest. At the time, it had been the only place she had wanted to be. Still did, truth be known, and that didn't frighten her half as much as it should, if at all.

Gray had chiselled his way into her thoughts and occupied far too many of them, just as he had since she had first encountered him.

Here.

The exact spot where she had headed at the crack of dawn to lick her wounds. That was only partly what she had been doing for the better part of two hours, when she couldn't glance at the water without picturing him in it and had probably come here with the express intention of doing so. Unhindered, unwatched and unjudged for her outrageous, lustful fantasies in which there was just her and him, cool water and a shocking absence of clothes.

'There you are.' He strolled into the clearing, making her jump, and stood a little awkwardly, eventually settling with his hands on his hips, taking in the whole clearing as if seeing it for the first time. How splendid. They were both beyond uncomfortable. 'Archimedes seems well. It's early days, of course, but so far so good. He has made excellent progress in just one day.'

'Yes. I saw. Thank you. Even our pessimistic stable master is hopeful.' She should probably apologise for her out-of-character and childish outburst, but had no earthly idea where to start without looking like a complete fool. Instead she stared back at her feet in the water, cringing, willing him away.

'I suspect we need to have one of those honest conversations you're so fond of.'

'I suppose so.' She couldn't look up, but sensed him move closer. Then heard him tug off both boots before he lowered himself on to the bank next to her. He sat quietly, his bigger feet idly swishing next to hers, clearly assuming she should start. It was time to bite the bullet.

'I'm sorry about yesterday. I got myself in a fluster.' A hysterical mess more like. Clinging on to him like a ninny. Irrationally inconsolable.

'A fluster?' She could hear the smile. She didn't need to humiliate herself further by looking at it. 'If that's what a fluster looks like, I'd hate to see you in a state. You scared the hell out of me. Do you want to tell me about it?'

'Not particularly. It was a shocking bout of useless self-pity that I am heartily ashamed of.'

'We all have our moments, Thea. Your horse was hurt and for a while things seemed grim.'

'And in the midst of the crisis, I was a hindrance rather than a help. I hate that.' Almost as much as she hated the hideous display of histrionics she had subjected him to.

'I disagree. It was you who suggested the cart. You who fetched it and organised the grooms. In the midst of the crisis you were a rock.' His hand found hers where it sat in her lap and he closed his fingers around it, instantly making her warm. 'Only once the crisis was past did you falter. Something you are entirely entitled to do. Nobody can be a rock all the time. I just came to check you are all right now. I hated seeing you so upset.'

'It's silly having such an attachment to a horse. He's just a horse.'

'I'd be devastated if anything happened to Trefor. I adore the useless mutt. And Archimedes isn't just a horse. He was your father's horse. I understand how much the things which link you to a lost parent matter. My mother's ruby means the world to me. I could never part with it. Fortunately, I never have to watch it age and die. Such attachments merely make us human, Thea, and, in case you were wondering, I certainly don't judge you for falling apart at the prospect of losing him yesterday. Grief is also human. It's real and it's visceral and it hurts.' Something he would understand more than most. 'What does concern me is the way you blamed yourself for what happened, when you were blameless and it was the droning, spitting Colonel who shot the gun. He just came around to apologise, by the way. I left your uncle reading him the riot act.' His other hand gently tipped her face to him. 'Why would you blame yourself for a freak accident?'

'It's ridiculous. You really wouldn't understand.'

'You understood how I lost my fortune thanks to my momentous fluster all those years ago. What makes you think I won't be equally as sympathetic?' Those unusual silvery-blue eyes were unwavering and kind. 'I am assuming it has something to do with your father... Your uncle told me the last words you exchanged on the day he passed were said in anger.'

'They were.' Thea considered lying, then discounted it. He would know if she lied. He was that perceptive. 'He wanted me to spend an extra hour with my governess perfecting my times tables. I wanted to climb Uncle Edward's apple tree. I told him I hated him and he never came back.'

'You were a child. He knew you didn't mean it.'

'Did my uncle also tell you that the last words I said to him before his stroke were also said in anger? Just like that awful day when my father was killed, I had given the rebellious part of my nature free rein and as a result my uncle and I butted heads worse than we ever had before. The eerie similarities are not lost on me.' He frowned, disbelieving. Who could blame him?

To her own ears what she was trying to articulate sounded daft.

'There was a man. An officer. He was a few years older than me, handsome, dashing and charming and like a dolt I believed all his flowery words. Uncle Edward saw right through him from the outset, but I wouldn't listen. Even when I was presented with evidence of the man's many debts I refused to consider such an experienced and intriguing gentleman would be so shallow to want only my money when he sounded so sincere. To cut a very short story shorter, being underage, I was forbidden from seeing my dashing soldier again and in response I was a total horror. I accused my uncle of being jealous, because his relationship with my aunt was so hideous he couldn't bear to see me find true love.' The next part was the bit she was most ashamed of, so turned her head away in case he also judged her as harshly as she judged herself.

'My uncle is not one to lay the law down, so the fact he had was unusual and I should have heeded him. But against his express instructions, I sent my *beloved* a note and crept out that night to meet him. He tried to seduce me, promising he would happily marry me once my virtue was gone, and alarm bells began to ring. We barely knew each other—three dances over two separate assemblies was the full extent of our acquaintance and already he was suggesting marriage? I was a dolt, but clearly still a suspicious one. It didn't ring true. I tested the theory by lying and telling him that I wouldn't receive a penny of my fortune till I turned thirty.'

'If he had loved you, he wouldn't have cared.'

'I know. But instead he said something which proved me to be the stupidest of fools and the most wilful of idiots.' She mimicked the scoundrel's overly sincere voice. 'Your uncle won't see you in the poor house, *my darling*. I am certain the terms of your trust can be altered.'

'Ah.'

'Ah, indeed. I ran home with my tail between my legs and walked through the door to chaos. My aunt was wailing about what was to become of her. Bertie was beside himself with grief and the physician said my uncle wouldn't survive the night.'

'Ergo, in your mind, you were somehow responsible for his stroke just as you were your father's carriage accident? When you weren't present for either event, nor witnessed the particular circumstances?'

'Both times I was lured by forbidden fruit.'

'Did your uncle know that you had disobeyed him?'

'No. He still doesn't.' Gray was using logic when all the tangled emotions inside her were completely illogical. 'I told you it was daft. But perhaps if I hadn't roused both of their tempers, neither tragedy would have happened?'

'And perhaps they still would have. None of us can fully control what fate has in store for us. How old were you?'

'Barely twenty and too green for my own good.'

'It's a dangerous age, twenty. You think you know it all when really you understand nothing of the world. As I know to my cost.' His foot brushed hers in the water and he stared down at it for a few seconds before moving it away. 'I suppose there were echoes of what had happened before. Enough for a vivid imagination to combine and jump to superstitious conclusions. But that doesn't explain yesterday's reaction. You never once lost your temper or rebelled. Did it churn all that misplaced guilt up again? All we did was have a perfectly pleasant morning ride to the village.'

'That Impetuous Thea orchestrated.'

Chapter Seventeen

'Impetuous Thea?'

'The part of me that refused to learn my twelve times table the morning my father was killed. The part that gorged on apples instead. The same part that ran off to meet the soldier. Was letting him kiss her at the exact moment my uncle was struck down.'

'The part that is obviously *entirely* responsible for two completely unlinked events, a decade apart, neither of which you were there for.' He smiled, his thumb tracing lazy circles on the back of her hand that were playing havoc with her pulse despite her misery. 'So you indulged in a bit of kissing? That doesn't make you evil, merely human. And the fact that you were not compliant and sought a little adventure hardly justifies fate punishing you. It makes you interesting. Flawed, as we all are. You were twenty. Barely an adult. And unlike your father, your uncle didn't die. If fate had truly wanted to punish you, that stroke would have killed him. It would have broken Archimedes's leg in two. Have you considered that?'

She hadn't. That night and yesterday could have been so much worse. 'Perhaps they were warning shots across the bow?'

'Or more likely it was an unfortunate coincidence. As so much of life is.' He leaned closer so that they touched from shoulder to hip. 'I am intrigued to know how Archimedes's sprain fits into this picture. What nefarious deed did Impetuous Thea do to make Colonel Purbeck fire off his gun at precisely that moment?'

She tugged her hand away because his touch was waylaying her from her guilt. 'I never should have been there in the first place! Impetuous Thea wanted to…' Thea sighed, feeling thoroughly embarrassed and ridiculous. 'The implausible long and the short of it is, I think fate punishes me for my wilfulness. That's why I keep Impetuous Thea locked in her box.'

He didn't laugh. That was something. But he was quiet for the longest time. 'If you were being scientific about it, you should probably test that theory.'

'Test it?' The idea was as daft as her fears were. 'How do you suppose I do that?'

'Tempt fate. Let Impetuous Thea out of the box for a month. Live in the moment, be a slave to her whims. Enjoy yourself. Eat every piece of forbidden fruit. If you are correct, then you are in for a horrendous few weeks and you can lock her up for good. If not, then life will continue much as it always does. There will be good things and bad things—because there always are. But unless there are significantly more bad things than usual, then I think you can safely and *scientifically* say it makes no difference if you cage the beastie or let her run riot. Life is far too short not to be yourself or to worry about what fate might throw at you, because in my experience it throws things at you regardless.'

'You make it all sound simple.'

'Not simple exactly, more philosophical. I'm all about leaving the past in the past where it belongs. It can't be changed, so onwards and upwards. Embrace the moment and follow the path it sends you on. That is what makes life exciting.'

'Is that another one of your mottos?'

'It's a bit long to be a motto in the strictest sense of the motto, more an edict to abide by. Let's take what happened with Cecily as a classic example. It was all very tragic at the time and losing my fortune was an act of desperate stupidity—but if those two awful things hadn't happened, I never would have joined the merchant navy. Then I never would have travelled the world and done all the things I've done. I wouldn't have Trefor and I wouldn't be here now. And you'd have been riding all alone with Archimedes and Colonel Purbeck might still have fired his gun—and without my hare-brained idea to truss him to the ceiling, the stable master would have put your old horse out of his misery and you'd be mourning him today instead of feeling sorry for yourself.' He laced his fingers in hers and sighed. 'My convoluted point is this, Thea. Things always happen for a reason, even if the reason for them is not immediately apparent. And if I may say, the last thing a woman with an imagination as vivid as yours should be doing is wasting time overthinking things. Nothing good can come of it.'

He stood and pulled her up with him. 'Out of interest, what *did* Impetuous Thea orchestrate yesterday?' She instantly felt her face burn with the shame of it all. Hell would have to freeze over before she admitted she had only wanted to see him.

'I can't recall.'

'That's such a pity. Because from the ferociousness of that blush, it's bound to be good. Never mind, I shall interrogate you all the way home to see if I can provoke...' Thea planted both her hands in the centre of his chest, pushed and giggled as he went flying backwards into the water. He emerged, coughing and spluttering, but smiling. 'What was that for?'

'Don't blame me! You're the one who told

me to give Impetuous Thea free rein.' Then she picked up her skirts and ran.

Gray found himself smiling as he fixed his ridiculously early morning coffee, then frowned when he realised he was smiling because of her. Again. Over the past week, he had been doing that a lot. Every morning he sprang out of bed at the crack of dawn filled with purpose, went to check on Archimedes, then used that as a flimsy excuse to call on her. Although yesterday she had been waiting for him at the stables and, instead of drinking tea in the company of her uncle, the pair of them had ended up chatting for more than an hour tramping across the meadow with Trefor as he followed whichever sniffing trail took his fancy in between adoring Thea as only a besotted dog could.

Lord Fennimore was delighted with Gray's progress, assuming he was ingratiating himself into Gislingham's circle diligently for the sake of the mission, when the mission had nothing to do with it. It was Thea he was actively seeking out and, while he asked the odd pertinent question which would help the King's Elite, the bulk of his time was spent getting to know her.

It was all very proper and platonic. All roughly within the parameters of their truce, but the fact that he didn't flirt with her did not in any way reflect how much he wanted to or how hard he had to work not to. Although yesterday there had been a moment, when she had been smiling and he had been walking alongside her trying to make her laugh, when their eyes had locked for far longer than they should have and he had almost kissed her before he'd stopped himself. Since then, he had given a great deal of thought to that moment and still wasn't entirely sure that *not* kissing her had been the right thing to do.

A sound outside pulled him out of his pleasant musings a second before Fennimore came through the back door and stopped dead at the sight of Gray.

'You're up early.'

He took in his superior's guilty-looking appearance and his face split in a grin. 'And you're apparently home late.' By the lack of cravat, ruffled hair and the crumpled evening clothes, the old man had either spent the night in a gaming hell—unlikely in this quiet corner of Suffolk—or unbelievably he'd spent the night with a woman. 'How was dinner at Lady Crudgington's?'

'Very pleasant.' But Lord Fennimore was glowing crimson. 'But all that rich food gave me indigestion, so I decided to take myself off for a walk this morning. Early. Very early. As it was dark, I pulled on the first clothes that came to hand.' It had been the old man himself who had taught Gray the art of spotting a liar. Liars, he was often prone to drone, always overembellished with too much detail.

'Of course you did.' Gray winked saucily. 'Rich food. A pre-dawn stroll and wearing the first clothes you could grab. Such excellent embellishment and so early... You *old dog*!' It had the most spectacular effect.

Clenched fists at his sides. Blinking and stuttering. 'Keep your filthy accusations to yourself, Gray! I went for a walk, damn it. I haven't seen her ladyship since I left her last night!'

'Of course, sir. And let's not forget the indigestion. Did the exercise help it in any way?'

The sound of horses outside prevented Gray's immediate murder. Two agents burst in without knocking and got straight to the point. 'There have been developments, sir. The Excise Men have captured a ship at Leiston! It's full to the brim, sir.'

'Do we have the crew?' Lord Fennimore snapped into action, his embarrassment and indigestion now miraculously cured.

'Every single one of them. And there's more, sir. Within the last half-hour, an express arrived at Gislingham Hall. The rider must have been minutes behind ours on the road from the coast.'

Nobody needed to mention how significant this coincidence was. It was their first tangible clue that The Boss and Gislingham were one and the same. 'I assume you are planning to check on Archimedes this morning?'

'I was heading there straight after breakfast.'

'Good. Observe the lay of the land, but tread cautiously. I'll head to Leiston to interrogate the crew.' The light of battle was in Lord Fennimore's eyes. 'The net is closing in, gentlemen. This is the most perilous time. Keep your wits about you and don't make any mistakes. One wrong move now and we destroy a year's worth of work.'

Less than an hour later, Gray trotted casually into Viscount Gislingham's stable yard with Trefor in tow, expecting to see some hint of uproar, but instead nothing appeared out of the ordinary. He dismounted and went directly to Archimedes, who was gingerly putting some weight on his newly strapped leg as he munched on hay. Only after he had given the animal a thorough going-over did he risk heading to the house to report the good news to Thea.

To his surprise, the ancient butler immediately invited him upstairs to the Viscount's private apartments where the old man was sat eating a jovial breakfast with his niece as if he hadn't a care in the world. 'Lord Gray! Sit! Sit. Cook has outdone herself with the coddled eggs this morning. You won't be disappointed. Will it be coffee or chocolate today?'

Next to him, Thea beamed and, despite his

important mission, everything else went out of Gray's mind as he basked in her smile. He sat in the chair directly opposite, allowing himself a surreptitious inhale of her sultry jasmine perfume as she lent down to make a fuss of the bouncing Trefor at her side, then caught the Viscount eyeing him with interest. 'Coffee, if you please.' He needed his wits about him today of all days. But, lord, she looked lovely this morning. 'How are you this fine morning, my lord?'

'Cannot grumble, young man. I slept like the dead and woke with the lark. And today promises to be most entertaining. Harriet is coming around to paint my portrait.' He chuckled, nudging Gray with his elbow. 'Is it wrong that I find myself delighted at the prospect? There is a disastrous inevitability about it, which appeals to my warped sense of the ridiculous. I am determined to hang the finished monstrosity in the gallery next to my father's portrait. Purely to vex the old tyrant. He always took himself far too seriously.'

Concentrating proved difficult as Gray felt Thea lean to pour his coffee and his eyes involuntarily flicked to hers. Locked. Held. They did that a lot nowadays. Lingering glances and knowing looks that negated the need for words. All very worrying, but equally as special. All seemingly as natural as breathing. 'I hope you two youngsters aren't going to waste this glorious day inside.'

'I have a basket to deliver in the village if Trefor would appreciate the walk?'

He needed to stay close to the hall. 'Trefor always appreciates a walk. And a good sniff. We'll happily accompany you.' He really needed to work harder at being a better spy. 'At least for a little while.' Where he would use the time to subtly interrogate her as well as thoroughly enjoy her company. He watched her rise and prepare a plate for him and tried not to wish she could be there for every breakfast.

'I suppose at some point I should ask you about your intentions, young man.'

'I'm sorry?' His head whipped around to find the Viscount grinning.

'One of those cringingly awkward man-to-man conversations which have been laid down in the statutes, where I stand like an admiral inspecting the fleet, rocking on my heels and piercing you with my overprotective and fatherly glare.' Gray felt the colour drain from his face, not at all liking the direction things were going. 'I shall enquire about your prospects and be generally intimidating.'

'Er…well…' Exactly how did he get out of this without hurting Thea, insulting the Viscount and jeopardising the mission? The plate of coddled eggs appeared in front of him alongside Thea's hand on his back. He felt that touch everywhere. Didn't want it to end.

'He's testing you. For his own wicked amusement. And you are failing abominably.' She sat down, her own cheeks a little pink, he noticed. 'He's been doing the same to me since you knocked me into the brook.'

'And I've got precious little out of her. It has both me and Harriet intrigued. The pair of you have been the source of much speculation.'

Thea pointed at her uncle with her fork. 'Desist or I shall tell Bertie you have been very lax with your exercises and I caught you smoking that cigar.'

'Talk of the devil and the devil appears.' The Viscount's manservant suddenly filled the door frame, still in his travelling clothes.

'Bertie! You're home early!' Yet another pertinent coincidence this morning. Thea tossed down her napkin and greeted the servant like a dear friend, kissing him on the cheek. 'We didn't expect you for another week at least.'

The manservant and his master shared an odd look, one that spoke volumes. 'I knew I was needed, so cut my visit short. Lax in his exercises, you say? Then I am glad I came home…'

Aside from that look, nothing else untoward happened in the next hour. Bertie disappeared and then reappeared just as quickly in fresh clothes. Neither man seemed in a hurry to do anything or seemed particularly perturbed. Harriet arrived with her easel and among much hilarity she began to paint. As they left, Gray took his time, watching the servants, the outbuildings and the drive for signs that something was amiss. But if The Boss was bothered about losing a ship loaded with brandy as well as its entire scurvy crew, he did a very good job of hiding it.

Chapter Eighteen

Gray was unusually quiet for the rest of breakfast, something Thea entirely blamed her uncle
for. Intentions and prospects indeed, when neither of them had discussed anything vaguely romantic since their truce! Although the past week
had been romantic as far as she was concerned.
She had never spent so much pleasant time with
a man. And although he never instigated any of
their casual walks or rides after he had attended
to Archimedes, he had never turned a suggestion
down either. Which she had decided to take as a
very good sign, despite the dire lack of flirting or
touching or incendiary heated looks.

If anything, he had been the perfect gentleman.
Rigidly sticking to the parameters of their truce
but allowing their new friendship to blossom. She
was glad for that—but wanted more. Especially
since Impetuous Thea had been out in the wild
for seven whole days now, too, and nothing un-

toward had happened at all. She never curbed her in front of Gray or Harriet and had twice told her uncle off quite forcibly. Once for the sneaky cigar she had caught him with and then briskly confiscated, and once for his shameless cheating at chess. Both times he had bristled and bit back, and neither time did he keel over. It encouraged her to be bolder, which in turn made her feel lighter and happier than she had in years. It also made her wonder if that boldness might be just what was needed to give Gray a gentle nudge to let him know she was open and receptive to more should he feel inclined. The more she got to know him, the more it seemed a shame that such a warm and passionate man was so averse to allowing himself to love again.

His was a big heart, filled with joy, and it was increasingly playing havoc with hers. With each meeting, a little more of her wariness melted away and she became more convinced he wasn't forbidden fruit, but the man for her. And she was the woman for him.

Yesterday, she had almost kissed him. They had been walking along, chatting amiably and laughing, then her eyes had locked with his and lingered. She had instinctively licked her lips and watched those wolf-like irises darken, found herself leaning towards him in invitation. Then lost her nerve at the last moment, fearing she had misread the signals or might push him away because he was adamantly wary of anything involving hearts. Particularly when one of the hearts was his.

They had discussed that a little this past week also, always at Thea's instigation, too, and although it was still clearly a very sore topic, he had opened up. Enough that she was now convinced it was the fear of heartbreak that made him keep his heart at arm's length, rather than his continued deep and abiding love for the awful woman who had broken it. In fact, he had confessed yesterday also that he now had to concentrate hard to properly recall Cecily's face. Something which had apparently surprised him, but made Thea's heart soar.

Because her wary heart was waning. Instead of being instantly suspicious or worried about his motives, she found herself thoroughly enjoying each and every moment in a way she never had before. She got butterflies before she saw him, tingles once she did and a delightfully warm feeling deep inside simply knowing they occupied the same planet. As well as a completely different sort of warm feeling every single time she looked at him or pictured him naked in the brook.

'Fetch the ball, Trefor!'

Shamelessly she feasted on the sight of him pulling back his arm and throwing the tattered ball, admiring the way the muscles in his shoulders and back bunched. He really was a very fine specimen of manhood. Once she plucked up the courage to kiss him again, she was going to allow Impetuous Thea to thoroughly explore those muscles. He glanced back, then paused to wait for her, his eyes fixed on Trefor as he bounded through the tall grass after his beloved cricket ball. 'I meant to ask—one of the grooms mentioned your uncle received an express early this morning. I trust it was not bad news.'

'He did?' That was news to her. 'He never mentioned anything, so I doubt it was of much importance.'

'Perhaps they were mistaken. He seemed in perfectly good spirits. It was good of Bertie to come back early, although I am not certain your uncle was as surprised to see him as you were. He looked relieved, though—as if he had wanted him back.'

'Bertie is his right arm. Always has been—but more so since his stroke. He's worked for Uncle Edward for all the years I have been alive and longer. Although I have no idea how many years. I've never thought to ask. Dear Bertie is the only person truly able to make my stubborn uncle do what he is supposed to.' Without his diligence, he might have died in those first dreadful weeks after the stroke.

'Really? He holds that much sway?'

'Much more than me, I'm sorry to say. But then Bertie doesn't have my fiery temper or my uncle's pig-headedness. He simply issues calm instructions and miraculously we all comply. It's his gift.'

'I wish I could manipulate people to do my bidding.'

'Me, too. Perhaps we both need to be more overt in our manipulations? Perhaps that is the secret. It certainly seems to be working for Harriet.' Something Thea was becoming more and more envious of. 'She seems to have your dour cousin Cedric eating out of her hand.' Gray grinned wickedly, then chuckled, but didn't elaborate as he picked up his pace. 'You know something, don't you?'

'I do.' Gray bent to wrestle the soggy ball out of Trefor's jaws and threw it again into the trees that hid the brook. 'But daren't tell you.'

'Daren't? Is it a secret? For if it is, I have to tell you Harriet will tell me herself.'

'I doubt that. It's not for delicate ears.'

'My ears are hardly delicate! And it shows how little you know Harriet if you think she would censor something. I have been privy to some eye-opening confessions.' Harriet was a great fan of *bed sport*, as she called it. 'Besides, it strikes me as grossly unfair that you should know something that I don't.' He had jogged on ahead after the dog, forcing her to sprint after him and catch him by the arm. 'Tell me, you wretch! Did you catch him stealing a kiss?'

He grinned and shook his head. 'So *innocent*...

Worse!' He was laughing, the deep sound doing odd things to her nerve endings.

'Worse?' He watched her puzzle it through, making no attempt to hide his delight when shock replaced curiosity. 'Oh, my goodness! They are...' She felt her cheeks heat as she struggled to find the polite term for the act she suspected.

'The word is *lovers*, Thea.' He raised his dark eyebrows suggestively. 'In truth, I've been itching to tell you all morning, because nobody is as shocked or thoroughly entertained by the situation as I am. But there is no doubt. He came home at the crack of dawn this morning, attempting to creep in in the exact evening clothes he went to hers to dine in last night—minus his cravat.'

'There might be a perfectly innocent explanation...' Harriet was incorrigible. She knew that in her bones. Although scandalous, part of Thea— the impetuous and wilful part—couldn't help but be impressed. Her friend didn't waste time with doubt or overthinking. When she wanted something, she leapt.

'There was nothing innocent in his guilty, convoluted excuses or the brilliance of his beetroot face. Consequently, I am left in no doubt that our older and wiser companions have...'

'Seen each other *naked*.' He roared with laughter and Thea found herself giggling. 'Oh, my goodness. Cedric and Harriet...do you think this is just an affair or something more...serious?'

He paused as if considering it for the first time. 'I have no idea. Cedric keeps his cards very close to his chest. They have been spending an inordinate amount of time together.'

'So have we.' The words had popped out before she could stop them and then she saw his shoulders stiffen. 'By which I mean, they might just be friends. As we are.'

His shoulders relaxed. 'Yes, but they have seen each other naked. There is a difference.'

'I've seen you naked.' What was the matter with her? Why was she intent on spoiling a perfectly lovely walk by pushing him into discussing something he really did not want to discuss.

'Again, there is a difference. You saw me in the altogether from a polite distance. Their nakedness was up close.' There had been nothing polite in the way her eyes had greedily drunk in the sight.

'Do you know, I was secretly rather jealous of you and Trefor that day? It's been so hot and that water looked so cool. Then, of course, thanks to Trefor, I got to enjoy it.'

'Fully clothed is hardly the same. You should give it a go one day when there's nobody around. A naughty bit of nude bathing sounds exactly like the sort of pursuit Impetuous Thea would enjoy.' She would. Except Impetuous Thea wanted to do it with him. An errant thought which made her suddenly peculiarly warm.

'I suspect it's something Trefor is currently enjoying.' Gray stared at the trees and shook his head. 'His absence suggests he's clearly been way-laid by the water again.' It was exactly then that Thea's toes reached the edge of the mystical preci-pice Harriet kept going on about and immediately all her friend's advice made sense. If there was any sort of future between her and Gray beyond this lovely friendship they shared, then one of them had to leap.

They found the dog swimming backwards and forwards with the ball clamped in his mouth, his tail swishing from side to side like a rudder. Gray tried to get him to stop, feeling slightly uncom-fortable that they were in this intimate, secluded spot when moments ago they had been talking about it and other wholly inappropriate things, and his mind was now filled with images of Thea floating naked in the water. Copper hair unbound and fanned out on the surface.

He never should have told her about old Fenni-more and Harriet. No matter how easy he found her to talk to, how frank and open and honest their conversations were, there were certain sub-jects a gentleman didn't discuss with a woman who wasn't *his* in the biblical sense. Now all he could think about was what it would be like to know her in a biblical sense and that was playing havoc with his senses.

Obviously, she wasn't similarly affected, because she made herself comfortable on the bank. 'Oh, to be a dog! Leave him be for a little while. I'm in no hurry and I'd hate to spoil his fun.' She patted the ground next to her, a place he really did not want to be. Not when his breeches were suddenly tighter and all he wanted to do was kiss her again—and more.

'I should check on my grooms. They claim they will have the exercise yard cleared by today.' Good grief, he sounded jittery. But his feelings regarding Thea were becoming more complicated with every passing day.

'Then leave Trefor with me. I might just allow Impetuous Thea to join him in the water.' She offered him a mischievous half-smile, peering up at him through her ridiculously long lashes which his rampant body responded to immediately. He really didn't want to know that. Or be beyond excited at the idea. Not when he was failing abysmally at being a better spy thanks to his overpowering need to be with her.

'I suppose I could linger a little longer.' Utter madness, but his feet were already making their way towards her. 'Keep Impetuous Thea on the straight and narrow.'

Gray sat, self-conscious and riddled with inappropriate lust, and decided the most sensible course of action was to change the subject back to what he was supposed to be doing. 'I wonder why Bertie rushed back? Do you suppose he was summoned by your uncle?'

'Uncle Edward isn't one to make demands.' She sat back on her hands, staring up at the dappled sunshine. The pose did wonders for her figure and served to further torture him. 'I think it's lovely that Cedric and Harriet have found one another don't you? I hope they make a go of it.' Her eyes flicked to his. 'In case you haven't already guessed, and despite my justified suspicion of fortune hunters, I'm a romantic at heart. I believe in true love. I know that you are jaded from the experience, but I like to believe that there is the perfect someone for everyone. I'm glad Harriet has been given a second chance.' She took his silence as disagreement. 'Don't you believe in second chances?'

'Of course I do.'

'Just not for you.' She tilted her face back towards the sun, making the obligatory loose tendrils of hair glow copper and gold to torment him. 'Because your heart cannot mend.'

'It's mended enough.' Unstable ground. 'But it's too scarred to risk again.'

'Liar.' She smiled up at the sky. 'At least be honest about it. This has nothing to do with the current state of your heart and everything to do with your silly fear history will repeat itself. You're no different from me for all your bold claims you like to live in the moment and leave it all up to fate. You claim to be full of life. Claim to embrace all its twists and turns and potholes and peculiarities, yet when you find a woman you are drawn to on a far deeper level than you care to admit—your words, Gray, not mine—you create boundaries and silly truces to guard your precious heart. You're a hypocrite. One who is too frightened to live life to the full.'

'You wouldn't understand.' And they were not having this conversation. He shot to his feet, not caring whether or not he looked outraged, because he was, damn it. This conversation crossed a line. He was not going to discuss them. They were friends. Nothing more. He couldn't allow there to be more. 'I need to get back.'

'Go ahead. Run away.' She was smiling wryly, but otherwise seemingly unbothered by his response. 'You're very good at that. But before you go, at least listen to some advice. It's good advice. Yours, in fact.' She sat forward and sighed, then smiled kindly, her dark eyes filled with an emotion he couldn't decipher. 'You were twenty. It's a dangerous age. You think you know everything, when in fact you are barely an adult. I should imagine what Cecily did, to someone with a vivid imagination like yours, would give you an irrational fear of trusting a woman ever again. But what you had with Cecily was one-sided. You loved her and the awful reality is she didn't love you enough back.'

'I know what the awful reality was, Thea. I lived it. And with the greatest respect, it is a subject you have little experience of. You have never been in love so are not in a position to offer me advice.' His hands had fisted at his sides and his poor damaged heart was thumping in his chest. He turned on his heel and began to stride out of the suffocating intimacy of the clearing and the perilous turn in an otherwise pleasant conversation.

'Then I suppose this odd feeling I have for you doesn't count?' At her words his feet stopped and those invisible cords forced him to turn around. She was stood now, proud but vulnerable. And more beautiful and tempting than he had ever seen her. 'The excitement I feel every time I see you. The overwhelming sense of rightness I feel when I'm with you. The affection. The friendship. The desire. You say I have no experience, but this…' both her hands went to her chest to cover her heart '…this certainly feels like what I've always imagined love would feel like.'

'Stop.' Although there was no conviction in his words. She loved him? Instead of making him want to run away, it tempted him to run to her. She loved him? That was…everything. She saw his hesitation and took a step forward.

'I am not Cecily. I don't care about titles. I have no need of a bigger fortune or greater standing in society. None of those things matter to me. I just want you.' She took another cautious step forward. 'If that makes you want to run, then go now before I humiliate myself further.'

Unbelievably, he was disinclined to run. He had promised himself he would never again allow another woman to get under his skin as he had Cecily. But while half of him was terrified by her unexpected confession, the other half—the half that couldn't resist the lure of the moment or the pull of the woman who stood next to him—was intent on staying exactly where he was. Because she had mined under his defences regardless and inexplicably he discovered he was exceedingly glad for the intrusion. His damaged, scarred heart was bursting with something which felt like joy.

'Oh, Thea...' He wasn't going to spoil the moment by considering the ramifications or all the many reasons why it was a bad idea. She loved him.

Him!

That was miraculous, all things considered. More miraculous was the way both relief and warmth bloomed in his chest. Instead of running, and because he was imprisoned by those invisible cords, he closed the distance between them and gently pressed his lips to hers.

It was an honest kiss. Slow, tender and brimming with all the complicated emotional attachments he had avoided for a decade. When she kissed him back, he wound his arms around her and gathered her close, carefully lowering them both to lie on the bank before he deepened the kiss.

Thea didn't hold back, slowly running her curious fingers through his hair, over his shoulders and down his spine before tunnelling under his shirt to find skin. He felt the dappled early morning sun on his back as she tugged his shirt off, then rolled him to lie beneath her so her fingers could explore his chest. Where they trailed, her lips followed, torturing him. Good grief, it felt perfect.

'This is dangerous.' Gray didn't have the strength to stop her, but then the panicked voice in his head came to the fore as he silently hoped she would come to her senses before he completely lost his. 'I can't make any promises.'

'I don't recall asking for any. I am simply following your advice and giving Impetuous Thea free rein. In this precise moment, she simply wants to kiss you.'

This was madness. He should put a stop to it. But his fingers had gone to her hair and were pulling out pins. 'Best not deny her, poor thing. Not when she's been shut in a box for years.' Not at all what he should have said for the sake of his heart—yet his heart was soaring. Beating with more purpose than it ever had before. What did that mean?

He kissed her again and she kissed him back.

A heated, open-mouthed kiss that blasted through what was left of his reserve. Let the cards fall where they may. With that acceptance came more relief and joy, both surging through him with such force they made him unsteady. Holding Thea steadied him and anchored him in the present and he realised his heart had not only mended, but was lost again. He wasn't entirely sure when that had happened, but knew it wasn't recent. Perhaps he had lost it that first day, when she had stumbled upon him in the brook. He didn't remember a thunderbolt, but he had felt a connection. One that had grown and thrived. One that felt perfect. So very different from what he had felt for Cecily.

The woman who didn't matter any more. The woman who paled into insignificance now that his heart had found Thea.

As moments went, it was the greatest he had ever experienced. He found himself smiling against her mouth as he accepted his fate and wrestled with veritable ironmongers nestled in her scalp. 'Exactly how many pins do you have in here?'

'A great many. Otherwise my hair is vertical.'

'I'd like to see that.' All her fiery hair loose; all her alabaster skin uncovered. Utter, utter madness, but those invisible cords were wrapping themselves around them, lashing them comfortably together, and he was powerless to fight them. Not when holding her felt so very right and he never wanted this perfect moment of clarity to end.

'It's not a pretty sight.' But she was smiling as she briskly and methodically plucked each pin out, then bent her head forward to shake out the curls. 'I have wayward hair, too.'

It was the first time he had seen it completely unbound and the sight of it had more impact than those few fallen tendrils he had glimpsed before that she was forever attempting to tame. He ran his fingers reverently through a long, copper ringlet, tugging out the curl until it was completely straight. To his delight it stretched way past her hips. 'It's beautiful. You're beautiful.' His hands smoothed their way back up her hips, briefly pausing to span her waist before moving up to cup her breasts. 'You've haunted my dreams, Thea. Have since the first day I met you. I am severely sleep deprived.'

'Me, too.' He loved her earthy giggle. Loved everything about her. Loved that the mere thought of loving her didn't make him want to run. 'But we are young and can sleep when we're dead.'

He kissed her again, their tongues tangling until his body wanted more. Far more than she might be prepared to offer. But he would wait...

Wait? That sounded ominously like he was ready to make plans. 'We should stop. Before this gets out of hand.'

'Very sensible. Is the brook cold?' She chewed

her lip shyly before boldly glancing up at him from beneath her lashes. 'Only in my dreams, you're back in there and I am swimming with you.'

There was no doubt he wanted her. Always had, but this was more than lust and so much more than one reckless moment. Unconsciously, he rubbed the spot in the middle of his ribs. Was she worth the risk? 'I'm not sure I can do this, Thea. Not again.' But the voice in his head urged him to gamble once again. It was tempting. She was tempting.

'I don't want to break your heart, Gray. I want to possess it. There's a difference. Unlike her, I shall treasure it and look after it.' Her fingers went to the laces at the back of her dress. He watched, helpless, as the front of her bodice loosened and fell to hang off her shoulders. 'Although don't take my word for it. To be completely sure, you should test the theory. Scientifically, of course. If I break your heart, you'll have the satisfaction of knowing you were right all along. And if I don't...' She stared at him intently. 'Onwards and upwards. It's your motto after all. Leave the past in the past where it should be...' She wiggled her shoulders and the bodice slipped down further, barely covering her breasts. 'And live in this wonderfully unexpected moment with me.'

Chapter Nineteen

Suddenly in a hurry, they both stripped off their clothes. Having never been naked in front of another person before and feeling self-conscious, Thea jumped in the water first, dipping quickly beneath so it covered her to her chin, and shamelessly watched him do the same.

His body was so different from hers. Broad where hers was slight. Angular where she had curves—and hard. The skin on his shoulders and flat abdomen covered intriguing muscles. He had thighs Harriet would approve of, she realised with a giggle. Strong and taut, as if he had spent many an hour in the saddle, but it was the wholly male part of him which appealed to her more. That, too, was hard. For her. And the prospect excited her and terrified her at the same time.

Should she be doing this? They barely knew each other, yet she wanted to be intimate with him. It would be the ultimate grand gesture. For the first time in for ever she had found a man she could trust. She felt giddy and euphoric and over-whelmingly glad she'd had the courage to leap.

Was it too soon?

Her heart said no. He was, bizarrely, every-thing she had ever wanted. And if she tweaked her essential attributes list, he ticked every one. Gray was prudent in his own way and gave sen-sible advice. For a purported scoundrel he was delightfully proper. In fact, he had been more of a gentleman to her than all the gentlemen she had encountered since her come out. Cautious with his heart, but adventurous in all else. It went without saying he was trustworthy and, while he wasn't completely above reproach, there were reasons why he had behaved as he had in the past. They had both been young and foolish and lived to rue the day. And they had both survived the experi-ence and emerged the stronger for it. She didn't care if he had no fortune because she knew in her bones he had no interest in such things. He em-braced her wayward nature. Enjoyed it. With him, Thea could be herself. He had always brought that out of her, even as she had tried to fight it. When you met the right person, fighting that powerful, all-encompassing emotion was pointless. She un-derstood that now. It was deliciously liberating.

And he wore his breeches well—although she much preferred him out of them.

He climbed in and swam towards her, then

caught his arm around her waist, pulling her close for a searing kiss. Wet bare skin next to wet bare skin was a revelation. Her body seemed to fit perfectly against his as if it had been made to do exactly that. Thea curled her arms possessively around his neck, flattening her breasts shamelessly against his chest, and enjoyed the way her pebbled, water-chilled nipples tingled at the contact.

He took his time kissing her. His big hands sliding over her body with aching slowness. Learning its shape and caressing the sensitive places she had not known she possessed until he touched them. Unable to stop herself, Thea's hands also went exploring, marvelling at the feel of the smattering of dark hair on his chest and the way he shuddered when her fingers grazed his nipples. It emboldened her to allow her palms to journey south, until she could tentatively trace the hard, hot shape of him with her fingertip. She watched his eyes close and his Adam's apple bob as he fought for control, until he could stand no more, wrapping his fist about her hand as he schooled her in how to hold him properly. Boldly.

Then he kissed her again, filling his hands with her needy breasts which were screaming for his touch, his thumbs doing wicked things to them which made her cry out in a voice she didn't recognise. A carnal, desperate sound that wanted more. So much more.

As if sensing that, he lifted her so that her over-sensitive nipples came level with his face and took one scandalously into his mouth, flicking the tip with his tongue and smiling against it as she moaned and writhed against him. Suspended in the water, all she could do was cling on to his shoulders as he thoroughly worshipped that breast before he moved slowly to the other. Torturing her with unspeakable pleasure until her legs were locked wantonly around his hips, her body throbbing with need, his hardness jutting against her with all the forbidden promise she had always secretly craved. So close, but yet so far from where she desperately needed it to be.

Of its own accord, her body positioned herself to take him, feeling the whole length of him harden further at the encouragement. 'There are other things we can do...we don't have to do this.' He voice was gravelly and breathless, laced with desire.

'Don't you want to?' Because she did. Thea had passed the point of no return and was ready to commit herself completely. There was no point executing a giant leap of faith to falter at the end. That wasn't a *grand gesture* when she was in the mood to be scandalously grand and shamelessly bold. She wanted to experience all of the things Harriet had alluded to. Wanted to feel such passion that she lost her head and he lost his.

'Of course I want to. But there are implications…'

'Forget them.' She moved her hips to caress him shamelessly, felt his fingers flex against her waist. Heard his laboured breathing as he fought the inevitable. 'Just make love to me, Gray.'

He hesitated for a second, clearly at war with himself. She recognised the second the lure of the moment won, because his beautiful, silvery, wolf-like eyes darkened and locked intently on hers. He watched her as he entered her, as he slowly lowered her body in the cool water to take all of him. His eyes closed only briefly as she winced slightly at the intrusion, as if he shared her pain, and she loved him for that, his strong arms holding her steady as the slight discomfort passed.

'I'm sorry.'

'Don't be. I trust you to make it right.'

He kissed her with such tenderness then that she knew she had made the right decision. 'I will. I promise.'

'I thought you could make no promises?' She didn't wait for his answer, knowing that it might not be at all what she wanted to hear or was ready to accept. Instead, she ignored his brief hesitation and the wary look in his eyes, kissing both away, then losing herself in his kisses and the blissful sensation of him moving inside her.

Neither spoke then. He offered her no promises and no flowery compliments, but he loved her body with such determined and sustained intensity, it didn't matter that so many important things were left unsaid. This was as daunting for him as it was for her. Nothing needed to be settled in the heat of this glorious moment—although for her so much was.

As the last rational thoughts fled from her head, she told him how she felt. If he was not ready to hear the words that was too bad, because she was ready to feel them and say them. 'I love you, Gray. I want to spend for ever with you.'

His answer was a kiss so intense it sent her over the edge. As she tumbled over the second, unexpected precipice, she wrapped her arms and legs tight around his body and dragged him with her. Through the roaring chaos in her head and through the powerful sensations which had possessed her body, she heard his voice. The quiet whisper so close to her ear, choked with emotion and desire.

'God help me, but I love you, too, Thea.'

It was late afternoon before he ventured home. Stunned, unsteady and shaken to his core. He was in love again and cautiously delighted to be so. He recognised all the signs, although despite some of them feeling familiar, they also felt different. It was that difference which occupied his mind now that he was alone and he tried to quantify exactly what had caused it in order to understand it.

Gray had always thought he had loved Cecily with every fibre of his being—but they had never been intimate. They had dabbled in pleasure—in an inexperienced and guilty way—but he had never seen her completely naked or been given the privilege of taking her innocence. In many ways, that lack of intimacy had been a barrier. With hindsight, he could see now that it was her insurance in case something better came along. Back then, he had accepted her reluctance to fully share her body with him as the way things were. They were both saving themselves for their wedding night because propriety dictated they did so. Similarly, as childhood had given way to adulthood, he could now see that his relationship with Cecily had been unbalanced. It was Gray who had done all the running and Cecily who controlled things.

It had always been Cecily who had stopped things getting out of hand, because as much as she had enjoyed his touch—and she had been quite selfish in the pursuit of her own pleasure—she had still had the rational and pragmatic ability to stop. In private she had used his affection and desire to manipulate him to bending to her will, so much so that in public in the latter stages of their relationship she had convinced him to behave as if there was nothing serious between them at all. She had rationed them to one dance at balls and happily allowed him to watch as she was twirled around the room by other men.

Now that he thought upon it, how many times had he watched her waltz with his brother? Certainly enough that he had come to think nothing of it.

In contrast, Thea had given herself with complete abandon. He had given her plenty of opportunities to hold back and she had dismissed every single one. Her trust and complete commitment had humbled him. Initially, it had been daunting. Terrifying, even, because he had known that the physical act of love between them was as much of a declaration as the words had been. She had been the first woman he had made love to with his heart as well as his body and the experience had been earth-shattering and earth-changing as a result. With entirely unscientific motives, he had made love to her twice more and both times the intensity of emotion had been there front and centre throughout.

What had really shocked him was how easy it all was. They had not only made love in the brook, on the bank and then back in the brook again— but they had laughed and chatted and relaxed with each other in between. She never asked him about the future, nor did he venture anything about it, but she had shared her body with impunity and delighted in sharing his. They had lived entirely in a moment that had lasted hours, both stripped naked in more ways than one and, despite not discussing what would happen next, Gray accepted they would have to. They would have to because he wanted to.

There was no turning back now. They were in love and there were plans that needed to be made. All he had to do first was work out how to remove the giant fly from the ointment. The enormous elephant in the room. Whichever path he took now was positively littered with potholes and, frankly, he had no idea what to do about it. Because it didn't take a genius to work out that Gray's mission, and all the secrets he was keeping from her, had the power to destroy it all and leave him alone and heartbroken all over again.

That horrendous prospect had occurred to him about an hour ago and had plagued him the second he finished their lingering goodbye kiss at the stables and he still hadn't worked out a way of fixing it. Casually dropping the fact that he was a spy into the conversation, one who had lied to her about a number of important details, one who happened to be searching for enough evidence to see her uncle hang for his crimes, wasn't an option. Nor was failing to do his sworn duty for King and country. Waiting for the cards to fall where they may, his usual answer to all life's problems, was also unappealing. He wouldn't trust fate with something of such importance. Somehow, he would find a way to negotiate the potholes because he couldn't and wouldn't live through all that misery again.

Trefor's barking interrupted his thoughts and it was then Gray saw the subtle signs—the amassed forces of the King's Elite had made it to Kirton House well before an agent came to tell him.

'Lord Hadleigh is waiting for you inside, sir.'

Of course he was. Now that an arrest was imminent, the lawyer would be chomping at the bit to get started. 'Is Lord Fennimore back?'

'Not yet, sir. We've received word he's staying overnight to continue his interrogations and see the prisoners secure. I'm to tell you that you are in command in his absence.' A responsibility which had now lost all of its appeal. One that meant he might be called upon to hammer the death knell into his and Thea's relationship. 'And to give you this.' The agent handed Gray a burned piece of what once must have been a letter. Remnants of a wax seal still adorned the charred back while on the other side were words which now made no sense because the rest of the sentences were missing, written in neat, tight handwriting.

Men will meet...
...payment in full...
...do not

'The captain of the vessel was in the process of burning this letter as the Excise Men found him. They managed to salvage this. It's not much, but Lord Fennimore wants you to do some subtle digging to see if you can find who wrote it.' A task easier said than done. It wasn't as if he could blithely stroll up to Gislingham and Bertie and demand they write something for comparison.

Wearily, because the full weight of the world now seemed to rest entirely on his shoulders, Gray headed to the kitchen where Hadleigh was calmly drinking coffee. 'What's going on at the Hall?'

'Nothing. To all intents and purposes, Gislingham and his right-hand man are behaving as if nothing is amiss at all.'

'His right-hand man?'

'Bertie. Or Albert Frederick Walsham, to give him his full name. Ostensibly his manservant but there's more to it than that. I can feel it.' The secretive behaviour. The knowing looks. Instinct told him there was something there. Something more than the bond between a master and an invaluable servant. 'The man watches everyone like a hawk and was the only person to dash back after the express arrived. He was *needed*, apparently.'

Gray shared everything they knew thus far, which was not a whole lot more than they had known when they had first arrived a few weeks ago. But at least they now had this tiny fragment of charred paper and the handwriting of somebody significant, even if they had no earthly idea whose. Then he gave Hadleigh all the papers he had taken on his midnight raid. The lawyer scanned each one silently and thoroughly before pushing them to one side on the old, battered table.

'There has to be more. The man never leaves the house! Did you search everywhere?'

'Of course not. It was too close to dawn, so I focused only on his study. I've thoroughly searched downstairs and, believe me, there is nothing of any interest down there.'

'What about the bedchambers?'

'Never set foot in one of them.' For very good reason. 'All of Gislingham's private apartments are on the first floor. Thea and the Viscountess sleep on the second.'

'Thea?' His friend quirked an eyebrow. 'That's very *informal*.'

They were long past informal. Gray had kissed every beautiful inch of her. 'Things are more informal here in the country.' Especially down by the brook.

'Do you think his niece is involved?'

'No.' And nor was he prepared to even discuss the possibility that she might be. 'But *dear* Bertie is in it up to his neck. And unlike Gislingham, he *does* leave the house. He's been gone weeks.'

'I concur. Maybe Bertie's room holds the key? I assume it is within the Viscount's private apartments. We need to urgently procure a sample of the man's handwriting.' The lawyer's eyes lit up. 'And in view of recent developments, I suggest we do that sooner rather than later. We don't want evidence destroyed.'

'Impossible. The man has eyes like a hawk. We can't go rifling around in his private quarters in broad daylight. Believe me, I've tried. I haven't even been able to return the letters I took from his desk! The Viscount is very particular about his privacy and Bertie is the hawk that guards it.'

'Even hawks sleep, Gray. And the longer we wait, the more chance we give them to cover their tracks. We have one tangible piece of evidence. This note.' He tapped the burned missive with his index finger. 'This could be our only chance to categorically link it to Gislingham.'

'You want me to break in again? Tonight? The day after his ship has been seized and they will be on their guard? That's utter madness. I won't do it.'

'Fair enough. I'll do it alone. I am an unknown entity here. I'll have a good poke around the bedchambers and if I'm discovered you'll be completely in the clear.'

Chapter Twenty

Several hours later and against his better judgement, Gray found himself picking the lock to the French doors while Hadleigh stood guard. Because the lawyer had the bit between his teeth and wouldn't be dissuaded and, because he had expressed his intention to investigate the trunks in Thea's room to sift through those accounts, too, Gray had reluctantly become involved. To his friend he hoped it looked like diligence and a desire to return those damned letters rather than a primal need to protect the woman he loved from the unsupervised gaze of another man as she slept. In fact, Hadleigh didn't stand a cat's chance in hell of setting one foot in her bedchamber. If that made him an irrational, jealous fool, then so be it. She was his and that was that. Irrational, protective jealousy went hand in hand with being in love.

God help him. This had been the most trying twenty-four hours!

Beneath his fingers, he felt the barrel of the lock click into place and tested the handle. The door swung open silently on its blatantly well-oiled hinges. They crept inside and diligently checked the hallways before moving on.

'There is a distinct lack of guards, don't you think?' Hadleigh whispered as they crept down the hall.

'There's a distinct lack of anything, if you want my humble opinion. Guards, papers, suspiciousness, motive...'

'You doubt Gislingham is The Boss?'

'I think there's as much chance, if not more, of him *not* being the man we suspect as there is the chance he is. Something doesn't add up.' Or he was becoming so desperate for a way to prevent the inevitable implosion and awful aftermath affecting him and Thea that he was purposely, yet unconsciously, missing things. 'I cannot shake the feeling that Gislingham is far too nice to be a master criminal.'

'That's what he wants you to think.'

'Yet if this house was his lair, the centre of all his nefarious deeds, then it might look like a house on the outside, but it would be a veritable fortress within.' To prove his point, they were able to slip up the stairs to the Viscount's private apartments completely unseen with not so much as a sleeping servant at the front door in case they were visited in the night.

They made a search of the sitting room Gray had happily sat in almost daily during the past week and found nothing one would not expect to be in a sitting room. Behind every picture was nought but blank walls and beneath the giant Persian rug every floorboard was secured with sturdy nails. There were no secret compartments, no hidden escape hatches, no nothing. Harriet's half-finished daub stood proudly on an easel near the window. A sorry effort which was little to show for the hours she had doubtless spent on it. Thea's unfinished book lay on the table. *Pride and Prejudice.* A romance, because his Thea was a romantic at heart, he now knew. When Hadleigh wasn't looking he traced his finger along the spine and allowed himself a little wistful smile. He hoped their romance had a happily-ever-after. She deserved it and perhaps so did he. If he could only navigate those blasted potholes.

They then searched the study where Hadleigh hastily stashed the rest of the love letters into his satchel and sat in the window seat, scrutinising the large leather account ledger by the light of the moon, with the burned note held aloft for comparison, while Gray hunted for hidden compartments in the furniture and floors.

'Anything?' Time was ticking along. They had been here an hour already.

'Nothing.' Hadleigh closed the book and returned it to its exact spot on Gislingham's desk.

'The handwriting is all the same, very curly and flamboyant, and very definitely not this.' He pocketed the charred remnant looking peeved.

'Thea acts as his secretary. The writing is probably hers.' She was curly and flamboyant, too. There was nothing staid or average about his Thea. 'Did you see anything amiss in the accounts?'

'He lives well—but well within his means. Exactly as you said.'

The next door led to a messy dressing room. A testament to Bertie's lack of talent as a diligent servant. Piles of Gislingham's bright silk waistcoats lay on a chair. Cravats hung from doorknobs. Plainer waistcoats that looked far too sedate and too small to still fit the Viscount sat folded on an ottoman in the corner. His plethora of cufflinks and stickpins jumbled together in a deep glass dish. Gray pressed his ear to the bedchamber door and heard the soft, rhythmic sounds of snoring. As there was no other way forward, they had to risk it.

He opened the door a crack and peered through. The large lump under the bed covers suggested the Viscount was sound asleep on his side. His two canes were propped haphazardly by the nightstand, their gold tops shining silver in the single sliver of moonlight that seeped through the tiny gap in the curtains.

In case they were spotted, Hadleigh went first,

his pocket stuffed with a silver candlestick and a diamond stickpin. If caught, he was going to claim to be a common, opportunist burglar so that Gray could escape with his cover intact. It wasn't much of a plan, but as he had point-blank refused to allow anyone to creep around Thea's bedchamber but him, it was the best they had and would jolly well have to do.

Hadleigh skirted the edge of the room, then stopped dead, frowning at the bed. Then he gestured and Gray followed and couldn't quite believe his eyes.

The Viscount was not alone.

Curled up next to him, their limbs intertwined in the tangled bedcovers, was Bertie.

Bertie!

Suddenly feeling guilty for the intrusion, Gray grabbed Hadleigh's sleeve and dragged him back to the dressing room as so many things fell into place. The secrecy. The knowing looks. The determined protection of his privacy. The dire state of the Viscount's sham of a marriage. The love letters that told the sad story, not of love lost, but of forbidden love. The most forbidden love.

I suspected you were the one. Now I know it.
I refuse to feel guilty for loving you.

Homosexuality could still be punishable by death, so this illicit love affair had had to be conducted well away from prying eyes.

It made him feel sad. Life couldn't have been easy for either of them, yet their love had survived twenty years of potentially giant potholes. But that didn't excuse smuggling and murder—if indeed they were smugglers and murderers. Yet stranger things happened, as this revelation was testament to.

'Well, I wasn't expecting that.' Hadleigh raked a hand through his hair as they both stood back in the sitting room, stunned. 'I think it's fairly safe to assume from the dressing room Bertie doesn't have his own room and if he does he rarely uses it.'

'We should go.' Gray felt queasy. Not at what he saw, because he had seen worse on his travels than that touching, affectionate display of what he now knew was enduring love, but at the ramifications for Gislingham and Thea on the back of it. Society, not to mention the authorities and the church, would be unforgiving. Ruthless even. He doubted even Thea knew exactly how much Bertie truly meant to her uncle.

'Not until we've searched that trunk in the niece's dressing room.' Hadleigh was already through the door before Gray could pull him back. 'We need to match that handwriting!'

'Only the dressing room! You do not set one foot in her bedchamber.'

'All right...' Hadleigh eyed him curiously. 'Any particular reason why?'

'This has nothing to do with her.'

'Is that based on feeling or fact?'

'I know her. And you don't.' Gray's feet took him to the third door along the landing, guided no doubt by those invisible cords and the intoxicating scent of jasmine. 'Her dressing room is the next door along.'

Hadleigh gently tested the door and poked his nose inside before turning to regard Gray blandly. 'Intuitive. It is indeed. And from a man who claims never to have set foot in any of the bedchambers here before…'

As there was no response that wouldn't condemn him, Gray set his jaw and followed the lawyer inside. Instantly, he was overwhelmed with her. The chemise and corset he had helped her back into only hours before lay on top of the trunk and he hastily moved them out of the way before Hadleigh touched the garments. Beyond the door he could sense her. Feel her breathing, her tender heart beating, his beating stronger as a result. Messy, complicated, wonderful feelings he was nowhere near getting used to.

While the lawyer searched through the discarded reports, Gray tried and failed not to drink in the intensely personal sight of her belongings. The huge pot of pins on the dressing table to tame her wayward, vertical curls. The fat hairbrush she must use to rid it of the inevitable tangles. The pretty perfume bottle filled with her imported fragrance from the Orient. He could picture himself here. Watching her dress or undress, comfortably chatting about their day. Their life. Perhaps even their children. The image so vivid and perfect he *had* to make it a reality.

The creaking sound next door had them both standing to attention. 'Gray?' The soft voice beyond the door was filled with sleep, but she sensed him, just as he had her. The bed creaked again, the mattress shifting as if she had sat up. '*Gray? Is that you?*'

In seconds she would come to the door and check. He knew that with the same certainty that he knew she would likely never forgive him for what he was about to do. He gestured frantically for Hadleigh to leave, feeling sick to his stomach and riddled with guilt at the only option fate had left him with, then answered, 'Yes, my love. It's me. I crept in. I hope you don't mind.' What else could he do but lie? As the lawyer hid in the shadows he grasped the handle and opened the door at the exact same moment as she did. She was smiling. Beautifully rumpled in the moonlight. 'You crept in?'

'Don't hate me.' He hated himself enough. This was the worst sort of betrayal. One she would likely never forgive him for if she ever found out. Their goodbye. 'But I missed you.'

'I missed you, too.' Feeling like the worst sort of chancer, ne'er-do-well and scoundrel, he opened his arms and she stepped into them, and in doing so he fell into the biggest, deepest pothole of his life.

Thea woke late and Gray was gone. She wasn't surprised. He was a gentleman despite his impulsive ways and he would want to protect her modesty. She could still see the indent his head had made on the pillow, still smell the lingering scent of his spicy cologne, so she wrapped her arms around it and hugged it close. It was a poor substitute for the man. She smiled as she pictured him unable to sleep and then doing the outrageous and coming to her in the night. It was such a spontaneous, devil-may-care, live-in-the-moment, Gray-like thing to do and hopelessly romantic. She still couldn't quite believe it.

Then he had climbed into the bed beside her and, at her instigation, made love to her with such aching, impassioned tenderness that it had brought poignant tears to her eyes. His final words before she had drifted blissfully back off to sleep in his arms had also been heartfelt.

'Just remember I love you. Always. No matter what. No matter how dire things are or how bad they seem.'

They made her sigh just thinking about them.

With an undisguisable spring in her step, she dressed and allowed her maid to fix her wayward hair loosely. Gray loved all her mad curls, so she would forgo the usual plethora of pins for him. She practically floated into her uncle's sitting room to find him sat on a chair striking a pose as Harriet stood behind her easel, measuring his angles with her outstretched paintbrush while Bertie stood by, looking highly amused at the ridiculous tableau.

'You look lovely today.' He eyed her up and down appreciatively. 'You've changed your hair. It's softer. Suits you.'

'Thank you. I feel lovely.' She did. Warm and ripe and thoroughly loved.

'Tuesdays will do that to a person.' Bertie's face was deadpan, but his eyes were dancing as if he knew she'd been thoroughly ruined and was happy to have been so. 'Tuesdays…and handsome gentlemen with soppy black dogs.'

'I don't know what you mean.' But her cheeks were heating at the memory of exactly how splendid her Tuesday had started. Harriet had never mentioned *that* particular bit of bed sport in all her descriptions, but it had been most enlightening. Her man had a very talented mouth.

Her man.

She wanted to sigh again at how marvellous that sounded, but withheld it because Bertie was grinning at her. 'How is the portrait going?'

'It's at a critical stage. Frankly, I think it's beyond saving. Your uncle, though, is quite delighted with it.'

'Good heavens, then it must be bad.' She wandered behind the easel and looked over Harriet's shoulder. It was a definite face—that was something—not her uncle's, but at least it had discernible features.

'What do you think, darling?' Her friend stepped back to admire her work, too.

'Fabulous colours.' The bold striped waistcoat jumped off the page, making her uncle's vivid choices seem tame, but part of Uncle Edward's hair was also apparently blue. Prussian blue, to be exact. She met his eyes and watched him stifle a chuckle. He really did have the most warped sense of humour. 'I think you've really captured his essence.'

'I've already had some footmen clear space in the gallery opposite dear old Pater. I decided he'd be able to avert his eyes if I was hung next to him and there's no fun in that. He can glare at me in disappointment for eternity now.' The chuckle escaped then and soon turned into raucous laughter. 'The old grouch will be spinning in his grave.'

'Has Lord Gray been to check on Archimedes yet?' Any hope that she had made the question sound casual died when she watched the three of them share a very unsubtle, but pointed look.

'Not as yet, darling. I'm sure he'll be here presently. He does seem rather devoted…to poor Archimedes, of course.' Harriet studied her thoughtfully. 'You look different.'

Thea drifted to the sideboard to fix herself some tea. 'It's the hair. I've decided to give my scalp a holiday and stop nailing my coiffure to my skull.' Once she was out of view of both her uncle and Bertie she couldn't resist beaming at her friend, then walked two fingers along the edge of the sideboard. Two fingers which hesitated at the ledge, then leapt off the end. 'Today, I am a quite different Thea from the one I was yesterday.'

Harriet grinned back, instantly understanding. 'How positively splendid. Did you *sleep* well?'

'I am thoroughly *rested*.' Although now that she thought about it, she wouldn't mind a passionate kiss to start the morning properly. 'I might wander down to the stables to check on Archimedes.'

But Gray wasn't in the stables and nor had he been there, which might have been odd considering he was usually up with the lark like Thea was, but, seeing as they had both used the bedtime hours for pursuits other than sleep, she wouldn't blame him for sleeping in. She had, after all, and *she* had worn him out. Alone, she made no attempt to stifle the grin of achievement and decided to saddle a horse to ride to Kirton House instead and be unapologetic about the reason. She wanted to see him. Wanted to kiss him. Wanted to drag him back to the brook for more shamelessly wanton lovemaking.

* * *

But as soon as Kirton House came into view through the trees she saw something wasn't right. There were strange men everywhere and lots of horses. Several wore uniform—she recognised it as that of the Excise Men—but Gray was nowhere to be seen. That made her panic and, recalling the overheard conversation from Ipswich, set her old, suspicious mind whirring.

Instinctively, she tied her horse to a branch out of sight and quietly picked her way through the copse by the brook to come level to the house without being seen. It was then she saw the guns. Big ones. Shotguns and pistols. So many of them in a huge crate, all being loaded and passed around like port after dinner to the forty or so strange men in the stable yard who appeared very confident handling them.

'Hurry up, you fools! We don't want to alert the whole of Suffolk to your presence. Unload and get inside!' She recognised Lord Fennimore's impatient bark and tried to pick him out from the crowd to no avail. Beyond, within the confines of the stable, were more men. She was certain she recognised the back of Gray's aged cousin as he quickly disappeared through the wide door frame, but she was too far away to be certain.

Sensing something was now very wrong, Thea crouched low, darting across the meadow from ragged bush to ragged bush, getting as close to the outbuildings as she dared without leaving the safety of the tall grass. When that proved fruitless, she darted towards the rear of the stable, sinking her bottom to the ground and pressing her back against the slatted wood to attempt to hear what was going on inside, while castigating herself for her suspicious nature. Gray was different. She felt it in her bones. He was good and kind and…

'I expressly warned him not to seduce the chit!' Lord Fennimore again. Angry.

'Well, if you don't mind me saying—' A new voice. Aristocratic. Deep. '—it's a damned good job he did. Their passionate little romance saved our bacon. We'd have been done for last night without his quick thinking.'

'Something that would not have been necessary if you had stayed put last night and not risked the entire mission with your carelessness!'

'Do you think it's a real romance?'

'Hard to say…' Two more strange males, their tones teasing. 'But from the look of him, there's something there. I've never seen him quite so angry.'

'Angry! Why, he's positively seething. He looks ready to punch one of us at any second.'

'Back off!' Gray's voice, accompanied by the noise of reins and buckles jangling.

'I think he's a bit taken with Miss Cranford.' Thea's hand covered her mouth a second before the wounded cry burst forth. She was the chit he had seduced? 'He called her *my love*…'

Bile rose in her throat as the world shifted on its axis. Last night had been a lie? It had all been lies! The two slices of toast a winking Harriet had forced her to eat to keep up her strength threatened to make an instant reappearance at the bitter aftertaste of forbidden fruit. She could hear fate laughing at her in the background. Realising Impetuous Thea had fallen for another vulture. A bounder. A ne'er-do-well. A scoundrel who would make calculated, premeditated love to her to cover up whatever it was he was really doing.

She stumbled, half-running, half-crawling, back to the trees blindly, silent, bitter tears streaming down her cheeks at the universe's cruel punishment. Her heart ripped callously in two.

Chapter Twenty-One

Gray had just slammed Hadleigh against the wall when he sensed her, then bolted from the stables like a man possessed to try to fix the unfixable. He frantically scanned the yard and the meadow, knowing she was there and that she was in pain, then saw the unmistakable glimpse of fiery copper hurtling through the trees. He tore after her, oblivious of the odd looks he was getting from his men and his friends. Nothing else mattered but reaching her and trying to limit the damage of whatever she had potentially seen, or, God help him, overheard.

'Thea! Wait!' He plunged into the trees, ignoring the branches that caught and tore his clothes and skin. 'Thea! Let me explain!'

She was fast. His lungs burned with the effort it took to come within touching distance. He reached out his hand, his fingers grazing the back of her dress. 'Please let me explain!'

She skidded to a halt then and finally turned to face him, small fists clenched, her face leached of all colour, the awful evidence of his betrayal etched plainly on her lovely face. 'Explain? What is there to explain? You are a liar! A barefaced, shameless, heartless liar!'

'I'm not…' Yet another lie when she deserved the truth. 'All right—I've lied, yes… But I had to… But not about the important things. I didn't lie about us.'

'Really? Then last night wasn't a lie. There wasn't someone with you when you claimed you couldn't bear to spend another second without me? When you climbed into my bed? Made yourself at home in my body?'

'There was, but…'

'How could you!' Her face crumpled, but she held back the sob. 'I trusted you! I gave myself to you believing you were genuine, yet you played me all along! Your own cousin forbade you from seducing me, because clearly you do this sort of thing a lot. How you must have laughed when I did your dirty work for you! Gave myself freely! What a stupid, ignorant fool I am!'

He reached out to touch her and the stinging slap across the face caught him unawares, although it wasn't anywhere near as painful as he knew he deserved. 'Don't touch me, Gray! Never touch me again!' She hugged her arms around her body and put six feet of distance between them. He couldn't blame her for that either. If he could have left himself standing somewhere and marched off in disgust, he would have, too. 'Why me? Was it sport? My fortune? The challenge?'

'I work for the government.' The least he could do was give the whole truth, no matter how unpalatable it was. 'For a covert agency called the King's Elite. Lord Fennimore is my superior, not my cousin. We created that story as a cover, to attempt to infiltrate a dangerous smuggling ring and bring the ringleader to justice. I wish I could have told you all that, I really do, but I couldn't. My mission had to take precedence over everything else—except it didn't. You kept pulling me away from it. I've always been drawn to you. That part wasn't a lie. All my background, everything about Cecily, all that is the honest truth, too. I've never lied to you about any of that.' His voice was desperate. 'In fact, I doubt you'll believe me in light of what you now know, but you are the only person on this earth who knows me that well. But I was tasked with befriending your uncle. Ingratiating myself into his circle.' He was spilling state secrets, breaking the law, but she was worth it. They were worth it. *If* he could make her understand.

'My uncle?' There were tears on her cheeks. More silently spilling over her long lashes. Tears he had caused. Each one like a knife to the chest.

'We have intelligence which leads us to believe he is the leader of that smuggling gang.'

She baulked, her face paling further. 'The cut-throat who murdered those men in Newgate?' She staggered backwards towards the brook, her head shaking with denial. 'That's preposterous!'

'Yesterday the Excise Men intercepted a smuggling vessel at Leiston.' The words felt like dust in his throat, but they now had a direct link to Gislingham Hall. The warrants had been issued. Her uncle's arrest was imminent. Sooner, seeing as she had overhead things their planned midnight raid would have to be brought forward. 'An express arrived at the hall within two hours of the raid. At roughly the same time, we were able to link the ship to a storehouse in Ipswich. It was heavily guarded. A few hours ago, we raided it and took every man within it prisoner. I am sorry to tell you that, as we suspected, it was filled with illegal French brandy.' The pretty, trusting mouth he had kissed just hours ago hung slack, disbelieving. 'But there was more. Guns, tea, tobacco…money. It hasn't all been counted yet, but we estimate there is in excess of twenty thousand pounds in coin alone.' There was no point sparing her from the most damning connection. The one he still struggled to come to terms with himself. 'According to the landlord, the storehouse is rented by a Mr Walsham.'

'Bertie?'

'And he's seen a carriage bearing the Gislingham crest there on more than one occasion in the last few weeks. Late at night. But while the witnesses cannot describe the passengers' faces, they all clearly remember the two canes he needed to lean on as he was helped out of the coach.'

'I don't believe it. I *won't* believe it! This is just more deception piled on your lies! Neither my uncle nor Bertie would ever do such things. They are not criminals!'

He rifled in his pocket for the charred piece of note, knowing she needed to see the proof with her own eyes. 'Do you recognise this handwriting?'

She stared at it, then flinched, recoiling at the sight, circling around him warily. He held it out. 'Look at it closely. It is a matter of national importance.' She took it and stared, her features frozen but her eyes tragic. She knew it. It went no way to making him feel better. 'Men have died. Too many of them. It's my job to see that nobody else does. Please, Thea—tell me. Do you recognise this handwriting?'

'No!' Then he felt her palms flat against his chest as she lunged, sending him flying backwards into the water. By the time he hauled himself up the bank, he heard the horse's hooves kick into a gallop and, sopping wet and utterly devastated, was forced to watch her ride like the wind towards her house, the precious, tiny, damning piece of evidence gone with her.

Thea had no memory of the short journey home. Not when her mind was reeling and the ground had been pulled from beneath her feet in more ways than one. But she miraculously made it in one piece and headed to the sitting room blindly.

'How could you?' Her temper so hot and bubbling above the surface, she swept her hand violently across the mantelpiece, sending all the tawdry silk arrangements flying.

Her aunt stared back at her blankly. 'Is everything all right, dearest?'

Thea held out the damning charred fragment. The one covered in her aunt's small, neat writing. Needing to piece together some sense out of the tempest of chaos swirling in her head. 'I know! I know all about your warehouse and the smuggling.'

Caro gently grasped the toxic piece of paper and stared at it silently. 'How did you get this?'

'The Excise Men retrieved it from a ship they boarded yesterday.' Her aunt sat up straighter. 'They've impounded all your brandy!'

All those meaningless lunches, all those shopping trips. Just lies. So many lies and all from people she cared about.

'But how did you come to have this?'

'They asked me if I recognised the handwriting! They caught the Captain trying to burn it.' Her aunt's calmness was staggering. Thea was accusing her of hideous, criminal acts and she hadn't even left her chair. Hadn't looked outraged or denied any of it. 'I snatched it and came here to confront you. I can't believe it...'

'Did you tell them it was mine?'

'No. I ran. I didn't want to believe it... But they can't be far behind me. They have a small army.' Good grief, this was all so surreal. Why didn't her aunt deny it? 'Is it true? Have you killed men?'

'Not personally.' Her aunt stood and began to pace, her eyes oddly blinking as she tapped the burned piece of paper against her other hand. 'This is all very unfortunate, but not entirely unexpected.' She sighed, as if it was of no matter rather than the most catastrophic and devastating news Thea had ever heard. For a woman who stressed about every wrinkle, her composure at the bombshell was staggering. 'Are you certain you never told them whose writing this is?'

'Not yet. I wanted to look you in the eyes. I wanted to understand.' But she didn't. Why anyone would stoop so low? And were Bertie and her uncle also involved? 'He said the warehouse is rented by Bertie. Is that true?'

'As it's in his name, legally it is.'

'What sort of an answer is that?' Thea gripped the other woman's arm hard, not caring that her nails bit into her skin. Caro tugged her arm away.

'Have they seen your uncle at the warehouse? The carriage?'

How did Caro know all this? 'Yes.'

'Yet only you know this handwriting is mine?'

Her face contorted into an ugly expression. Calculated. Cruel. Completely mad. 'Interesting...'

'Interesting?' Thea's world was falling apart. Blown to smithereens. And it was just *interesting*? For the first time, Thea saw through the brittleness and the self-absorption to the woman beneath the ageing face she fought so hard to keep youthful. Her uncle might well be a criminal, too, something she still couldn't quite believe, but he had been right. Her aunt was every inch the cold, callous, self-serving and unfeeling witch he had always accused her of being. 'All this time, I tolerated your vanity and made excuses for your affairs, yet they were apparently the tip of the iceberg. You're a criminal. A murderess...'

Her aunt caught her expression and snarled, 'How dare you judge me, Thea! You are the last person in the world who can judge me! I had no alternative. Not when you and your uncle forced me into it.' She saw it then. Blind, unadulterated hatred burning in the other woman's eyes. Hatred for her. Hatred that made no sense.

'Forced you?'

'He ruined everything. Years of planning. Years of sacrifice...yet he gave you everything and left me with a pittance!

'Everything that isn't entailed or cannot be nailed down was legally bound to you in trust the day before we married! Out of sheer spite! When he dies, which he will sooner rather than later, this house will go to some distant, faceless male relative and then where would I have been left? All the money has already gone to you! It was Edward's petty act of revenge. One I should have foreseen!' Out of nowhere her hand shot out and something hard and blunt struck Thea on the temple.

She saw stars and staggered backwards, catching herself on the sideboard before she crashed on the floor. Dazed, it took several moments before she could focus properly on the pistol pointed at her. 'You're a *monster*!' Why hadn't she seen it before? 'But they are coming for you!'

'No, dearest. They are not. They are coming for Bertie and Edward. I have made very sure of that.'

Chapter Twenty-Two

~~~~~~~~

The King's Elite stormed Gislingham Hall within twenty minutes of Thea's mad dash home. Thanks to his carelessness, they had little choice. Powerless and ravaged with guilt and wretchedness, still soaked to the skin, Gray rode silently alongside Lord Fennimore and Hadleigh. His friends Seb Leatham and Jake Warriner rode close behind along with fifty agents and half of Suffolk's Excise Men. He supposed they made an impressive sight. They were all fully armed and prepared for a full-scale battle. One he was more than happy to die in if he couldn't make Thea understand.

Except, when they thundered up the drive, the grooms and the gardeners all stopped work to come and investigate what all the fuss was about. They dismounted and were met at the front door by the equally perplexed ancient butler, still clad in his brown apron, a silver candlestick in one hand and his polishing rag in the other. He took in all the strange new faces and then settled on Gray. 'Has something happened, Lord Gray?'

'Where is his lordship?'

'I believe he is resting, my lord. Bertie insisted he take a nap before Lady Crudgington returns this afternoon to finish his portrait.' It felt rude to simply barge past him when the man had never done a thing wrong, but before he could reply, both Leatham and Warriner were halfway to the stairs. 'Wait! You cannot go up there now! His lordship won't be decent!' But it was too late. They had.

Gray followed, taking the stairs two at a time in his haste to catch up. Although to do what, he wasn't sure. His duty, probably, but he had stopped caring about that the second he had seen Thea's tears. Now, all he cared about was her. Her and him, and whatever dregs of their love he could salvage, dreading the thought that there was nothing left to salvage and already mourning the loss of her.

He arrived at the door to the sitting room where he had been such a welcome guest seconds before Leatham flung it open. It crashed hard against the panelling.

Bertie stood alone in front of a chair, blinking at the unexpected intrusion. The book he had been reading hung limply from his hand. 'What the blazes is going on?'

'Albert Frederick Walsham.' Hadleigh's deep

voice boomed over Gray's shoulder. 'I have a warrant for your arrest.' Every bit of blood drained from the servant's face as he backed towards the farthest door. 'Where is Gislingham?'

The door opened and the man himself appeared. Hair on end on one side of his head, shirt-tails untucked, but leaning proudly on his two canes. Something about the scene didn't sit right. In fact, it made loud alarm bells clang in Gray's mind. 'What is the meaning of this, gentlemen?'

'Where's Thea?'

'I thought she was with you.' Gislingham stared Gray dead in the eye. Unwavering. But accepting. 'And I shall ask again—what is the meaning of this rude intrusion, gentlemen?'

'It's all right, Edward.' Bertie used his body to shield the Viscount. 'It's me they want.'

The older man tossed one of his canes to the ground and took his lover's arm. 'Over my dead body. If we are to hang, then we'll hang together. We always knew this day might come.' They smiled at one another. Wistfully. It was the single most poignant display of affection Gray had ever seen. 'Yet I would not have a changed a second of it. You were worth it.'

Bertie's hand closed around his. 'As were you.'

'Gentlemen, it is not your unconventional relationship which brings us here.' Hadleigh stepped forward with the papers in his hand. 'These arrest warrants are for high treason. There is one for each of you.'

Neither Gislingham nor Bertie said a word. If their flabbergasted expressions were anything to go by, the power of speech had temporarily left them both.

'Treason?' Both men seemed to Gray to be genuinely confused.

'We have evidence you have been smuggling brandy into these isles for years.' Hadleigh had no sympathy for their denials. 'Furthermore, we suspect you have colluded with subversive French nationals, paying them in guns in return for your contraband. Contraband you have had your minions distribute with impunity while you reap the handsome rewards.'

'You are mistaken, sir.' Gislingham's tone was measured, reasonable, but it was obvious he was scared. 'We might be criminals in the eyes of the law, but I can assure you, neither one of us has ever smuggled a thing.'

'Furthermore, you are both charged with murder in the first degree.'

'Murder? Who has been murdered?' As the Viscount wobbled, then crumpled, Bertie supported his weight and guided him to a chair. The Viscount then gripped Gray's arm, the mobile half of his face a mask of grief. 'Not my Thea? Please God, not my Thea!'

'No, of course not Thea!' At Gray's impassioned answer the old man slumped in his chair with relief. Not at all the behaviour of a selfish, callous man who had just been charged with treason. 'Excise Men, government agents. Viscount Penhurst and the Marquess of Deal.'

'The two men murdered in Newgate?' Gislingham shook his head in denial. 'I've never even met them, let alone murdered them! This is lunacy! On what evidence are these scurrilous charges brought?'

'We have witnesses.' Again Hadleigh's tone was matter of fact. 'The lease to your storehouse in Ipswich. And that is just what we have managed to find in the last day. Once news of your arrest spreads, I'm sure more poison will seep out of the woodwork.'

There was a shriek downstairs and what sounded like a scuffle. Lady Crudgington's outraged voice. 'I have every right to go upstairs! Unhand me, sir! Or you will answer to my fiancé!' Lord Fennimore instantly went to the door in time to see her frogmarched in. 'Cedric!' She shrugged off the agent and clung to the old man. 'What's happening? What's going on? Has this got something to do with you being a spy?' Unlike Gray, his superior had at least been honest if he had confided that much.

'There, there, my dear.' Leatham, Warriner and Hadleigh all stared open mouthed at the sight of the old curmudgeon kissing Harriet's hair. 'I shall explain it all in due course.'

'We've been arrested, Harriet,' said Gislingham, still shaking his head in disbelief. 'For *treason* and *murder*.'

'I don't understand? That's...ridiculous.'

'We know. The world has plainly gone mad.'

'Have you seen Thea?'

'I thought she was with you, Lord Gray.'

'She went to find you.' Bertie was still soothing the Viscount with a calming hand on his arm. 'At least an hour ago.'

'She found me.' In the worst way possible. Lord only knew what she had heard or thought. 'She learned all about this and fled home. In a state. I expected to find her here.'

'Then perhaps she went to Caro? She dealt with her last upset quite well...' He turned to Bertie with obvious concern for his niece when he should have been thinking about himself, casting more doubt in Gray's mind as to his ability to commit the heinous crimes he had been accused of. 'Is the *boss* here today?'

His blood ran cold. 'What did you say?'

'That for all her many faults, my wife managed to calm Thea after Archimedes's accident.'

'Not that. The name. Why did you call her *The Boss*?'

Bertie and Gislingham shared a look, before Gislingham shrugged. Defeated. 'Well, I suppose the cat is well and truly out of the bag regarding Bertie and I... You should know she's been blackmailing us for years. Since well before I married the witch. It's our private name for her. Makes us feel better about dancing to her tune.'

Thea had been constantly aware of the cold press of the pistol throughout the short walk across the deserted lawn. She had expected to be dragged to the stables and the carriage, not across the boundary meadow to the old and disused ice house at the back of Colonel Purbeck's estate. Now, sat on the damp, cold floor, she kept one eye on her aunt and the gun while the other scanned for objects to use to aid her escape. The choice was limited to a rickety table and a three-legged milking stool. Both well out of reach.

Caro was agitated, despite her claims to the contrary. And as every minute passed she became more so. She might have her own escape planned to within the last detail, but it all hinged on her men carrying out the plan to the letter of her instruction and Thea doubted cut-throats could be trusted on their word.

But as her aunt paced, waiting to be rescued, Thea kept asking her questions, hoping that she would have enough time to give someone—anyone—the shocking answers that would save her uncle, before her aunt put the promised bullet between her eyes. The witch wanted no messy loose ends linking her to her crimes once she was safely ensconced in France with all her ill-gotten gains.

Yet, as bizarre as it all was, Thea had heard too much to be shocked any longer. One dreadful crime after another had been unveiled. Unspeakable things that made no sense, but peculiarly made perfect sense to her crazed aunt.

'Does Uncle Edward know you murdered his first wife?' Something Caro had apparently plotted and meticulously planned for years before she carried out the crime because she had always had her heart set on huge wealth and a title. And after some scandal during her one and only Season involving a married French *comte*, there was no chance of her snaring a suitable candidate in the capital. That's when she had turned her greedy eyes on the only viable option while she had languished in virtual exile in Suffolk—poor Uncle Edward.

'Of course not. He still thinks it was a mystery illness which killed her.' As opposed to the arsenic their then young neighbour had slowly fed her during her frequent social visits. 'Your uncle can be very naïve sometimes.' Because clearly, poisoning a man's wife to take her place was the most natural thing in the world. Especially to a woman who had then used blackmail to force the grieving husband down the aisle. Caro had had lofty plans of birthing his heir swiftly and then dispensing with him, too. Except he had thwarted her on that score and never set foot in her bed-chamber. Hardly a surprise, really, in view of the other revelation.

She still couldn't quite believe that her uncle and Bertie were lovers, although alongside today's other earth-shattering and tawdry discoveries, it was the secret that bothered her the least. At least he'd had the wherewithal to transfer the bulk of his fortune to Thea before he had been forced into marriage, something which her crazed aunt was clearly still enraged about. She had hoped to retain the entailed half upon the birth of her first son, but despite the many lovers she had taken to her bed over the years to provide her with one, Caro's womb had remained as barren as her cold, black heart.

Her aunt smiled, regarding Thea in an odd, de-tached way as if the madness which consumed her had now completely taken over. 'Nor has he any idea that it was me who facilitated his brother's accident either.'

Fresh betrayal and grief ripped through Thea. All these years, she had blamed herself and all these years her aunt had let her. 'You murdered my father?'

'It was necessary.'

'Necessary?' Poor Papa! Every second of that awful day surged to the fore, making Thea relive each moment with agonising clarity. The argu-ment. The dreadful news. Aunt Caro comforting her afterwards, knowing full well his blood stained her hands. She lunged, an animalistic cry coming from her lips.

'I'm going to kill you!' Her nails bit into her aunt's cheek until Caro pressed the gun to her temple and forced her back down to the floor, the barrel digging into her temple painfully.

'Now, now, dearest. Go sit down. There's a good girl. You cannot die yet, I might need you as insurance.'

'What did my father ever do to you?'

'He was in the way. He'd met a woman. He thought himself in love. After everything I'd suffered, I couldn't allow him to remarry and father a son before I did. Another hideous brat to inherit what should have been mine.' She shrugged. Once again flipping to the cheerful assassin devoid of any and all conscience. 'Once I had a son, I knew it wouldn't matter, but then your uncle exacted more petty revenge and had his stroke.' As if her poor uncle had almost died on purpose! 'With the clock ticking, I had to have a contingency plan.'

Tick-tock. Tick-tock.

'And wide-scale smuggling, treason and more murder was the obvious choice?' Thea wanted to laugh at the absurdity of it all, except nothing about it was even remotely funny.

'I had the connections.' Caro never had stopped seeing her scandalous French lover. 'And it's not as if everybody doesn't buy from the free traders.'

She wished Gray were here. She hated him, but he was strong and resourceful and she still loved him despite her broken heart. He worked for the government. His mission was to have the perpetrators brought to justice after all, except they were going to hang two innocent men for her aunt's many crimes. Because Caro hated Bertie and her uncle more than she loved money.

Chapter Twenty-Three

~~~~~⊱❦⊰~~~~~

They had searched everywhere. Scoured every inch of the grounds and the surrounding country-side. Nothing had passed through one of their road blocks and nobody had seen a blasted thing. To all intents and purposes, Thea and her aunt had disappeared off the face of the earth.

As Leatham and Warriner turned their horses back to the hall to regroup with the others to plan their next move, Gray couldn't bring himself to turn back. She was close. He could sense her.

'It'll be dark soon. We won't find her in the dark without lanterns.' Leatham's accurate assessment was unwelcome.

'You go back and get lanterns. I'm going to check the grounds again.'

'Gray—this is madness. We are going round in circles. If she was here, we'd have found her if…' His friend's voice trailed off. He didn't need to finish the sentence. Gray had been wrestling the awful possibility to the back of his mind since the search had started. *If she was still alive.* 'I'm not suggesting we give up. I know how much she means to you. I'm just suggesting we take a break and fetch lanterns.'

Fetch?

Before pausing to reconsider the unlikely idea that had popped into his head, Gray kicked his horse towards Kirton House, leaving his friends to trail clueless in his wake. Trefor had a nose for Thea. He adored her. Was besotted. He always knew where to find her.

He burst through the door to find his dog jumping with excitement. 'Trefor—fetch Thea!'

The dog tilted his head and Gray repeated his desperate instruction again, swiping away the errant tear which was making its way down his cheek. As if understanding his master was heartbroken, Trefor nuzzled his hand. Licked it. 'Please fetch Thea, boy. Fetch Thea!'

Finally, the animal seemed to have an epiphany and dashed out the door, his black nose inches from the ground. Miraculously, he started moving and Gray followed, trying not to hope, but praying for a miracle regardless. When they came within sight of Gislingham Hall, Trefor sped up and then bounded towards the door.

He was sat patiently on the threshold as the three friends finally caught up with him. His tail wagging. Proud of himself that he had understood such an important instruction, while not understanding it at all.

'It was worth a try.' He felt Warriner's hand on his shoulder. 'Come on. Let's get those lanterns.' His friend's enforced optimism was not mirrored on his face.

Inside the house, it appeared everyone was back and, judging by the grim expressions, nobody had located her. Someone pressed a glass into his hand. 'We'll find her.' Harriet's voice, lacking its usual certainty, cut through the silence of the room. 'Remember, Thea is fearless.'

She was. She'd been braver than him. And now, thanks to him, she was in danger. His eyes wandered around the room. Gislingham sat with Bertie, utterly distraught. Hadleigh, Warriner and Leatham in the corner, talking in hushed voices. Trying to spare him from hearing the potential truth. Harriet…

'What the blazes!' Lord Fennimore almost fell over Trefor, who was sat in the middle of the room. 'Why does that blasted dog always sniff the air?'

'Come here, boy.' But Trefor refused to budge. His head was tilted back, his shiny black nostrils were twitching and he was inhaling deeply almost as if he was in a trance. 'Trefor!' Gray patted his thigh. 'Come here, boy.'

Instead of obeying, the dog began to bark. Agitated and pawing the ground, he stared at Gray for several seconds, then he was off like a shot down the stairs, barking all the way. Trying not to hope, Gray followed him to the Viscountess's sitting room, watched the dog circle the room with his nose to the rug, then sit and whine outside one of the concealed servants' doors in the panelling.

Praying for a miracle, he pulled it open. 'Fetch Thea, boy!' He watched transfixed as the dog hurtled along the passageway as if he knew exactly where he was going, when Gray knew for a fact neither of them had ever set foot here before. 'This way!' he bellowed the instruction to Hadleigh, who had followed them downstairs. 'Bring lanterns! And guns!'

Alone, Gray followed his dog, trying not to get impatient each time the animal paused and quietly sniffed the air, instead making a fuss of him while repeating the command, *Fetch Thea*, in case he got waylaid by any other scent or distraction as he was prone to do. At the boundary of the spitting Colonel Purbeck's vast estate, Trefor sat, then began to pace a slow circle, his sensitive nose never leaving the ground.

As the others all arrived bearing light and weapons, and, in the Viscount's case, canes, he motioned for them to stay well back, not wanting their scents to contaminate whatever trace of Thea's intoxicating jasmine remained.

After an eternity, during which Gray's heart loudly hammered in his head because he was too frightened to breath out, Trefor set off again. He ran for a good quarter of a mile towards the strange house, then Gray watched the animal disappear down what appeared to be a genuine pothole.

Caro froze at the sound of an animal's whining. 'What's that?'

'A fox, I think.' Or, please God, a dog. A black one with floppy ears and an irritating, deceitful master who Thea had been silently willing to find her since she had been frogmarched out of Caro's cloying, soulless sitting room. Now that it was dark outside her aunt was becoming more twitchy, craning her ears at every sound and constantly unlocking the heavy oak door, checking outside for her rescuers.

'It's a long way from midnight. They won't be here yet. Why don't you sit down?' They were apparently coming along the brook, an irony that was not lost on Thea, and would smuggle Caro out on the water. A plan that had been made over a year ago. A plan that had been rehearsed repeatedly. How could such things happen in such a quiet corner of Suffolk and someone with as suspicious a nature as Thea's not notice? Clearly, she had atrocious instincts all around.

Caro began to pace again, her finger never leaving the trigger. 'I hate foxes. I wish the damn thing would shut up.' Absently she tossed the heavy key on the rickety table where the only lamp burned. The key Thea had been desperate to get her hands on since they had arrived. 'They'll be here! It's more than their scurvy lives are worth to double-cross me! They know that.' Another mantra the woman kept repeating, as if reassuring herself of her own power. 'I'll have the lot of them killed!' She pulled out the timepiece again, stared at the dial and then snapped it shut, oblivious to the scant few inches Thea had managed to move closer to the table in the brief bit of time. 'They'll be here. They'll be here.'

The animal whined again and her aunt instinctively started towards the door to investigate, allowing Thea to shuffle closer to the key.

'Not so fast, dearest!' The barrel raised again as her aunt spotted what she was up to. 'Sit still and stop being a nuisance, there's a good girl.' The key disappeared back into her pocket again accompanied by a smug smile.

'Gray will come for me.' Despite wanting to hate him, Thea knew that in her bones. 'His men have probably blocked every road. They will search every property.' At least that is what she guessed government agents did. 'They'll have boats on the water, too. I've never seen so many Excise Men.'

'He'll be too busy clapping your uncle and his molly in irons to give you a second thought and, by the time he does, I'll be long gone. You were a means to an end, dearest.'

True, but aspects of his behaviour last night kept niggling. The fervency. The selfless passion. He had thoroughly adored every inch of her and not allowed her to repay him. The intense emotion swirling in those troubled, wolf-like eyes. Almost as if he hated himself for lying.

Just remember I love you. Always. No matter what. No matter how dire things are or how bad they seem.

Well, things were about as dire as it was possible for them to be, so dire that she was now clinging on to the pathetic hope that he at least cared enough about her to come looking. In the meantime, all she had to do was stay alive and find a way to get either that key or the gun.

'If Gray doesn't come, then Mr Hargreaves will. He's in love with me.' Seeing as patience, cunning and obedience had failed to give her any chance to escape, she might as well try riling Caro. The woman was already quite irrational. In anger, she might make a mistake and provide an opening. Thea knew only too well how irrationally an angry mind behaved. 'He told me so only last week at your garden party. He wants to marry me. Which is odd, considering he warms your bed, don't you think? Perhaps it's your age that's putting him off?' A gentle kick in her Achilles heel. 'Men always prefer a younger woman. Especially as they all want to sire a son.'

'Shut up!'

'Why? I have nothing to lose, do I? Seeing as you are going to kill me regardless, I might as well be honest in my final hours. I have no cause to spare your feelings now, nor am I particularly inclined to. Let's face it, you were a means to an end to Mr Hargreaves. He wanted a way to get close to me and your pathetic desperation to be adored by any man in possession of a pulse allowed him to do it. He mentioned he hated your wrinkles…'

'I said shut up!' Her aunt had stalked forward, the pistol pointed menacingly. Refusing to be cowed any longer, and mindful that she couldn't make any sort of move glued to the floor, Thea stood defiantly.

'Do you know you're pitied by all our neighbours? They all whisper about you behind your back. The *poor* barren Viscountess. How *sad*. Nothing going for her except that *once*-pretty face. If only they knew the whole truth. That the only way you could get any man to marry you was by blackmail! Do your loyal men know that? I'll bet none of them turns up to save you. Why would they? You were nothing but a means to an end.'

As Caro lunged, Thea went for the gun, holding her aunt's arm to the side to avoid getting shot. She felt the other woman's fingers in her hair, felt them twist and pull hard, heard the ominous click before the trigger was squeezed, then saw bright light as her head was smashed against the wall.

Except the bright light never went. Out of it came Gray. He barrelled into her aunt and sent her sprawling on the floor amid what sounded like frantic barking alongside the ominous gunshot.

Thea couldn't see what happened next through the streaming army that followed him into the icehouse. Lanterns, noise, more barking as she swayed, struggling to focus on the sea of moving faces swarming in front of her.

'We've got her!' A stranger. Her aunt's howl as she struggled. Muffled as they overpowered her.

Trefor's pitiful howling.

'Good grief, is that blood?' Her uncle.

'He's wounded!' Lord Fennimore. 'Leatham! Get a physician!'

Finally, the scene came sharply into view.

Gray. Face down. Unmoving.

Time stood still.

Chapter Twenty-Four

Thea threw herself on the ground to get to him. 'Gray! Wake up! Wake up!' A crimson circle of blood was blooming through his coat at his shoulder. He groaned and it was the most perfect sound she had ever heard. 'He's alive! Somebody help him.'

Two men stepped forward who seemed to know what they were doing far more than she did and reluctantly she stepped back and watched impotently as they gently cut off his coat and turned him around. Twice his eyes fluttered open and twice she watched them close again, his normally tanned face waxy pale.

'Is he dead?' Please God, don't let him be dead. Not when it had taken so long to find him.

'Not yet.' But Hadleigh's expression didn't hold out much hope as the man she loved was loaded on to a stretcher and carried away, his loyal dog practically glued to his side.

* * *

'The bullet has gone straight through.' Lord Fennimore patted her hand reassuringly on the sofa several agonising hours later. They had locked her out of the bedchamber. For the best, with hindsight, because Thea had been an inconsolable mess.

'Is that a good thing?'

'In my experience, they're better out than in.'

'But will he survive?'

'He'd better. I'm too old and too busy to command the Invisibles.' He turned as the lawyer stepped into the room. 'How's the patient, Hadleigh?'

'Awake and in high dudgeon. He wants to see you.' The blond man gestured for Thea to come closer, pointing to his ruined cravat. 'He demanded it, actually. Quite forcefully. He's been in a dreadful state since you went missing. Something he will undoubtedly blame himself for when it is me who should shoulder it all. It was my idea to break into the Hall last night. Gray was dead set against it and only came to protect you. It was also my clumsy, disrespectful words you overheard this morning. I was playing to the gallery and had no idea how he felt about you or that you would ever overhear. I apologise wholeheartedly for all the distress I have caused you, Miss Cranford. If it is any consolation at all, I think he loves you.'

'Oh, I know he does,' said Harriet with a dramatic sigh. 'The man leapt in front of a bullet meant for her. A true leap of love. He was prepared to sacrifice himself so that Thea lived. As grand gestures go, they don't get much grander than that.'

'Indeed they don't. Don't you remember what I've always said? True love is the greatest joy in the world and worth all the hideous turmoil in the long run.' Uncle Edward gripped Bertie's hand and the pair smiled a little watery-eyed at one another, still not quite over the trials of the day, but obviously relieved they would not have to stand trial themselves. Lord Hadleigh and Lord Fennimore had given their word. 'He loves you, Thea. Trust me—nothing else matters more.'

Thea dashed from her uncle's sitting room to the bedchamber beyond, emotion clogging her throat as she saw him propped on pillows, deathly pale but thankfully alive. Their eyes locked and then his dropped.

'I'm so sorry. For everything.'

He reached for her hand and squeezed it hard, reassuring her that he had plenty of life left in him, thank goodness. 'Don't be.' It had been a grand gesture after all. The grandest. The sort that melted away all doubt. 'Things always happen for a reason, even if the reason for them is not immediately apparent. If you hadn't lied, then we wouldn't have fought. And if we hadn't fought, my uncle and Bertie would have been accused of crimes they didn't commit and you wouldn't have caught the true criminal.'

'I don't care about any of that. All I care about is you... And me. If there is *still* a you and me.' He tugged their entwined hands to rest possessively on his chest. Beneath her palm she could feel his heart beat, sure and steady, secure in the knowledge it beat solely for her.

'You lied to me.'

'I had to. That doesn't make it right. If I could do it all again...'

Thea silenced him with a kiss.

'You forgive me?'

Her uncle was right, true love was the greatest joy in the world and worth all the hideous turmoil in the long run. That didn't mean she couldn't make him sweat a little. She sat back and disentangled her hand from his. 'Lord Gray, I have found no reason to reappraise my initial assessment of you. You are a chancer and a ne'er-do-well. A man with scant regard for the proper rules of society. A man who lives wholly in the moment without any thought to the consequences. A disgraceful scoundrel of the first order...and I speak for both myself and Impetuous Thea when I say we wouldn't have you any other way.'

She watched her words sink in. Watched him smile that cocky smile he did so well. 'Then I have a question for you.'

Her heart danced. 'What sort of question?' He

was going to propose. She could feel it in her bones.

'An important one...' As his voice dropped to an intimate whisper, Thea found herself leaning closer. 'One that frankly terrifies me... One I've been running away from for the better part of ten years...but the thing is, I've recently had cause to re-evaluate everything I've come to believe, face my fears and...'

'And?' Her lips were inches from his, so close they heated with awareness and longing.

'I was wondering if you would...?'

'Would what?'

'Consider...' She had dreamed of this moment. A perfect proposal from her perfect mate. 'Consider making some plans?'

'Plans? *Plans?*' His eyes were dancing with mischief, the wretch, because he knew exactly how to vex her. 'I want more than plans, you scoundrel. At the very least, I want promises. Blood-sworn, granite and solemn promises. Of the forever kind.'

A wet black nose appeared from nowhere and sandwiched itself between them. Two big, manipulative chocolate eyes gazed adoringly up at them before he wiggled on to the mattress and presented his belly to the ceiling for a rub.

'And I want Trefor. That is not negotiable. And a summer wedding. And babies. Plural. Disgraceful dark-haired boys and fiery redheaded girls.

And I want to see some of the world. Have a few adventures. With you, of course. And I want an exercise yard full of horses. And long summer days filled with laughter and long winter nights wrapped in your arms.'

'That's a great many ands. Is that all of them?' His finger had begun to wind itself in one of her vertical curls.

'And I'd like to see you naked and cavorting in the brook again, but I'm prepared to make Impetuous Thea wait till you're better for that one.'

'I might struggle with the brook, but I can't deny poor Impetuous Thea the rest of her request. Not when she's been shut in a box for years.' Despite being pale, weak as a kitten and clearly in no fit state to be indulging in anything energetic, her man always found tremendous joy in the moment. To her delight, he whipped back the sheet and then lay back with a wolfish grin, mirroring his charming mutt's scandalous pose. 'For the record, in case there is any doubt whatsoever, I would be delighted to have her vouch for my credentials whenever she sees fit.' Something she did as soon as he was better. Rather a lot.

* * * * *

MILLS & BOON

Coming next month

THE EARL'S COUNTESS OF CONVENIENCE
Marguerite Kaye

'We're alone now.'

It was absurd, the way Eloise's stomach lurched when he said that, as if he'd told her something she didn't know. Something exciting, that made her pulses flutter and her mouth go dry. 'There are probably at least two footmen guarding the ballroom doors. And gardeners—there are bound to be gardeners out there, looking up, catching a glimpse of the newly married Earl and his Countess surveying their domain.'

'The newly married Earl and his Countess enjoying a rare moment of privacy together,' Alexander said. 'Relishing the opportunity too, because once they launch themselves into the preparations for their wedding ball, they are not likely to have many more such moments.'

One of his hands was resting lightly on her waist. The other was at the nape of her neck. Heat was radiating from the point where his fingers made contact with her skin. If they were being watched, it would seem odd if she simply stood there like a wooden mannequin. Eloise put her hand on Alexander's shoulder. Her legs brushed his. She reached up, feeling the smoothness of his freshly shaved jaw under her palm, curling her fingers into his hair. It was as silky as it looked. Her heart was hammering, but she was acting, that was all, she was playing her part as the recently married Countess of Fearnoch, deeply in love with her husband.

She stepped closer. Her breasts brushed his chest. His hand tightened on her waist. If she really was alone with her husband for the first time that morning, she would…

His lips touched hers before she had finished the thought, and her heart began to beat wildly. There was a pause, an aching pause, and she realised hazily that Alexander was giving her time to draw back, but a newly married countess would not draw back from kissing the husband she loved, so she did not. And he kissed her.

Continue reading
THE EARL'S COUNTESS OF CONVENIENCE
Marguerite Kaye

Available next month
www.millsandboon.co.uk

COMING SOON!

We really hope you enjoyed reading this book. If you're looking for more romance, be sure to head to the shops when new books are available on

Thursday 2nd May

To see which titles are coming soon, please visit

millsandboon.co.uk/nextmonth

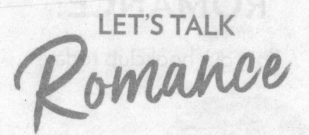

LET'S TALK
Romance

For exclusive extracts, competitions
and special offers, find us online:

 facebook.com/millsandboon

@MillsandBoon

@MillsandBoonUK

Get in touch on 01413 063232

For all the latest titles coming soon, visit
millsandboon.co.uk/nextmonth

Leabharlanna Poiblí Chathair Baile Átha Cliath

Dublin City Public Libraries